"Lady, you bother me."

"You prance around in that slinky thing and expect me to ignore it. Well, I'm doing my damnedest. But I'd find life a lot easier if you'd either put more clothes on or join me on my bed."

The last suggestion hung between them. "I don't think that would be a good idea," Sally said.

"I don't, either. As long as we both agree, we should be all right." Diamond didn't move.... She wondered if she ought to kiss him, just a little. "Don't look at me like that," he warned.

"Like what?"

He moved closer, so that his mouth hovered just over hers. "Like you're asking for trouble. I'm a man with too much history and too many problems to mess with a woman like you, and even if you're on the verge of forgetting it, I'm not."

He was so close. "I'm not forgetting it," she whispered. "You are."

ABOUT THE AUTHOR

When asked to tell us about herself, Anne Stuart sent in the following: "Anne Stuart has written lots of books in lots of genres for lots of publishers. She lives in the hills of Northern Vermont with her splendid husband and two magnificent children, where it snows so much, she hasn't much else to do but write."

Books by Anne Stuart

HARLEQUIN AMERICAN ROMANCE

311–GLASS HOUSES
326–CRAZY LIKE A FOX
346–RANCHO DIABLO
361–ANGELS WINGS
374–LAZARUS RISING
398–NIGHT OF THE PHANTOM

ANNE STUART

CHASING TROUBLE

Harlequin Books

TORONTO • NEW YORK • LONDON
AMSTERDAM • PARIS • SYDNEY • HAMBURG
STOCKHOLM • ATHENS • TOKYO • MILAN

Published November 1991

ISBN 0-373-16413-0

CHASING TROUBLE

Printed in U.S.A.

Chapter One

Sarah "Sally" Gallimard MacArthur had been in sleazier, scrungier, dirtier places in her life, but not many. And usually not on her own accord. This seedy office building in the worst part of the Tenderloin District of San Francisco should have been condemned years ago. The green-painted hallways were littered with trash, the offices seemed to be rented by one-room venues with names like Novelty Toys and Rubber, Inc., and that faint scuffling overhead had to come from little rodent feet. The windows were so dirt-engrimed that nobody could see out into the decaying city street, and the whole place reeked of grime, sweat and despair.

Sally absolutely loved it.

Even at eleven o'clock on a hot September morning, the place was dark and dank. The halls were deserted—their usual denizens had probably slunk out into the daylight, blinking. It took her longer than she expected to find the third-floor office, but it was worth the trouble. It was perfect.

The rippled glass door was cracked, a jagged lightning streak through the stenciled name. James Diamond, Private Investigator. She took a deep breath of pure pleasure. Sam Spade himself would have been at home there.

For the first time in days—weeks, maybe—her luck had taken a turn for the better. She'd been right to go with her instincts. When the chips were down, those instincts came through for her every time. With a brisk knock, she turned the door handle and stepped into the office.

"What can I do for you?" The man stepping out from the inner office was somewhat of a disappointment, but then, she couldn't expect everything to be like an old movie. He was too clean-cut, for one thing. He looked more like a seminary student than an ex-cop turned private detective, with his neat polyester suit, his short hair, his phony smile and his wary eyes.

"I need a private detective," she announced. "I've got this little problem that I need some help with."

He reached out and took her hand in his own soft ones. "There, there. Why don't you come into my office and tell me all about it? I'm sure I can help you deal with whatever it is."

"I'm not so sure about that," she said doubtfully. Private eyes shouldn't have soft hands, should they? There was certainly a lecherous expression in his slightly bloodshot eyes, and that was reasonable enough, but still...

"Get out of here." The voice was rough, hostile, coming up behind her, and she jumped in panic, ready to run. Instead, however, the seminary student turned a bright red and began slinking toward the door.

"I didn't mean any harm," he muttered. "Just trying to be helpful."

"The day I need your help, Frankie, is the day they put me under. Take your pal with you."

"Not my pal, Diamond. I think she's a client. Better not be too rash. You need all the work you can get." With that, the seminary student disappeared out the office door, slamming it behind him, widening the crack that speared through James Diamond's name.

It took all Sally's self-control to hide her smile of pure pleasure when she saw him. This was what she'd been hoping for. This man was unshaven, his dark hair needed cutting quite badly, his suit was rumpled, as if he'd slept in it, and his expression was sour and unfriendly. If his face was a little too handsome beneath the day's growth of heavy beard, if his body was a little too tall and lean to be quite right, she was willing to overlook those deficiencies. This was her down-and-out detective, like something out of Raymond Chandler. This was her savior.

"You a client or one of Frankie's girls?" Diamond asked, eyeing her up and down as he lit a cigarette. His hands shook slightly, but they didn't look soft. Not soft at all.

"One of Frankie's girls? You mean he's a . . . ?"

"That's right." He blew the smoke in her direction. "Although he calls himself a 'talent manager.' I guess that's as good a job title as anything. All right, you weren't here to see him. That means you must be here to see me." He glanced at her again. "You from the IRS? The telephone company? Pacific Gas?"

She'd really tried to dress down. She should have known a private investigator would see through her pathetic attempts. Even with a cheap dress and bargain-basement shoes she couldn't disguise a two-hundred-dollar haircut. Though why a down-and-out detective should recognize Antonio's best work was a question in itself.

"You heard Frankie. I'm a client."

"Oh, yeah?" He didn't sound promising. "Well, I don't do drug buys for spoiled rich girls, and I don't make blackmail drops. You can't be in the midst of a divorce—

you look too cheerful for that—and you look too clean for kinky sex, so that rules out just about everything."

"I want you to find my sister."

For a moment, he didn't move. "Your sister's into drugs and kinky sex?" he asked finally, as if the question bored him.

"Not that I know of."

"Then what's the problem?"

"Do you suppose we could go in and sit down?" she asked, choking slightly as another stream of cigarette smoke made a beeline for her. "I think better sitting down."

"I think better standing up."

"Frankie said you were in need of clients, and looking around me, I can believe it. Don't you think you ought to make an effort to get me to hire you instead of trying to chase me away?"

"No," said James Diamond, moving past her into the inner office. She followed him before he could shut the door in her face, almost choking on the thick, stale air in the room. It reeked of old cigarettes and whiskey. Perfectly in keeping with what she wanted, but it was hard to breathe in there.

"Mind if I open a window?" Without waiting for an answer, she headed for one grime-coated one and began tugging. It couldn't have been painted shut—there'd been no fresh coat of paint on these windows since the Korean War, but it was proving almost as stubborn as the man she'd come to hire.

"I mind," he said, dropping down into a chair behind the cluttered desk and tipping back, putting his feet on top of a pile of papers. That was one thing she didn't like. He was wearing sneakers. Sam Spade wouldn't wear sneakers.

Sally gave one more shove, the window jammed upward and the glass shattered. "Oops," she said.

Diamond didn't move. "Why don't you go away before you destroy my office?"

"It would take more than me to destroy this place," she announced, looking around her. There was one other chair, something that looked like Mission Oak. Pretrendy mission oak, just something found at a junk store and dumped there. James Diamond was clearly the kind of man who'd sell it in an instant if he had any idea of its value.

The sofa was sagging Naugahyde, one that had obviously provided its owner with more than one good night's sleep. Sally wondered for a moment whether it had had other, more energetic uses. No, rampant sexuality wasn't part of this particular fantasy. The hard-boiled detective wasn't someone who tumbled clients on his office couch. Even if he did have sinfully beautiful blue eyes.

"Tell me what you want and then leave," Diamond said in a world-weary voice, lighting another cigarette from the end of his old one before stubbing it out.

"Do you always smoke so much?" Sally questioned artlessly, sliding onto the top of his desk beside his large, sneakered feet, dumping half the papers on the floor at the same time. "It's no wonder your voice sounds like gravel and your office smells like toxic waste. If you keep this up, you'll die young."

He just stared at her, as if he couldn't quite believe her gall. She'd seen that expression often enough—she didn't let it slow her down. "It's too late," he said. "I've already missed dying young by at least five years. You, however, might make it under the deadline if you don't tell me what you're doing here."

She let her long legs swing back and forth under his patently uninterested gaze. She had wonderful legs—long and shapely, and she was wearing a skirt made for the express purpose of exposing most of their length. Private eyes were supposed to be fascinated by legs, but Diamond didn't seem to care. Maybe she should have unbuttoned another button or two on her dress.

"Why don't you want to take me on as a client?" she asked instead.

He let out a long-suffering sigh, tipping back farther to stare at her out of those sinful eyes. He should have been wearing a fedora, but then, no one wore a fedora in the 1990s, more's the pity. Maybe if she bought one, stomped on it a bit to give it some character and then gave it to him, he might be persuaded to wear it.

"You're trouble, lady. From the tips of your brand-new shoes to the top of your up-scale haircut, you're the kind of client I do my best to steer clear of."

She glanced around the seedy office meaningfully. "Obviously. I pay very well."

"And I have scruples. Standards. I know those things might be foreign to someone like you, but I don't break the law for anyone."

"How do you earn a living?"

He hesitated, but it was clear she wasn't moving from her perch on top of his old desk, and short of throwing her out the window she'd already broken, he wasn't going to get rid of her. He had enough sense to know that. "Divorces," he said finally.

"Pretty sleazy."

"Hey, it's a living. So why don't you tell me what you want from me, and I'll steer you in the direction of someone who can help you."

"What makes you think you can't help me?" She swung her legs back and forth and was pleased to notice his eyes followed the movement of her long legs.

"Instincts. You learn to trust 'em when you get to my age."

"Ah, yes, your advanced age. That's the second time you've mentioned it. You're thirty-eight years old. I hardly think that qualifies you for a wheelchair."

She'd gone too far this time. He sat forward with a snap, and his formerly impassive face looked downright dangerous. For the first time, Sally wondered whether she was as much in control as she'd thought.

"How do you know I'm thirty-eight?" Diamond demanded.

"Simple. I had you investigated once I decided I wanted to hire you."

He sat back, momentarily stunned. "You had me investigated? Why the hell would you hire investigators to investigate an investigator? For that matter, why didn't you use those investigators to investigate whatever the hell it is you want investigated?"

"You're confusing me."

"Good. You've done nothing but confuse me since you waltzed in my door."

"Maybe you're easily confused," she pointed out. "I didn't mean that I had someone investigate you. I mean I checked with the licensing bureau to see whether you were someone reputable before I contacted you."

He seemed to believe her; at least he didn't call her an outright liar. "And why did I have the honor of being chosen for your problem? I don't advertise on buses or park benches. I don't do much to drum up business."

"But you are in the Yellow Pages."

He just looked at her. "The Yellow Pages," he echoed faintly. "There are over two hundred private investigators listed in the Bay Area directory. Why me?"

"Isn't it obvious?" she said cheerfully.

"Not to me."

"Your name. It just sounds like a private eye's." She gave him a beatific smile. "The moment I saw your name in the Yellow Pages I knew you were the one for the job. I mean, how could I hire someone like Edwin Bunce or Liebowitz, Inc., when there's someone with a name like James Diamond?"

He shook his head. "Trouble," he muttered under his breath, stubbing out his cigarette without lighting another one. "Just plain trouble. Why don't you tell me about your sister so I can get rid of you once and for all?"

"It's not going to be so easy." She swung off his desk, deciding he'd had enough time to appreciate her legs. She figured the rest of her wasn't really his style, even though her looks were something she usually took for granted. A hard-boiled P.I. like Diamond wouldn't be attracted to porcelain skin, silky black hair and blue eyes, and he wouldn't like her slightly voluptuous body. He'd like reed-slim women with platinum hair. "I already told you, I need you to find my sister."

"And what's happened to your sister, and why can't the police help you, and what the hell are you doing?"

"Making coffee," she said cheerfully, not quite sure how to handle the electric kettle. "And I haven't gone to the police."

"Why not?"

"It's a family matter. My sister—actually she's my half sister, Lucy. My mother went through three husbands and unfortunately, Lucy's father was the only one without money. Anyway, Lucy got involved with an unsavory character and took off with something she shouldn't have taken. I need to get her back, return the item before it's missed and get rid of her boyfriend. It's really quite simple."

He stared at her, clearly fascinated despite himself. "Simple," he muttered. "You expect me to kill this boyfriend?"

She smiled at him. "I don't suppose you'd consider it? It would certainly solve most of our problems."

"I would not."

She dished out some lumpy instant coffee into two disposable cups. "I didn't think so. We'll have to figure some other way around it. Did you know fish choke on plastic foam? It's one of the worst ecological disasters..."

"I don't give a rat's behind about the ecology," Diamond said flatly.

That stopped her cold. "You don't?"

"Nope. I'll be dead and gone by the time the ozone layer disappears, and I'm certainly not going to have any family to leave behind, so who gives a damn?"

"You're not going to have any friends to leave behind, either, if this is your usual attitude," Sally said sternly.

"Since I won't be here, it won't matter."

"God, you're cynical. I love it."

"I beg your pardon?"

"Never mind." Sally poured boiling water from the kettle and then set it back with an ominous crack that didn't bode well for its future use, handing Diamond one of the polluting cups. "Drink your coffee, and I'll give you the details about my sister."

He stared down at his cup, at the nuggets of crystallized coffee still floating in the foam on top. "I need milk and sugar."

"Don't be ridiculous, a man like you would drink it black," she said flatly, dropping onto the aging sofa. It was surprisingly comfortable despite the deep sag in the middle.

"A man like me drinks it with milk and sugar."

She didn't bother arguing. She'd already checked the supplies. The sugar bowl had ants in it; the coffee creamer had hardened into a lump. Let him deal with it. "Lucy's been gone for five days. I figure we have maybe another five days to find her without the manure hitting the fan."

"What happens in five days?"

"My father comes back from Asia, finds his prize Chinese figurine missing and raises holy hell. He's a stern man—it wouldn't matter if my sister was the culprit. It wouldn't matter if I were the culprit. He has a Biblical sense of justice, and Lucy would end up behind bars before she could blink. Lucy wouldn't be able to survive."

"You'd be surprised at how many people survive prison," Diamond said, taking a sip of his black coffee. He probably knew all too well the condition of his cream and sugar and had only been trying to bait her.

"Not Lucy. She's not like me. She's flighty, impractical, a little silly."

"Not like you," he murmured wryly. "I bet she talks too much, too."

Sally nodded. "A regular chatterbox. As a matter of fact, I'm surprised Vinnie can put up with her. I used to drive him crazy—" Her own runaway tongue had tripped her up again.

"You used to be involved with your sister's unsavory character?"

Sally considered lying, something she was quite adept at, but saw no point in it. She only lied when she thought she could get away with it or if she was bored. As long as she was in James Diamond's cynical company, she wasn't the slightest bit bored. "I was engaged to him. Until I realized he was more interested in my father's collection than in me, and then I dumped him. Next thing I knew, Lucy had stars in her eyes and the figurine was missing. And then Lucy and Vinnie were gone, Father was on his way home and I had no choice but save the bacon."

"In five days," Diamond said faintly. "I don't suppose you have any idea where they went?"

She drew herself up straight. "Of course I do. I don't expect the impossible. I have a very good idea exactly where they went. I'm just not sure how to find it."

"But you're going to share your information with me."

"Even better. I'm going with you."

"No, you're not. If I take this job, I'll do it alone."

"Don't be ridiculous, you wouldn't be able talk Lucy into coming home and throwing herself on Father's mercy. You'll be too busy dealing with Vinnie. Did I happen to mention that Vinnie has connections?"

"What kind of connections?"

"Organized crime. That's another reason why I picked you. You used to work for the police force. You must have dealt with thousands of gangsters."

"Thousands," Diamond agreed faintly.

"So you'll know exactly what to do to get rid of him, even if you won't kill him. I'll talk Lucy into coming back home, and everything will be absolutely wonderful."

"Except for one thing." He pulled out his crumpled pack of cigarettes and lit another one, blowing the smoke in Sally's direction.

She gave a meaningful little cough. "And what's that?"

"I'm not taking the case."

She stared at him nonplussed. This was a lot harder than she'd ever expected. Humphrey Bogart didn't turn down cases, particularly when Lauren Bacall showed up and swung her long legs in front of him. Of course, Sally was no Lauren Bacall. And James Diamond was too young and too pretty, even beneath that stubble, to be the great Bogie. But he was a start, if he just wouldn't be so damned stubborn.

"Why not?" she asked.

He didn't hesitate. He didn't strike her as someone who hesitated in this life. "Because you're lying to me."

"I am not—" she began hotly.

"Then you're not telling me the entire truth. And I don't walk into situations blindfolded, lady. Speaking of which, what's your name?"

"My name?" she asked blankly, her mind working at a feverish pace. She'd hoped to get a commitment from him without having to go into all the sordid details. She'd hoped she could manage to rescue Lucy without having to tell him much at all. If he really wasn't going to take the case, and she didn't believe that for a minute, then it would be better if he didn't know who she was.

"Your name, lady," he said, pushing back from the desk and standing up. He was too tall for Sam Spade or Philip Marlowe, but he looked suitably seedy in that rumpled suit and unshaven, too-handsome face.

"Bridget O'Shaunessy," she said promptly, not bothering to rise from her seat on his sagging couch. If he wanted to get rid of her, he was going to have to throw her out. "I'm a costs analyst at Wells Fargo." She didn't actually know what that was, but it sounded properly impressive.

James Diamond had skirted his desk and strode over to her. "Bridget O'Shaunessy, is it?" he said. "Which branch of Wells Fargo?"

Sally blinked at him. "The downtown one," she said.

He reached down, caught her hand in his and hauled her upward. "Sure, lady. But my name's James Diamond, not Sam Spade, and I don't believe a word you're saying. Now take your pretty little upscale butt—" he pushed her toward the door "—and go away before I have to get real hostile."

She held back as much as she could, but he was strong and not possessed of any gentlemanly scruples about using that strength to get rid of unwanted visitors. "But what about my sister?" she demanded.

"Go back to the Yellow Pages. Maybe you'll find a listing for Philip Marlowe." And with that, he shoved her out the front door, slamming it behind her.

She stood there for a moment, disheveled, rumpled, as she listened to the sound of the door being locked. For a moment, she considered bashing her purse through the cracked smoked glass window, then thought better of it. She'd lost the first skirmish, but she had no doubt whatsoever that she'd get him to do what she wanted. People were seldom able to hold out against her once she made up her mind, and she'd made up her mind about James Diamond. She only hoped she could convince him in time.

BRIDGET O'SHAUNESSY, James thought, leaning back in his chair and lighting another cigarette. Who the hell did she think she was kidding? If there was a private investigator alive who hadn't seen *The Maltese Falcon* he'd eat his hat, if he wore one. She'd probably escaped from some lunatic asylum. Her connection with reality was extremely iffy, and he'd be surprised if she even had a sister.

Still, she did have absolutely wonderful legs. Just the kind he liked, long and shapely, the kind that could wrap around— No, he'd better not start thinking like that. His infallible instincts had taken one look at that dizzy female and decreed that she was nothing but trouble. If there was one thing he'd learned during the last tough years, it was that it was better to trust his instincts than his hormones.

She was right about one thing, though. He had a definite lack of clients, and he had an overdue rent bill, gas bill, electric bill, and the IRS was getting edgy. Maybe he shouldn't have been so quick to turn down her offer. Her clothes might have been department store, but her hair and the way she held herself projected big money. He could baby-sit her for a couple of days and have enough to at least crawl out of the hole he'd managed to dig for himself the past few months.

She was too pretty, though, with that silky black hair and porcelain skin. Her mouth looked tempting, if it stopped talking long enough, and her eyes were absolutely wonderful. It was no wonder he didn't want to get anywhere near her.

Still, it might be an interesting game to find out who she really was and where she came from. It wasn't as if he had anything else to do on this damnably hot morning but recover from his hangover. He could make a little bet with himself. If he knew who she was by five o'clock, he'd consider himself still in fighting trim. If it took longer than that, then his skills were in poor shape and he'd better give up his passing acquaintance with the whiskey bottle.

He knew that already. But maybe Miss Bridget O'Shaunessy would be able to distract him enough to forget about it. Maybe once he found out exactly who she was, he'd reconsider her offer. After all, what else did he have to do?

If only she weren't so damned pretty.

Chapter Two

James Michael Diamond was everything a private investigator should be. He'd grown up in a boisterous Irish Catholic family in Boston, had got a scholarship to Berkeley and had stayed in the area ever since. He'd taken his degree with him into the police force, hoping to do some good, but it hadn't taken long for his ideals to be knocked out of him. The police force in the 1970s didn't take kindly to Berkeley graduates, and he'd had the stuffing pounded out of him a number of times before he learned to keep his mouth shut.

Fifteen years in the department had been more than enough. Enough to make him so damned cynical he wouldn't trust the Pope himself. Enough to make James so burned out that it was only a question of when, not if, he was going to explode. After Kaz died, it was only a matter of time and choice. Whether he'd go back to law school, get his degree and try to change the world for the better and make a pack of money. Or whether he'd go into business as a private investigator, slide deeper into the human cesspool he'd been wading in and manage to scrape by each month.

It had been no contest. The world wasn't worth saving, and James didn't give a damn about the things money could buy. What he could do, and do damned well, was find the truth behind lies. Find the people who were missing, find out who was cheating whom, find the dirt, find the filth, find the lies. Why give up a God-given talent, he'd decided with his usual cynicism. It wasn't as if he had anyone to answer to. His wife had decamped seven years ago with their joint savings account, and once he'd satisfied his curiosity and discovered where she'd gone, he hadn't thought about her since. She was happily remarried with two kids, and he didn't give a damn.

Kaz was a different matter, as James's ex-wife had known. They'd been partners for years, and when Kaz died, a part of James had died, too.

It would have been better all around if someone had shot Kaz. The survivors' benefits would have been a lot better than a simple pension for Marge and the kids. And James would have had a purpose in life, a villain he could go after, hunt down and wipe out.

Instead, he could just think about something as irrationally stupid as a strep infection that moved so fast, his best friend was dead in three days from his first sniffle. And all James could do was crawl into a bottle and hide there for a while.

By the time he crawled out, James was feeling decades older than his thirty-eight years, and the sleazy environs of Hubbard Street felt like home. Besides, that was the kind of neighborhood in which most of his business originated or ended, so he might as well make himself comfortable, he thought. He'd got his drinking under control again, except for the occasional bad night, and if he smoked too much, there was no one around to complain.

Unless someone like his recent visitor made the mistake of bothering him. He didn't trust the yuppie types—they wouldn't seek out someone in his part of town if they didn't want something sneaky pulled. He'd assumed the fictitious Bridget wanted something like that done, but now he wasn't so sure. She was just flaky enough to have gone for his name in the Yellow Pages. He didn't think anyone read Dashiel Hammett or Raymond Chandler anymore, but maybe his recent visitor was offbeat enough to do so.

Maybe it was his hangover. Maybe it was just his skills getting rusty. He told himself if he didn't discover who and what the so-called Bridget O'Shaunessy was by five o'clock, he'd take the job. At quarter past seven that night, he was driving his decrepit little Volkswagen Beetle up the winding driveway of the MacArthur mansion, cursing under his breath.

WHEN SALLY CRASH-LANDED her Alfa Romeo in front of her father's imposing mansion, she was out of her car in a bound, kicking her shoes off in the marble front hall and racing toward the kitchen at her usual breakneck speed. She seldom walked when she could run, drove when she could race, was quiet when she could talk. Energy bristled out of her like a jagged aura, and the vast, echoing emptiness of her father's house was enough to drive her crazy.

Jenkins was in the kitchen, his proper butler's coat off and his sleeves rolled up as he polished the silver that no one ever used. He didn't bother to look up. He'd been with the family since before Sally was born, and he knew that any noise would have to come from his rambunctious mistress.

"Any word?" she demanded breathlessly.

"None, miss. Were you expecting any?" Jenkins was concentrating on the coffee urn, but Sally wasn't fooled. He was just as worried as she was. The two of them had watched over Lucy since their mutual mother had dropped her off in San Francisco on one of her round-the-world jaunts and then simply failed to reappear. Together, they'd brought Lucy up, covered up for her minor peccadilloes and rescued her from her major ones. This latest mess, however, seemed to be proving beyond even their abilities.

"One can always hope." Sally plopped herself down on the stool next to Jenkins and took the heavy silver creamer and a polishing cloth. "Things didn't go too well with James Diamond."

"I can't imagine why you wanted to hire him. Wouldn't we be better off with Blackheart, Inc. or one of the bigger agencies?"

"The bigger agencies would tip Father off, and you know it. Besides, I know James Diamond is the man to help us. You wouldn't believe his office, Jenkins. It's like something out of an old 1930s movie. And he fits the part, or almost. If only he were a little bit older. And if he didn't wear sneakers," she added truthfully, staring at her reflection in the silver.

"I don't suppose that matters if he won't take the case. Who are you going to ask?"

"He's going to take the case, Jenkins. I simply haven't managed to talk him into it yet."

Jenkins looked up from the urn and his expression was severe. "We don't have much time, miss."

"I know, Jenkins, I know. I have to figure how to plan my next attack on the surly Mr. Diamond." She set the creamer down and reached for the sugar bowl. "Don't worry, you old darling, there's no reason why anyone has to find out the truth."

"If you say so," he said gloomily. "I wish I had your faith."

Sally grinned at him. "Frankly, so do I."

Jenkins turned his head at the sound of the electronic beep from the security system, and with a sigh, he went to the bank of sinks to wash his hands. "Someone just drove in."

Sally slipped off her stool, dumping the polishing cloth onto the floor. "I'll check and see who it is."

"Your father didn't spend a fortune on security systems without reason, Miss Sally. Don't be foolish enough to open the door without checking the security monitor."

She grinned. "I promise." She heard Jenkins's disapproving sniff as she headed back out into the hallway, bypassing her discarded shoes without a glance, secure in the fact that Jenkins knew well enough not to try to stop her. Besides, the entire place was absolutely riddled with security devices and cameras. He'd be watching any visitor, wanted or otherwise, in any place in the house, short of her bathroom or bedroom. And there'd be no one she'd be taking upstairs to her bedroom. Particularly not James Diamond.

She knew it was Diamond even before she opened the wide front door without even glancing at the video screen discreetly placed behind a curtain. She stood framed in the doorway, frowning slightly as his beatup VW pulled up the winding drive.

She waited as he unfolded his long body from the small car and started up the wide, marble steps. "You don't look surprised to see me," he said in that low, sexy rumble of a voice.

"You're a private detective. You wouldn't be worth hiring if you couldn't see through a simple alias and find me."

"Simple is right. You think I never saw *The Maltese Falcon?*"

She let her gaze slide down his length. He was wearing the same clothes he'd been wearing before—a dark rumpled suit, a flamboyant tie that was pulled loose and those damned sneakers. Still no fedora, but not bad. "You've seen *The Maltese Falcon,*" she acknowledged. "You couldn't be this close by accident."

"This close to what?"

"To the quintessential hard-boiled detective," she said. "I've already explained it to you—that's why I hired you. I just wish I could figure out what kind of car you should be driving. That Beetle won't do."

"You haven't hired me—I haven't said I'll take the case. And what do you mean by that crack about my car? I'll drive what I can afford, and that means a 1974 Super Beetle with the bottom rusting out."

"Of course I've hired you," Sally said, serenely self-confident. "Why else would you have gone to the trouble of finding out who I am and coming to the house? A nice black Packard would be the perfect car if this were fifty years ago, but..."

"No, it wouldn't. The Packard was a luxury car. No self-respecting private detective would be driving one. Philip Marlowe drove a Chrysler."

Her mouth dropped open. "Diamond, I'm in love with you," she breathed, starting toward him. "Any man who understands Philip Marlowe—"

He put up a restraining arm. "Keep your distance, Miss MacArthur. I didn't come out here to fulfill your kinky sexual fantasies."

Those words stopped her more effectively than his outstretched arm. Lauren Bacall would have slapped Humphrey Bogart, but then, Bogie would have slapped her back. So would James Diamond. Sally settled for glaring at him. "They're not kinky, and they're not sexual. If anything, I tend to romanticize things a bit, but you're not here to fill my bed. You're here to find my sister."

"Wrong. I'm here to tell you I'm still not taking the job."

Her momentary anger vanished in the sheer enjoyment of the situation, the bantering. Sally leaned back against the door frame, stretching one long leg across the other. She saw his gaze drawn to that bit of byplay and watched him quickly look away, over her shoulder. So he wasn't as immune to her long legs as she'd thought. There was definitely some hope in the situation.

"Any particular reason why you came all the way out here to tell me that? You already said as much before you kicked me out of your office. Didn't you think I got the message?"

"I think nothing short of a brick wall falling on you would make you get the message."

She glanced around her. "The walls around this place are in no danger of tumbling down, more's the pity. I'm sorry I overestimated your abilities, Diamond. I should have realized this would be too difficult—"

"Don't give me that crap. I won't fall for it. I could find your sister in twenty-four hours if I had a mind to do so."

"Then why don't you? You surely aren't overloaded with work, and I can pay you extremely well. You wouldn't be breaking any laws, you'd be doing everyone a favor, and you'd end up with your rent paid up and money besides. You could even buy a better pair of shoes."

"What makes you think my rent's not paid up?"

If she told him how much she knew about it, she'd have blown her last chance. "Lucky guess," she said. "Philip Marlowe was always behind on his rent."

"I'm not Philip Marlowe," Diamond snapped.

"No, you're not. He wouldn't refuse to help a lady in distress," she shot back.

"Is that how you see yourself? Someone in need of being rescued?"

"No. I need help, plain and simple, and I'm smart enough to ask for it, and to ask for it from someone who knows what he's doing. I just can't figure out why you're not smart enough to take the job."

He hesitated and she knew she had him. Had known it, as a matter of fact, since he drove up the winding driveway to her father's house, but now all that was left was preserving his dignity. She was willing to do that, as long as he'd do what she wanted.

"You can buy me a cup of coffee," he said finally, "and explain exactly what's going on with your sister and your ex-boyfriend. And maybe I'll consider it."

"But I already told you—"

"I want details. Every last little thing you can think of. And I'm expensive. Five hundred dollars a day plus expenses, with no satisfaction guaranteed."

"You forget that I had you checked out before I came calling. You usually charge between two and three hundred a day," she said. "Think you can take a rich girl for a ride?"

"Nope. My standard fee is three hundred dollars a day. I'm adding an extra two for the irritation factor."

"Irritation factor?"

"You annoy the hell out of me, lady," he said, and his eyes momentarily strayed to her long legs. "I figure that's worth a substantial bonus. Take it or leave it."

"Can I talk you into wearing a fedora?"

"I already have a hat."

"Would you get rid of those fancy running shoes?"

"Nope." He lit a cigarette, took a deep drag and blew the smoke in her direction. He used one of those old-fashioned lighters, silver, and the smell of lighter fluid, pungent in the afternoon air, mixed with the smoke of his filtered cigarette.

She sighed. "It's a deal. Come on in and meet Jenkins."

"I'm already here, miss." Jenkins appeared from behind the open door. He'd put his fancy coat back on and had slicked back his thinning white hair. He looked every inch the proper English butler, and Diamond stared at him in astonishment.

"You come from Central Casting too?" he drawled, moving past Sally's lounging figure into the huge front hallway.

"Mr. Isaiah doesn't approve of people smoking in the house, sir," Jenkins said with a faint cough.

"But Mr. Isaiah's not home. And if his ditzy daughter wants my help, she's going to have to put up with my cigarettes. She wanted a hard-boiled detective, and they usually come with a three-pack-a-day habit. Just be thankful I try to keep it to one and a half."

"Yes, sir," Jenkins said dutifully.

"Would you bring us some coffee into the library, Jenksy? Lots of cream and sugar for our guest—he's a major wuss when it comes to coffee."

"You're treading on thin ice, lady," Diamond muttered.

She smiled up at him, finally secure that she'd got him hooked. "And dig out the ashtrays. We're in for a long siege."

JAMES WANTED TO PLANT the toe of the sneakers his new client disdained into her saucy little butt as Sarah MacArthur led him into a walnut-paneled library that looked like something out of a movie set. He still couldn't understand why he'd come out to her place, why he'd ever allowed himself to be drawn into a conversation with this silly female and why he was finding himself agreeing to take a job that he knew was pure poison.

He didn't like doing irrational things. He was the only thing he counted on in this life, and when even he started acting strange, that was the time to worry. Maybe he was merely enamored of Sarah MacArthur's long legs. She looked like she had a luscious body underneath that baggy dress, but he was smart enough not to get involved with someone like her. Wasn't he? Or maybe he was just so damned burned-out and bored that he didn't mind playing Philip Marlowe for a few days. Especially since he was going to be well paid for the privilege.

"They're somewhere up north," Sarah was saying, flinging herself down onto the leather sofa and ignoring the fact that her skirt had slid halfway up her thigh. Or maybe she knew exactly what she was doing and how he was reacting to it, despite his poker face.

He stared into the cup of coffee Jenkins had provided him with. Fancy, wafer-thin cups, thick cream, probably fresh-ground beans. Now if only he had a shot of Scotch to go in there....

"Up north where?" he said, taking a drink. It wasn't coffee, it was the best thing he'd ever tasted. Even without the Scotch.

"Vinnie said his uncle used to go fishing at some lake near the Oregon border. Lake Judgment. He always promised to take me up there sometime."

"I don't suppose you went?"

"Heavens, no. I don't like fishing, I prefer the ocean to lakes, and by that time, I didn't care much for Vinnie, either. The thought of being holed up in some rustic cabin with him was enough to make me break the engagement."

"How many men have you been engaged to?"

"What's that got to do with my sister?" she demanded.

"Nothing. I'm just curious."

"Be curious about my sister. She's never been engaged before in her life. She has a more cavalier attitude about men. Love 'em and leave 'em. That's why I'm so worried about Vinnie. He's a little more old-fashioned. And she's never threatened to marry anyone before."

"Whereas you've been engaged six times in the last five years?" She glared at him. James liked her blue eyes, even at their frostiest.

"If you knew, why did you bother asking?"

"How do you define 'love 'em and leave 'em' as opposed to six engagements? I'm asking because of your sister," he added quickly, when it looked like she was going to object.

"At least I'm trying to make a commitment."

She drained her coffee with the same respect he gave the instant slop he was used to. *So much for the difference between the classes,* he thought. "Not doing too good a job at it, are you?" He wanted to linger over his own coffee, but she was already pouring herself another cup and he figured he'd better move fast if he didn't want her to hog it all. "So what makes you think that's where they'd go? Just because he wanted to take you up there doesn't mean he'd necessarily take your sister."

She hesitated, a bare second, long enough for James to know that she was about to lie to him. "Instinct," she said with enough promptness to fool most men. "Besides, it's a place to start. Got any better ideas?"

"Of course, I do. I'm a professional, remember? You can give me a list of Vinnie's friends and acquaintances, his full name and address, his place of business, and I can run a check in a matter of a couple of days."

"We don't have a couple of days."

"Why not?"

Again that infinitesimal hesitation, the shift in her wonderful blue eyes that signaled a lie. "Because my father's due back soon, and if he finds she's gone, and taken his damned sculpture, he's going to be furious. This time, she'll have gone too far, and I want to protect her from the consequences of her behavior."

"You can't spend your life protecting people. When they make mistakes, they need to pay for them. Otherwise, they'll never learn not to make mistakes." His voice was flat, matter-of-fact.

"Life isn't that simple, shamus," she said, looking at him over the rim of her coffee cup.

"Shamus?" he echoed, aghast. "Give me a break. Listen, lady, I expect you know as well as I do that I'm simply an ex-cop out to make a living the only way I know how."

"I love it when you talk that way," she murmured happily.

He glared at her. "I'm not Philip Marlowe or Sam Spade or any of your other lurid fantasies. I'm a private investigator. I investigate things that don't necessarily come under the jurisdiction of the local police, and I know how to be discreet and look the other way if need be. If the matter isn't too serious. But I'm not, repeat, *not,* something out of a 1930s novel."

"I was thinking more of a 1930s movie," she said, totally unrepentant.

"This is the 1990s."

"I'll work on it," she said, and he didn't believe her for one minute. "In the meantime, when can you start?"

"I still haven't said I'm starting."

"Diamond, you're sitting in my father's drawing room drinking Kona coffee and lecturing me about our professional relationship. Of course, you've taken the job. When can we leave for the mountains?"

"We?"

"You'll never find it without me."

"Lady, I work alone."

"Do you always argue this much with your clients?"

"Always," he said gloomily. "That's why I'm months behind on my rent."

"Well, I'm tolerant," she said with a breezy smile. "Let's leave first thing tomorrow morning. I need to get Lucy back before my father shows up. I don't quite know what he'd do if he found she'd taken the falcon."

"The falcon?" he echoed, filled with sudden foreboding. "This sculpture is a falcon?"

"Yup. Made of jade. But don't worry, it didn't come from Malta."

"Thank heaven for small favors. Where did it come from?"

"Tenth-century Manchuria."

"God help us. We're after the Manchurian falcon," he said with a groan.

"And I know you'll do a wonderful job finding it. While I take care of my sister."

"I'm going alone, Ms. MacArthur."

"Call me Sally," she said in dulcet tones. "And we'll see about that.

"We certainly will," James said grimly. Knowing with the unerring instinct that had saved his life more than a dozen times and solved countless unsolvable riddles that Sally MacArthur was going to be breathing down his neck if and when he found her damned jade falcon. If he had any sense at all, he'd drain his second cup of magnificent coffee, get up and walk away without another word, another question, even a moment's hesitation.

He looked at her, at those magnificent blue eyes, her charming, elfin face, her eagerness, and yes, the damned lies lurking behind the charm. And cursing himself for a major sucker, he leaned back against the sofa, lit another cigarette, and said, "Okay, tell me about Vinnie the Viper."

Chapter Three

Sally wasn't sure whether she was relieved or disappointed when James Diamond left her. If she hadn't come up with her contingency plan, on the off chance that he wouldn't take the case, then she would have been perfectly happy sitting there drinking coffee and breathing in the fragrant odor of his filtered cigarettes. That was another little touch she was uncertain about. Of course, any hard-boiled detective would smoke heavily. Diamond smoked Marlboros, but they were low tar and filtered. Bogey wouldn't have been caught smoking anything as wimpy as a filtered cigarette. But then, Bogey had died of lung cancer, hadn't he?

Maybe she'd work on Diamond to forego that little aspect of his persona. He could be hard-boiled without a cigarette dangling out of his mouth, couldn't he? They'd use her car tomorrow. The VW didn't suit his image or his long legs, and she'd simply inform him she didn't allow people to smoke in her car.

She could just imagine what he'd inform her right back. Maybe she'd better concentrate on one thing at a time. He didn't even want her coming with him when he headed up to Vinnie's fishing camp. She could fight the battle of the cigarettes later.

Though there was a good chance that either they wouldn't need to go at all or that it would simply be a quick jaunt to fetch her sister and the falcon. After all, she wouldn't be going ahead with her plan tonight if she didn't think it had a good chance of working. Salvatore Calderini was a human being, just like everybody else. He must have a decent side to which she could appeal. Sally had squirmed her way through the violent *Godfather* movies often enough to know that family was important to even the most hard-bitten criminal. She intended to fling herself on Don Salvatore's mercy. And if he resisted, she'd simply try a little bit of blackmail on her own.

If Diamond had given her half a chance, she would have told him about her plan. Maybe included him as a little backup protection. Except that he probably would have insisted on doing it his way, and besides, one of his many assets was the fact that he looked exactly like what he was. A tough, down-on-his luck ex-cop turned private detective. Albeit a too-handsome one. Salvatore Calderini and his army of henchmen—at least Sally assumed he had an army of henchmen—would see through Diamond immediately.

No, tonight would, of necessity, be a solo performance. If Don Salvatore refused to budge, then they'd do it the hard way. Go in search of Vinnie's rustic little fishing cabin and break up the romance of the century. Before it turned into the crime of the century.

It would have been nice if she'd been able to be honest with someone other than Jenkins, she thought as she stepped into her room-sized shower and let the tiny needles of water sluice down over her. If she felt she could trust Diamond enough to tell him everything. But she knew how he'd react to the unvarnished truth. He'd make her go to the police and the FBI, and probably the CIA, and if she refused, he'd go in her place. She didn't trust all those alphabet-soup organizations to do the right thing in such a tangled mess of a situation.

No, for the time being, she'd play her cards very close to her chest, starting with bearding the old lion in his den, she thought, pleased with her mixed metaphors. Salvatore Calderini spent his evenings at the Panama Lounge and Supper Club. She knew that from her short tenure as Vinnie's fiancée. She'd even met the old man once, at a family wedding that looked like something out of *The Godfather,* though she doubted he'd remember her.

She did know he had a soft spot for pretty young women, and she had every intention of dressing to the nines. If she couldn't appeal to his heart, maybe she could appeal to his aging vanity. Or if worse came to worst, for her sister's sake and her own culpability in the current situation, maybe she could appeal to his lust.

The turquoise-beaded dress was too tight on her, purchased after she'd just emerged from a bout with Slimfast. That nice ten pounds hadn't stayed off for long, and soon, she was back to her own pleasantly rounded form, but she kept the dress on the off chance that maybe she'd manage to flog the weight off again. She could zip it up, just barely, and it made her breasts plump out over the low neckline. The dress clung so tightly, it made her figure look far more hourglass than it was, and the hem crept up higher than it was supposed to go, exposing another two inches of her long legs. With any luck, Don Salvatore would be drooling.

Of course, there was always the possibility that he'd be as immune to her as James Diamond. No, scratch that. Diamond wasn't immune to her. She'd seen the flicker in his dark blue eyes, the slight twisting of his mobile mouth. He'd noticed her legs, he'd noticed whatever admirable attributes she had. He'd just been tough enough to discard whatever wayward attraction had crept in.

Just as well. She wasn't Lauren Bacall, even though she wore her hair in a page boy and had a husky voice. She was a little too rounded, and much too energetic. Still, it was fun to fantasize. Maybe once they got the mess with Lucy settled, she could talk Diamond into a Fedora and wing tips. She could wear great-aunt Betty's suit, and they could go dancing.

Hell would freeze over first, Sally thought, grabbing her beaded purse and heading out the front door. James Diamond was determined to resist her, and it would be a waste of time trying to break down that resistance. Besides, why should she want to? Apart from the fact that he was sinfully handsome and seemed to fulfill all her deepest fantasies.

She shook her head, pausing beneath the light on the front steps. Tonight wasn't a night to think about fantasies. Tonight was a night to make one last-ditch effort to rescue Lucy from the consequences of her folly. Not to mention the consequences of Sally's folly. She could fantasize when she got safely back in bed.

She ran down the steps, jumped into her Alfa and started the engine. It made its usual brave roar, then settled down into a sensual purr. Maybe she could talk Diamond into using her car, after all. What man in his right mind could resist an Alfa Romeo?

JAMES SANK DOWN LOWER in the sagging front seat of his VW and stubbed out his cigarette as Sally sped past him. That was one hell of a car, he thought with a trace of envy. He hadn't thought much about cars since he was seventeen years old, but a hunter-green, late-model Alfa Romeo was enough to engender most adolescent fantasies.

So, for that matter, was the woman driving it. He'd had a good look at her as she paused beneath the light over the front steps of her father's mansion. That dress would have been banned in Boston. He hadn't realized she was so voluptuous. She'd made certain he'd noticed her legs, but the rest of her had been shrouded in loose-fitting clothes. It was just as well. He'd already had a hard enough time ignoring those legs. If he'd been as aware of the rest of her, there would have been no chance of him seeing through the web of lies she'd spun him.

He wasn't sure if he could tell where the truth ended and the lies started. He expected they were all twisted together, and unraveling them would be one hell of a chore. He already knew her well enough to guess she had something planned for tonight, and he'd simply decided to sit and watch for her.

It had taken her maybe an hour and a quarter to go from upscale debutante to the hot little number who'd just squealed out of the curving driveway. He was going to be disappointed as hell if he found she was simply going out on a date, maybe on the prowl for fiancé number seven.

But he didn't think so. He counted on his instincts—they'd saved his butt more times than he cared to remember, and he trusted them implicitly. Lying Miss Sally was up to no good. Something rash and dangerous, and if he didn't look out for her, she was going to end up in deep trouble. Worse than she already was.

He shook his head in disgust as he sped after her, his VW making its usual chirping noise. If he still had any doubts as to the level of his involvement, he might as well accept the fact that he'd jumped in, hook, line and sinker. She'd asked him to help her find her sister and the jade falcon and bring them both back. She hadn't asked him to play nursemaid and/or bodyguard.

Within a couple of blocks of her destination, he knew where she was going and he cursed, pounding on the steering wheel in impotent fury. It couldn't be coincidence that the Panama Lounge and Supper Club was nearby. The moment she'd mentioned Vinnie the Viper's full name, Vincenzo Calderini, James had been filled with misgivings. Salvatore Calderini was becoming a name to reckon with, an éminence grise of the San Francisco underworld. Word on the street had it that he was involved with the Chinese in a new gambling operation. Not the San Francisco Chinese, but the real thing, a branch of mainland criminals who were eager to rake in some profits from the New World. Salvatore was doing his best to make that happen, and the San Francisco police were doing their best to stop it. So far, Salvatore had the winning hand.

There was no way James was going to get into the Panama looking like he did. And there was no way he was going to simply go home and ignore the fact that idiotic Miss MacArthur had just walked into a mess of trouble. He was going to have to do something about it, and fast. Before things moved to a point at which even he couldn't fix it.

No one knew San Francisco better than James Diamond. He knew where he could get a dark tie and a pair of size-ten, narrow-width shoes within a few minutes, not to mention an electric razor to shave the stubble he'd been ignoring for several days. Within half an hour of the moment Sally MacArthur had sashayed her beaded hips through the front doors of the Panama Lounge, he was after her, hoping no one would have the misfortune of remembering where and when they might have seen his face before.

He knew half the people working there. It was a busy night and the place was crowded, a faceless blur of high rollers and big spenders mixed in with insensate tourists and a few slumming yuppies. The security people, the bartenders and most of the waiters had police records he could practically recite from memory. At the moment, they were all too busy to notice him. Even if they did, each and every one of them had been arrested often enough that they wouldn't necessarily remember that at least once, they'd been arrested by James Diamond.

He'd been in the Panama before, on a vice bust. They'd cleaned it up a bit, and most people wouldn't know that there was high-stakes gambling going on one floor above the big dining room. But then, he wasn't most people. They'd added a band and a dance floor, probably hoping to drown out the occasional shouts of triumph that sometimes filtered down from a craps game, or the thud of a body hitting the carpeting. He squinted through the smoke, trying to avoid the maître d' bearing down on him. He'd never arrested Tony the Cannon Delmaggio, but that didn't mean James didn't recognize him and know his rap sheet better than he knew his mother's birthday. And there was a damned good chance Tony would know James.

His eyes caught the glitter of blue beading and he focused, suddenly intent. She was at a table in front, on the edge of the dance floor, too near the band. And she wasn't alone.

Even from a distance, James could see the carefully controlled panic in those terrific eyes of hers. He could see the rapid rise and fall of her chest as it tried to squeeze out of the too-small dress. And he wished to hell he hadn't left his gun in the glove compartment of the VW.

"As I live and breathe, if it isn't Detective Diamond," Tony the Cannon said in his ear, an unpleasant smile wreathing his unpleasant face. "To what do we owe the pleasure of your company tonight? And all dressed up? Surely this isn't a social call?"

James turned slowly, giving Tony an icy glare that had quelled many lesser souls. "You're not as up on things as you ought to be, Tony," he said mildly. "You should know I quit the force more than a year and a half ago."

"So I heard. I just don't believe everything everyone tells me."

"Smart man. This time it's the truth. I work on my own."

"Doing what?"

"This and that. Do I have to pass a test to get a table, Tony?"

"I don't know that you're welcome around here." Tony's tuxedo was tailor-made. For some reason, it didn't seem to fit as well as it had a few moments ago. James noticed the perfect manicure on Tony's hands as he tugged at his collar. He didn't trust a man with a manicure. But then, there'd never been any question that he'd trust a jumped up hoodlum like Tony.

"Discrimination, Tony? On what grounds?"

Tony's instant smile exposed two rows of badly discolored teeth. "Don't get me wrong, copper. Of course, we're happy to have you here. We just wondered why you decided to grace us with your presence tonight. And where's your date?"

"Who's 'we,' Tony?"

"The boss. And me."

James nodded. "That's what I thought. As a matter of fact, I'm meeting my date here. I believe she already arrived. Don't do it." His hand shot out, grabbing Tony in a vise-like grip before the man could make a move. "You know as well as I do where she is. But I expect your boss doesn't realize she had any backup. She does, Tony. And you know I can be a mean son of a bitch if you get in my way."

It took a fair amount to scare a hardnose like Tony. James was pleased to recognize that he still had the ability to do so. Tony nodded, swallowing. "You mean the babe in the blue dress."

"I mean the babe in the blue dress," James echoed. "Am I going to have any trouble taking her out of here?"

"No, man. At least, I don't think so. I don't know what's been going on between her and the boss, but if you get her before she puts her foot in her mouth, you should be okay. I won't stop you."

"Even if Salvatore orders you to?"

Tony shrugged, an edgy look in his eyes. "Hey, man, I'm just doing my job."

"I can do my job, too," James said, very softly. "And you know it."

"I know it."

James released him. "Now you be easy, Tony, and let me take care of things. Salvatore will understand that you weren't able to deck me." Tony was approximately four inches shorter than James's own six-foot-two height, and twenty pounds lighter. He was well armed, but he was also a convicted felon. There was no way he'd flash a gun around even a retired police officer unless his life depended on it. James was counting on that.

"Hey, man, I'm cool. Just take the bitch out of here."

James's eyes narrowed. "Lady, Tony. She's a lady."

"Sure, Diamond. Sure thing." He backed away, into a waiter, almost precipitating a crash.

James looked back at the table. Sally looked like a butterfly, pined there by an avid collector. He'd never seen the estimable Salvatore Calderini up close. He was about to get his chance.

THIS, SALLY THOUGHT, was definitely a dumb move. It had all made perfect sense when she'd been planning it. All she had to do was bat her eyelashes and plead prettily, and Salvatore Calderini would be moved to humanity.

A nice enough idea, but she hadn't seen the man sitting next to her up close.

She'd been expecting Marlon Brando, of course. Someone avuncular, faintly sinister but approachable. When Don Salvatore arrived at her table, she'd been momentarily relieved. And then frightened.

He was a small, spare man with thinning white hair combed over his scalp, slightly bulging eyes and a curiously childlike face. Impeccably dressed and groomed, he sat down beside her at the table and listened with utmost courtesy as she outlined her request.

Even to her own ears, it had sounded disconcertingly brash. "Let me understand this," Calderini had said in his eerily soft voice, once she'd finished. "You want me to call Vincenzo home, have him break off his relationship with your sister and relinquish all interest in the falcon. In return for this, you offer absolutely nothing. Was there anything else?"

"I didn't say I'd offer absolutely nothing. I promise I wouldn't mention this unfortunate incident to anyone. Like the police." The moment the words were out of her mouth, she realized she'd made a tactical error. Don Salvatore had been amused, perhaps even considering her request. Now that she'd threatened him, she'd sealed her own fate.

"You're trying to blackmail me, Miss MacArthur?" he asked softly. "You're a very foolish little girl to think you could do such a thing. I'm afraid I'm going to be forced to teach you a lesson." To her horror, he placed his hand on her knee, under the damask-covered table.

She squirmed away, but there wasn't anywhere to go on the banquette seating, and his small hand was like a taloned claw, squeezing into her flesh. "Such a pretty little thing you are," he murmured, ignoring the fact that she was several inches taller and a few ripe pounds heavier than he was. "I never realized what a looker you are. I don't know why Vinnie prefers your little sister when he could have had an armful like you."

"I dumped Vinnie."

Salvatore frowned. "No one dumps Vinnie. Not unless he wants to be dumped. You're smarter than your sister, that's the problem. Though you haven't shown much sign of it in coming here tonight and threatening me. I think we'll go back to my office."

"I'm not going anywhere."

"Of course you are." His fingers were massaging her silk-covered leg, and she vainly tried to slap his hand away and pull the hem down at the same time. "We'll have a little champagne supper and I'll teach you a thing or two about Calderini men."

"Please..." Sally hated that frightened little moan. She wasn't used to being frightened.

"There you are." If ever there was a deus ex machina, the man who suddenly appeared at the table was it. James Diamond wore a dark tie and dark shoes, and he'd even managed to shave. He looked devastatingly attractive and very dangerous. It didn't matter how attractive he was at that moment. To Sally, even Bigfoot would have been gorgeous. "I thought you were going to wait for me."

"I...I..."

Diamond's hand was on her arm, pulling her up from the banquette and toward him. Salvatore's hand was still on her leg, and for a moment, Sally wondered dizzily whether they were going to have a tug of war, yanking her apart like a rag doll. "Let go of her, Mouse."

Salvatore's face froze into an angry glare and his fingers still dug into Sally's knee. "Who the hell do you think you are, coming into my place and assaulting my guests?"

"She's not your guest, she's mine," Diamond snapped. "This is the last time I'm telling you. Let go of her."

One of the elegantly dressed waiters leaned over and whispered something in Salvatore Calderini's ear. The old man's face took on an even more glacial expression, but the clawlike grip on her knee loosened and Sally scuttled out from behind the table with indecent haste, half hauled by Diamond's grip on her bare arm.

She was going to have an interesting set of bruises tomorrow, she thought, tugging uselessly at the bulging neckline and climbing hemline of her stupid beaded dress.

"You should have told me you had protection, little lady," Salvatore said in a gentle voice. "I would have had you dumped in a back alley instead of wasting my time with you."

"I still want to make a deal...." she said breathlessly, but Diamond was already dragging her away.

"No deal," Salvatore said flatly.

"No deal," Diamond said, just as immovable.

She had one last glance at the old man at the table as Diamond dragged her through the maze of crowded tables. Don Salvatore was sitting there, staring after her, a phalanx of dark-suited men behind him. Sally knew that all he had to do was snap his fingers and she and Diamond wouldn't be taking one step farther. A sudden, bone-shaking cold swept over her, and she began to shiver.

Diamond was paying no attention to her sudden reaction. He simply continued dragging her out of the place, not even bothering to look back at the very dangerous bunch of men he was leaving behind.

The night was cool, with a damp fog off the bay hanging thick in the air. She had no idea where her Alfa was, and obviously, Diamond didn't care. He was pulling her down the sidewalk in the direction of his beat-up VW when he noticed her hanging back.

He stopped, turning to stare at her with obvious impatience. "What the hell's your problem now?" he demanded. "If you're worried about your car, don't be. We have more important things to deal with."

She opened her mouth to deny it, but to her horror words refused to form themselves. "I—I—I—" she stammered. She could feel hot, wet tears begin to tumble down her face. She never cried. She certainly wasn't going to cry in front of Sam Spade.

The tears splashed down the front of her cleavage, but she was beyond trying to tug it up. She was shivering, her teeth chattering, and all she wanted to do was curl up in a little ball and howl like a baby.

Diamond took one look at her, let out a long-suffering sigh and scooped her up in his arms. The sheer romantic gallantry of such an act effectively shocked her into a momentary calm, but by the time he'd angled her into the front seat of the Beetle and started down the road, she was shaking and crying again.

The drive back to the MacArthur mansion was endless. He turned the heater on full blast, but it failed to warm her. He handed her a wad of napkins filched from a fast-food restaurant, but they couldn't stem the tears. By the time they pulled up in front of the huge house, Sally was so distraught and so disgusted with herself, she could barely move.

Once more, he scooped her up into his arms, moving up the wide front steps with seeming effortlessness. Jenkins was there, and Sally caught a brief glimpse of his worried face as Diamond sailed past him heading for the long, curving stairs.

"Where's her bedroom?" he demanded, starting up.

"Third door on the right," Jenkins replied. "Shall I bring her anything?"

"A brandy," Diamond said, panting slightly from the exertion. Sally immediately regretted the cheesecake she'd had for lunch, but the anxiety was finally beginning to vanish, and she was starting to enjoy herself tremendously.

He didn't bother to turn on her light when he kicked open the door. He headed straight to the huge, canopy bed, pausing there for a moment with her beaded body still held tight in his arms.

She looked up at him, eyes swimming with tears, her lips damp and trembling and slightly parted.

"What are you looking at me like that for?" he demanded irritably.

"I don't just like detective movies," she said. "I'm also quite partial to *Gone With the Wind.*"

She couldn't believe it, the man actually smiled. It was a revelation in his darkly handsome face, and she told herself that if she was really as ditsy as people believed, she would have fallen in love with him at that moment.

"Yeah," he said, "but you're forgetting one thing. I'm Philip Marlowe, not Rhett Butler." And he dropped her onto the bed.

A moment later, he was gone. No good-night kiss, but then, Sally didn't necessarily need one. No man had ever been strong enough or forceful enough to carry her up to bed. It was more than promising. It was downright hopeful. With a blissful sigh, she snuggled down into the bed, wondering what Diamond would look like dressed like Rhett Butler.

Chapter Four

James passed the butler on the stairs as Jenkins headed toward Sally's room with a dark glass of brandy on a silver tray. James scooped up the crystal snifter, drained the brandy and set the glass back down with a snap. "That was for me," he said.

Jenkins's severe face showed just the glimmer of a smile. "Does Miss Sally need anything?"

"Not that I know of. It wouldn't hurt to check." He watched the butler disappear at the top of the stairs. He was in a hell of a bad mood, and he wasn't quite sure why. Part of it had to be the certain knowledge that Sally MacArthur was lying to him. Another was the fact that this simple little time waster was going to be a bit more complicated than he'd first imagined. Earning his five hundred a day wasn't going to be as easy as he'd thought. Not only did he have to deal with the dizzy female upstairs, he also had to run up against a crowd of people who had every reason to hold their own assorted grudges. The Calderini family wasn't as dangerous as some of their East Coast counterparts, but it wouldn't do to underestimate them, either.

There was one other, more basic reason for James's rotten mood, and that was the way Miss Sally MacArthur felt in his arms, the way she looked up at him when he held her over that ridiculous bed. If he'd been a different man, in different circumstances, he wouldn't have left quite so quickly. Hell, he might not have left at all.

It didn't do any good to start thinking that way. He made it a hard and fast rule never to get involved with a client, and he certainly wasn't dumb enough to get involved with someone like Sally MacArthur. Even if her legs were outrageously wonderful, her mouth delicious looking, her body...

"Hell and damnation," he muttered aloud, sprinting down the stairs two at a time in his hurry to get away from temptation. He'd just reached the bottom when the telephone rang.

He was going to ignore it, figuring Sally had to have a phone in her bedroom. If she did, it was either not working or a separate line, for the phone kept up its insistent buzz. James headed for the door, then stopped, turning back and grabbing the phone on a last-minute impulse.

"Yeah?" he barked into it, not wasting time with amenities.

"Is this the MacArthur residence?" a fairly stuffy voice demanded.

"Who wants to know?"

"Isaiah MacArthur, that's who!"

The ogre Sally wanted to protect her sister from. "You were supposed to be in the Far East," Diamond said accusingly.

"I got back early. To whom am I speaking?"

James considered it for a moment. "James Diamond. I'm a friend of your daughter's."

"Which one?"

"Which friend?"

"Which daughter?"

That didn't sound like a man who was too hard on his unwanted stepdaughter. "Sally's friend."

"Oh, God, not another fiancé," Isaiah moaned.

"We're not engaged."

"Not yet," he said in a resigned voice. "But you will be. That girl collects fiancés the way I collect jade. Could I speak to her, please?"

"She's gone to bed."

"What about Jenkins?"

"He's not around."

"Then what are you still doing there?"

"I was on my way out the door," James replied. "You want me to track Jenkins down?"

"Damn it, I need a ride home from the airport. I've got terminal jet lag, twelve pieces of luggage and the worst case of Montezuma's revenge this side of Acapulco."

"No problem. I'll be there in twenty minutes." The decision was automatic. If Sally was going to lie to him, maybe he could ferret out some of the truth from her monster of a father, a man who sounded far more reasonable than she'd suggested.

The other man hesitated. "Are you sure it wouldn't be too much trouble?"

"If you think I'm going to end up being engaged to Sally, I might as well meet my future father-in-law."

"Oh, she never marries 'em. As a matter of fact, I think she gets engaged as a way of ending her relationships. I'll be at Gate 53 in the Pan Am terminal. The sooner you get here, the happier I'll be."

"I'm on my way."

San Francisco airport was relatively empty at a little past midnight. James walked past the sourdough racks and bookstores without even glancing at them, intent on finding Isaiah MacArthur and discovering exactly what Sally was covering up. The old man had sounded bad tempered and fretful, but not the oppressive ogre Sally had described. James had every intention of scoping him out, and if necessary, explaining to him exactly what was happening with his wayward family.

There was only one man waiting at the Pan Am counter, and James had a moment to survey him and quickly discard any notion of telling him what Sally was up to before he crossed the industrial carpeting.

He was quite old and frail looking. Of course, the digestive problems he'd picked up while traveling would be bound to take their toll, but James realized the man was easily seventy years old and not in the best of health. He glanced up at James as he approached, then looked away, dismissing him.

"Mr. MacArthur?" James said with more courtesy than he usually bothered to exhibit.

The old man looked up again, his faded blue eyes narrowing in disbelief. "You couldn't be my daughter's latest fiancé!"

"I told you, we aren't engaged."

MacArthur's perusal was leisurely. "You're certainly a far cry from the type she usually attracts. She tends to like 'em a bit on the pansy side as far as I'm concerned. How did you two meet?"

James blinked. "At a party." The lie was automatic, instinctive.

"Whose party?"

"Want to wait till we get to the car before you give me the third degree?" James drawled. "Or do I need to past muster before you do me the great honor of allowing me to drive you home at 1:23 in the morning?"

MacArthur cackled. "Yup, you're a far cry from Sally's usual wimps. You might just be the making of her."

"I have no intention of making her."

"Oh, really?" The old man managed to look both exhausted and arch at the same time. "Maybe you're a pansy after all."

James wasn't in the best of moods. For one thing, he needed a drink. For another, he needed a cigarette and there was no smoking in the San Francisco airport. For another, he was feeling tired, restless and edgy. And he couldn't get this old man's feckless daughter out of his mind.

"Old man," he said with specious patience, "I'm going to give you to the count of ten to start out toward the car with me...." His voice trailed off as an airport cart zoomed in their direction, beeping needlessly in the deserted terminal. MacArthur struggled to his feet, swaying slightly, and James told himself he didn't feel the slightest bit guilty as he quickly put a supporting hand beneath his frail arm.

"Want a ride, hotshot?" MacArthur demanded as he settled onto the seat of the cart. "Or are you going to jog along side to show me how macho you are?"

"You're going to give me your claim checks, I'm going to pick up your baggage and meet you at the south entrance," James said in a deceptively calm voice. He glanced at the driver. "That okay with you?"

The driver shrugged, clearly bored. "What else have I got to do?"

James cursed all the way to the baggage claim. MacArthur wasn't kidding; he had twelve pieces of luggage. Four of them were matched leather suitcases. The rest were boxes and bundles wrapped with the excessive string that seemed to characterize the packages of all old men James knew, whether they were multimillionaires like MacArthur or retired cops in Oakland. He loaded everything on a cart, wheeled it out to the VW and used every bit of his ingenuity to squeeze it all in. By the time he got to the south entrance of the Pan Am terminal, more than half an hour had passed and he expected MacArthur to greet him with a tirade.

Instead, MacArthur and the cart driver were smoking cigarettes on the front sidewalk, deep in conversation about the Oakland A's. "Should you be smoking those things?" Diamond demanded as he climbed out of his car.

MacArthur was eyeing the VW with deep misgivings. "You actually expect me to ride in that thing?" he demanded. "Why didn't you bring the Bentley?"

"Because I thought you needed to see how the other half lives." James helped the old man up, filching the cigarette from him and dropping it in the road.

"Hey, that was the first cigarette I've had in days," MacArthur protested.

"And I'm sure you weren't supposed to have that." James palmed a generous tip to the operator before heading around to the driver's seat.

"Not according to my daughter," MacArthur said with a sniff. "But that's not your problem, is it? The state of my health? If anything, you should hope that I kick the bucket. Then Sally and Lucy will inherit a tidy little piece of change."

"Since Sally never marries her fiancés, I don't think that will matter," James said, heading out of the airport.

"True enough. But you're not her fiancé. I find that a very hopeful sign. Maybe she'll just skip a step and marry you without an engagement."

James shuddered. "I don't think so. What are you leaving to Lucy?"

"Fancy her, do you? Forget it. She's fallen in love with that quasigangster that Sally dropped."

James glanced at the man beside him. "How do you know that?"

"Hell, I know a lot more than my daughters give me credit for. It makes 'em happy to think they're keeping me in the dark, and I want to make them happy."

Interesting, James thought. "I thought Sally was your only child. Isn't she going to inherit the bulk of your estate?"

The old man's eyes glittered in the darkened car. "Lucy's been around so long, I tend to forget I didn't breed her. She and Sally split the pot. There's more than enough for both of them, and neither one is what I'd call a down-to-earth, practical type. They need the cushion of a little money."

This was the judgmental old devil who'd send this unwanted stepdaughter to jail, James thought, wishing Sally MacArthur were there so he could wring her neck. Of course, her neck and a great deal of her chest were exposed in that damned beaded dress, and if he put his hands on her, they probably wouldn't end up in the vicinity of her throat.

He cleared his own throat as he pulled up to the toll booth. "Fond of them, are you?"

"What father wouldn't be?" MacArthur demanded, blinking slightly as James opened the tiny glove compartment and pulled out his stash of tokens.

Too late, he remembered he'd left his gun in there. MacArthur was staring at it as though he'd found a tarantula sitting in front of him, and James shut the little door with a snap.

"I've got a license for it," he said.

"What else have you got a license for?"

"I beg your pardon?" They were heading toward the city, the VW whistling away as it picked up speed.

"I should have known Sally wouldn't have the good sense to pick a real man. You're either a weasel like Vincent, or you're on the other side of the law. Either way, I don't like it."

"I'm not police."

"No, but you were, weren't you?"

James didn't bother to deny it. "You got any reason to avoid the police?"

MacArthur cackled. "Hell, boy, I've broken my share of laws along the way. Show me a rich man who hasn't. But most of my crimes are petty ones. I can't imagine you'd be after me. So I guess it must have something to do with my daughters."

"I'm not a cop," James said again.

"Are you going to tell me who and what you are?"

For a moment, James actually considered it. Client confidentiality was a basic tenet in his business, but he was also a maverick enough to bend the rules when need be. That particular trait had been responsible both for his success in the police department and his ultimate undoing.

But nothing would be accomplished by telling Isaiah MacArthur exactly what was going on. It would make Sally so mad, she'd fire him, and there was no way she could go after her sister on her own. Her precipitate meeting with the senior Calderini that night was proof of it.

And there was no way this elderly, querulous man would be able to help her, much as he doubtless thought he could.

James couldn't toss Sally MacArthur to the wolves known as the Calderini clan. Nor could he abandon this fractious old man or even the unknown but flighty Lucy. At least, not yet.

He'd give it a few days. Five, he thought at random. Five days to track down Vinnie Calderini and his upscale fiancée. Five days to find out where Sally's lies ended and the truth began. Five days to do his best for the MacArthur clan and make enough money to keep Pacific Gas off his back.

"I told you who I am. My name's James Diamond and I'm a friend of your daughter Sally." He used the voice most effective at stopping impertinent questions.

He was dealing with a millionaire, not a two-bit street thug. "What do you do for a living?"

"This and that."

"This and that what?"

James glanced at the fuming old man. "Actually I'm a fortune hunter," he said. "I'm after your daughter for her inheritance."

MacArthur sniffed in patent disbelief. "I'll just have to ask her myself. Not that she'll tell me the truth. That girl tells more stories than Sheherezade. Don't know where she got such an imagination from. Probably her mother."

"Speaking of which, where is her mother?"

MacArthur snorted. "You don't need to worry about having to share my fortune. Marietta is out of the running. She's been through so many husbands since she dumped me that she probably doesn't even remember she ever married me. She's off in Europe somewhere—doesn't stay put more than a week at a time. I think the last time the girls heard from her was Christmas 1989." The VW pulled to a stop and the old man looked around him in surprise as he recognized his own imposing mansion. "This little car does pretty good for something that sounds like a cricket and rides like an oversized roller skate. Come in and join me for a drink."

James preferred to drink alone. He'd taken to sitting in the dark, at his desk, quietly making inroads on a bottle of first-class Scotch. When he had to switch to second-rate, he knew he'd be in trouble. That time was coming closer and closer.

"Not tonight," he said, and was surprised to find he regretted his decision. "I'm making an early start tomorrow."

"Where are you heading?"

"I was planning to go fishing up near the Oregon border," he said, glad he didn't really have to lie. He was going fishing, all right, but for Vinnie Calderini and his hostage.

"I see," MacArthur said. "Sally going with you?"

"Not if I can help it."

The old man laughed. "How the hell are you going to find Calderini's fishing camp without her along? Besides, she's like a big, fat, juicy tick. Once she catches hold, she's not likely to let go."

"Old man, is there anything you don't know?" James demanded, exasperated.

"Not much." Jenkins was opening the door with solicitous care, and MacArthur gave him a playful jab in the shoulder. "The girls are in trouble, I take it."

"I couldn't say, sir," Jenkins said dolefully, helping him out of the car.

"Won't say, you mean. What do you think of Diamond here?"

Jenkins glanced at him over the rounded top of the Beetle, and James found himself suddenly curious as to the butler's opinion.

"He'll do, sir," Jenkins said briefly.

Faint praise, but MacArthur seemed satisfied. "That's what I thought, Horace. We'll get Sally settled yet."

"Wait just a damned minute..." James said, horrified.

The two elderly men were making their way slowly up the broad front steps. "Just leave the luggage on the porch, sir," Jenkins called over his shoulder, ignoring James's protest. "I'll deal with it later."

"Not all the luggage, fool!" MacArthur protested. "That small box carries the most beautiful jade peregrine I've ever seen. Not as fine a piece as my falcon, but she'll make a good companion piece."

Once more, Jenkins's eyes met James's, and a silent warning was passed. So the old man didn't know quite as much as he thought he did. "I'll leave it in the hall," James said quietly.

JAMES HEADED STRAIGHT for his office. He had more food in the tiny little refrigerator there than he had in his one-bedroom inefficiency apartment near the Embarcadero, and his bottle of Scotch was residing in the bottom drawer of his desk. Besides, he needed to make a few phone calls before he took off toward the Oregon border, and the people he intended to call were the type to work all night and sleep all day.

As far as he knew, the Calderini family didn't go in for cold-blooded murder, probably for two reasons. Number one, it attracted too much attention. Number two, their position was secure. There were no incipient gang wars. The Calderinis knew how to keep things prosperous and well-ordered, and the various territories in the Bay Area were well-defined. They didn't encroach on the tong districts in Chinatown, and the Chinese gangs left the Calderinis strictly alone.

Which didn't explain the Calderinis' involvement with the mainland Chinese who wanted a piece of San Francisco action. Why were they dealing with the Calderinis, not the tongs? He hadn't paid much attention—it wasn't any of his business anymore, except if a case happened to overlap. Which certainly seemed to be the situation. Isaiah MacArthur collected Oriental jade, Vincent Calderini had run off with a MacArthur daughter and a piece from MacArthur's collection, and there was no reason on this earth why the Calderini family would be interested in jade. Unless they were planning on handing it over to the their new Asian confederates. James couldn't imagine why the mainland Chinese crime lords would be interested, but he'd bet his last ounce of Scotch that they were behind it.

So why wasn't Sally telling him the truth? She'd spun him a bunch of lies and half truths, and the only thing he knew for certain was that Lucy MacArthur, if that was even her last name, and the Manchurian falcon were off somewhere with Vinnie the Viper.

He could hear the distant scuffle of rats as he moved through his darkened office building, and the slightly noisier movements from the two-legged variety that roamed the halls after midnight. Frankie was probably out and about, drumming up trade. He just damned well better not be drumming it up in James's office.

The third floor was relatively quiet, and James wrinkled his nose as he let himself into his stale-smelling office. The air was filled with ancient cigarettes, and in self-defense, he lit a fresh one, inhaling with a grimace. He'd spent so much time running around after his client tonight that he hadn't smoked in hours. Even now, he could still remember the exotic fragrance that had clung to Sally's lush skin. Something rich, far from subtle and frankly erotic.

There'd been nothing erotic about the fear in her eyes when he'd first appeared at the table. Nothing erotic about her obvious panic. He owed old man Calderini something for that. Sooner or later, he'd get the chance to put the fear of God into the head of the Calderini family. He'd take a great deal of pleasure in doing just that.

In the meantime, he needed a stiff shot of whiskey and a few quiet minutes on the telephone. And then just enough sleep on his sagging old couch to make sure he'd be able to head out toward Oregon by first light. Long before Sally MacArthur crawled out of that ridiculous bed with the soft white sheets.

He groaned, picturing her all too vividly lying in those sheets. He'd told her she was trouble from the moment she walked into his office.

He was beginning to realize just how much trouble she really was. And to know that he'd be damned lucky if he got out of this with everything still in working order. Particularly his armor-plated heart.

Chapter Five

Coffee. Rich, delicious coffee wafting under his sleeping nostrils. There was nothing, absolutely nothing, that smelled better than fresh-brewed coffee. Not single-malt Scotch, not fresh-baked bread, not roast turkey on Thanksgiving. Not even that teasing, tantalizingly erotic scent that clung to Sally MacArthur's ripe skin, though that came a close second.

The coffee he was smelling through the rapidly disappearing fogs of sleep had to be the best coffee he ever smelled. Probably because it came accompanied by the tang of Sally's perfume....

His eyes shot open, immediately focusing on long, stockinged legs. She had her back to him, and she was leaning over his desk. For a moment, he allowed himself a brief, lustful appreciation of her wonderful legs and ripe curves. By the time she turned around, a mug of coffee in each hand, he had his own reaction back under control.

"What the hell are you doing here?" he grumbled, giving vent to his irritation and the headache that was plaguing him. Though this time it was more the result of too little sleep than too much Scotch. "And how the hell did you get in? I keep the doors locked. And what the hell...?"

"That's three hells," she said primly, squatting down beside him. The skirt hiked up, exposing even more of her legs, and he almost groaned. "You forgot to lock the door last night, and I'm here to bring you coffee and generally make your day start a little easier. We have a lot to do, and Lake Judgment is at least six hours' drive, most of it on twisty back roads where you can't do more than forty without risking life and limb. I could tell that you didn't have a secretary, so I thought I'd show up here with coffee and doughnuts and see if I couldn't put you in a better mood. You aren't really going to smoke that, are you?"

He'd already lit his first cigarette of the day. He glared at her. "Yeah, I'm really going to smoke that." He took the coffee from her, swallowing half of it in one gulp. It was too hot, a marvel in itself, but he didn't even flinch.

Clearly, Sally decided, now was not the time to fight the battle of the coffin nails. "I checked the weather report, and it's supposed to be rainy up north. I thought we should get an early start, so as soon as you shower and change, we can head out. I brought my car—it's newer and faster and it probably gets better gas mileage, and besides, every man I've ever known has wanted to drive my Alfa, so I decided that you might be more agreeable to having me come along if you could..."

"Shut up!" James roared suddenly, slopping some of the coffee onto his knee and burning himself.

She subsided, staring at him with those huge eyes of hers. "I suppose you're one of those people who wake up grumpy," she said in a subdued little voice.

"I am one of those people who hates being yammered at before I've had at least three cups of coffee." He drained his ceramic mug and held it out to her for more, telling himself he should be feeling guilty. It wasn't his fault that she suddenly looked like a wounded fawn.

She poured more coffee for him from something that looked more like a pitcher than a thermos, and the aroma went a little ways toward improving his mood. Except that he didn't know how he was going to get rid of her while he went in search of her sister.

She handed the mug back to him in hurt silence, but James steeled his diamond-hard heart. "You're not coming with me," he said, knowing he had to get this perfectly clear.

"You'll like the Alfa, Diamond," Sally said, sliding onto his desktop, her pert little rump displacing all his notes. "She's very fast and smooth, even on the bumpiest roads. And she has a terrific sound system—"

"Why do you call it a 'she'?"

"I feel we're soul mates," she said, picking up her own mug of coffee and taking a delicate sip.

"So you've both got great headlights," he grumbled. "I'm driving the VW, and I'm going alone."

"Have some more coffee," she said in an affable tone of voice. "I can wait."

He stubbed out his cigarette and drained the mug. "I hate to tell you this, babe, but my office doesn't come equipped with a shower. I'll have to go home, pack a few things and meet you."

"Just like that?" She took another delicate sip. "I thought I was going to have to convince you for another hour or two."

"Hell, I've been around. I know when it's a losing battle. Listen, it'll take me a couple of hours. Let's say three. I'll come by your place and pick you up."

"No! I mean, I don't think that would be a good idea. My father came home unexpectedly last night, and I don't want to have to answer any questions. Besides, I don't want you two to meet."

"Why not?" So the old man hadn't told her about his ride home from the airport, James thought. Obviously, here was a family that kept secrets.

"Because I don't think he'd like you."

James grinned. Score one for him—the old man had definitely approved. "What makes you think that?" he said. "Don't you think he'd be bowled over by my personable charm?"

Sally snorted. "You have as much charm as a rattlesnake."

"You can find yourself another private investigator."

"Not one who's so close to Philip Marlowe," she said. "Besides, I'm not too fond of charmers. Vinnie the Viper was full of charm."

"Which reminds me, what the hell did you think you were doing, going off to the Panama like that? And how did you get your car back? Last I knew, the parking valet had the keys and you were in the midst of a Victorian swoon all the way back to your father's house."

Sally sat up stiffly, affronted. "You really can be a swine," she informed him. "If you think I wasn't scared—"

"Oh, you were scared, all right. Just not scared enough. How did you get the car?"

"I got a taxi."

James said a few pungent things about the brain power of certain women as he lit another cigarette. "So you went back there alone?"

"I had another set of keys."

"You know you aren't dealing with the Rover Boys. They could have wired your car."

"You mean so they could follow me?" she asked, fascinated.

"No, lady. So they could blow you up."

For a moment, she looked faintly green, and once more, the damnable guilt cropped up in the bottom of James's gut. Maybe he shouldn't have tried to scare her, but damn it, someone had to make her see reason.

She managed to smile. "There's no reason to kill me. I don't know anything that I shouldn't, I don't have anything they want. I may be a nuisance, trying to get my sister and the sculpture back, but they don't kill people simply because they're being a nuisance."

"You want to bet? I've seen people killed because they belched at the wrong time. You're still living in a fantasy world, kid, and you're going to be a very unhappy young lady if you don't smarten up."

She slid off the desk, crossing over to him, and her lush hips were at eye level. Some men might find her hips a little too round. Personally, James liked a woman with curves.

"But Diamond," she said, squatting down in front of him and reaching out for his loosened tie. "That's why I hired you. To protect me from the baddies of this world."

"Then why don't you do as I tell you?" he said, ignoring the impulse to catch her hands in his. "Why don't you go home, stay put and let me protect you?"

She hesitated, looking up at him, her hands on his tie. Nice hands, he thought. No gunky rings or bright red polish. Long-fingered, deft-looking, capable hands. He wondered how they'd feel on his body.

"You promise you'll come get me?" she asked in a low voice, suddenly very serious. She was giving him a chance; she was willing to trust him, just a little.

Which is more than he could say for himself. He wasn't going to trust her farther than an inch. "I promise," he said, and told himself it wasn't guilt eating away at his stomach, it was his hangover.

He wasn't sure if she believed him, but she dropped his tie and rose. "I'll be waiting for you just outside the gates," she said. "Eleven o'clock?"

He wasn't going anywhere in the vicinity of the MacArthur mansion, but he had to keep up the pretense. "I told you it would take me three hours. . . ."

"It's quarter to eight."

"In the morning?" His voice rose in an indignant shriek. "You came down here to wake me up at seven in the morning?"

"Or thereabouts. I thought it would be wiser to get my car before everyone was up and about." She smiled brightly. "Besides, you wanted to get an early start, didn't you? This is the best portion of the day."

Diamond glanced out into the smoggy, overcast morning, and something halfway between a growl and a snarl issued from his throat. "I'll meet you at eleven."

THE SLEAZY STREETS OF Diamond's neighborhood were blessedly deserted at that hour of the morning. The half hour or so Sally had spent in his office hadn't made an appreciable difference on the denizens of the area. Apparently, people didn't work nine-to-five jobs around here, which came as no surprise to her. These were night people, including James Diamond. She half expected him to throw his coffee at her when she told him what time it was.

She glanced up at the windows of his third floor office, half hoping he'd be watching her. The filthy glass was blank and empty—apparently she'd been dismissed from his mind as easily as if she were a one-night stand.

She knew perfectly well he'd dismissed her for the next few days. He wasn't going to show up at the gates of her father's house—at least, not until he had her sister and the falcon in tow. If she could count on him to do just that, she would have, she told herself. She'd sit back and twiddle her thumbs. Or she might have.

If her father hadn't come home unexpectedly, throwing all her plans into disarray. Things had been complicated enough; Isaiah's precipitate return had been the final straw. She had been counting on five more days. When Jenkins had woken her from a sound sleep that morning with the dreadful news, she knew she had no choice but to hightail it out of there as fast as she could and leave it to Jenksy to cover for her.

If only she could trust someone, anyone. The only one who knew most of the truth was Jenkins, and he'd be home, baby-sitting her father and keeping him from working himself into a fatal apoplexy. He was going to have at least a minor fit when he went into his library and found his beloved Manchurian falcon missing.

How did things get so complicated? It hadn't really been her fault. Certainly she'd been a fool to be bowled over by Vinnie Calderini's elegant looks and solicitous charm. She'd learned by now that charm was a greatly overrated commodity. It was no wonder she was finding Diamond to be a refreshing change.

But she'd already begun to be uncertain about Vinnie's masterful performance. It had been sheer luck that she'd overheard his conversation with his driver, when they'd discussed how long it was going to take them to retrieve the Manchurian falcon.

No, scratch that. She could lie to everyone else, but she couldn't lie to herself. It hadn't been luck at all. She'd seen him deep in conversation, and she'd deliberately moved closer with the express intention of eavesdropping.

She couldn't remember what she'd expected to hear. Maybe something a little shady—she was more than aware of Vinnie's family connection, and she had expected the mild thrill of hearing about some gambling operation, maybe bookies or something.

Instead, she had found out that the pride and joy of her father's collection, the Manchurian falcon, was the object of the Calderinis' current quest, and that she was simply the means to the end.

She'd listened in growing fury, hugging her arms around her body to keep from shaking apart. It wouldn't have come as such a shock, except that she'd decided she'd been too flighty. That she really ought to make an effort to marry this, the sixth of her fiancés.

Her damaged pride, which was far more battered than her armored heart, would have been bad enough. Until the other shoe dropped and she remembered that the Manchurian falcon wasn't simply her father's finest sculpture, one treasured and hoarded and loved; it was also stolen, taken from the mainland Chinese during the debacle that engulfed China at the end of the Second World War. And no one outside the family even knew Isaiah owned it.

He kept it locked in a series of vaults, taking it out to gloat over it at odd occasions. He never said much about it, but Sally, who was possessed of an excellent brain despite her flighty tendencies, had been able to put two and two together and come up with a nefarious four.

The fact that the Calderinis knew about the falcon was bad enough. That Vinnie was willing to court her to get it instead of having someone just breaking in and stealing it made things worse. And there was no one she could go to for help. She couldn't very well call the police and tell them she thought the quasigangster she'd been fool enough to become engaged to was going to steal her father's already stolen art treasure.

So she did the only sensible thing. She ran.

She sent a vague letter breaking off her engagement before she took off for Europe. She'd had enough practice dismissing unwanted fiancés, and that part had been particularly easy. Getting her hands on the falcon before she left wasn't much harder—the MacArthurs had a tendency to underestimate each other and it was simple enough to find the various combinations to the vaults and to wheedle the others out of Jenkins.

It was getting the copy made that proved the real difficulty. Unfortunately, the Yellow Pages didn't have a listing for art forgers and the only criminal she knew was Vincent Calderini. She certainly couldn't ask him for help.

She'd finally had the inspiration to head to a local art school, hoping a struggling young student could manage to make a creditable copy. Instead, the teacher had taken the commission, providing a matching Manchurian falcon that was so like the original, it took Sally's breath away.

She'd replaced the real one with the phony, hiding the priceless original inside an empty box at the back of her cluttered closet. And then she'd taken off, content in the knowledge that even if Vinnie didn't take his dismissal well, even if he decided it was time for direct action and had someone try to steal the falcon, they'd end up with the phony one.

Unfortunately, Vinnie still had more tricks up his sleeve. Sally had been sunning herself on the Riviera, smugly content and only faintly bored, when her sister had called, breathless with excitement and not listening to a word of caution. She was getting married. Right away. To Vincent Calderini. And taking a dowry of sorts, one that Isaiah would never miss.

The phone went dead before Sally could start screaming. In the time it took for her to get back to San Francisco, jet lagged and exhausted, Vinnie and Lucy had already had a head start. It was no wonder that the phony Manchurian falcon was missing from its perch behind a series of five locked doors. The only surprise was that Lucy had figured out how to get to it.

Sally had hoped, had truly hoped, that Lucy had found the real falcon and taken that, too. But it was still safely ensconced in the welter of Sally's closet, gleaming in all its malevolent beauty. Sally set it back on its pedestal and wondered how in God's name she was going to be able to get her sister back safely.

If the Calderinis knew they'd been stiffed, Lucy's life wouldn't be worth a plug nickel. Vinnie might not actually be the killer sort—his hands were too soft and his smile was too practiced. But he had access to any number of people who'd do the dirty trick, up to and including his driver. Vinnie had taken Lucy along with the falcon, but Sally couldn't imagine why.

Once he had what he wanted, why had he bothered to take Lucy with him? Why hadn't he simply abandoned her, dumped her as her sister had dumped him? Did he have doubts about the authenticity of the falcon? Was he holding Lucy for ransom?

One thing was clear, it was up to Sally to get her feckless sister back. And there was only one obvious way to do it. She had to trade the real falcon for the phony one and her sister's life.

But she didn't know who could help her. Not the police. Not her father, who'd have a stroke if he realized he was going to lose his precious falcon. Who'd also have a stroke if he knew Lucy was in the hands of a mobster.

Sally needed an outsider to fix things, someone who could get her where she needed to go and then step back and let her negotiate. James Diamond had been that man, but he had an alarming tendency to think he could get Lucy back without Sally's help.

If she told him the whole truth, he might be in a better position to help. But he might also walk away in disgust. And besides, her simple plan of exchanging the real falcon for Lucy had run into a major snag. Someone had stolen the real one.

She'd been a fool to put it back in its original place behind the five locked doors. But she'd assumed Vinnie had gotten what he wanted and that, for now, the falcon would be safe.

It wasn't. Three mornings ago, the day she'd first found Diamond's name in the Yellow Pages, she'd gone to check the falcon and found it missing. She'd stared at the empty pedestal in horror, shrieking for Jenkins. But while his reaction had been equally aghast, there was nothing they could do. There were no clues. No sign of forced entry. Nothing else was missing. A ghost had simply waltzed through the walls of the MacArthur mansion, picked up the real Manchurian falcon and then disappeared.

For an agonizing day, she'd hoped and prayed it had been Lucy and Vinnie going after the real thing. Lucy's breathless late-night phone call had dispelled that particular hope.

She and Vinnie were at Lake Judgment on the California–Oregon border. They were breathlessly happy and hadn't left each other's side in the five days they'd been there. Lucy hoped Isaiah wouldn't mind about the falcon, but Vinnie needed it for a business deal with some Chinese importers, and surely it should have stayed in China in the first place.

Before Sally could come up with questions, objections, warnings, Lucy had rung off, and Sally had cursed her sister's brainless chatter, chatter that even outdistanced her own.

She'd had to admit defeat, then, and her need for help. If Vinnie was planning to hoard the statue just as Isaiah had, it wouldn't have been as great a problem. He might never discover it was a newly minted fake.

If he was presenting it as a goodwill gesture to some Chinese importers, who were probably Chinese gangsters, then someone was going to find out, and find out right quick, that the falcon was a fake. And then Lucy's ersatz honeymoon was going to be over.

Sally had to get to Lake Judgment and confront Vinnie. She had to get Lucy back. Originally, she'd hoped to bring back one of the falcons, it didn't matter which, and hope that Isaiah would never look too closely. That option was now closed to her.

So she had to rescue Lucy any way she could before Vinnie found out he had the phony falcon. And she was going to need James Diamond's help to do that.

Sally eyed her beloved Alfa with a trace of doubt. She'd seen enough movies to know that cars could have bombs set in them, but the Calderinis would have no reason to do that. Still, there had been no sign of Diamond while she was woolgathering on the cracked pavement outside his sleazy office. She knew she'd better get moving if she intended to follow through on her plan.

James Diamond wasn't going to come by the house at eleven o'clock and pick her up. He was going to keep as far away as possible, heading straight to Lake Judgment before she realized what was going on. Her plan was simple. Find an out-of-the-way place near his apartment, wait for him to come out and follow him up north. By the time he realized she was behind him, it would be too late for him to do anything about it.

IT TOOK JAMES less than an hour to shower, scrape a dull razor across his stubble and throw some clothes into a battered, old suitcase. Sometime between three and five in the morning, he'd gotten the information he'd needed from the people who lived by night and slept by day, and he was ready to take off after Vinnie the Viper and his hostage bride without a dark-haired distraction by his side.

He controlled his instinctive shudder as he glanced at the digital clock on his way out the door to the VW. Nine-fifteen. He usually wasn't even awake at that hour, much less on the road. Clearly, Sally MacArthur was having a dangerous effect on him. He needed to find her sister and find her fast before he got further entangled with someone who was far too great a distraction.

Such a distraction that he didn't even notice the car tailing him until he reached the outskirts of the city. His instincts told him it couldn't be. He'd convinced her. He'd looked up into her vulnerable, baby blue eyes and sworn he'd come by the MacArthur house and fetch her. And she'd trusted him.

Not far enough. There were a number of hunter green late-model Alfa Romeos around San Francisco, and possibly a fair number of them were driven by young women. But the creature in the scarf, oversized dark glasses and intense, hunched posture could only be one person.

It would be child's play to lose her now that he'd emerged from his abstraction to notice her. It was possible she could find her own way to Lake Judgment, but he was willing to bet she was the sort of woman who couldn't read a map and who always took at least five wrong turns. If he pulled a few smooth moves, he wouldn't see her till it was all over.

James pressed his foot down on the gas pedal, hard, and his trusty little VW shot forward. He made a sudden, unheralded right turn, zipping forward, but she was still doing her best to keep up with him.

She should have known she'd be no match for one of San Francisco's finest, even with her Alfa pitted against his old rust bucket. He had one last glimpse of her face, pale mouth beneath the dark glasses, before he disappeared around another corner, then another, finally losing her. And it was only then that he realized there was a faint sheen on her face, one that might have come from sweat on this cool autumn day. But more likely came from tears.

He cursed loud and long. He hit the tiny steering wheel with his large hand, called himself every kind of stupid, sentimental name. And then he pulled over to the side of the road and waited for her to catch up.

Chapter Six

The Alfa Romeo pulled up beside him. James had slouched back in the driver's seat, hands draped loosely over the steering wheel, waiting with infinite patience as Sally switched off the engine, pulled off her scarf and sunglasses and opened the door.

He was still half tempted to make a run for it. From what he'd discovered in the small hours of the morning, this little excursion wasn't going to be the piece of cake he'd first envisioned. She might sulk and rage if he left her behind, but at least she'd be safe.

And then he remembered her rash visit to Don Salvatore. And he knew, deep in his heart, that the only way she was going to have any chance of being safe was either by being under lock and key or by his side.

He should have called Jenkins and enlisted his aid. If Isaiah MacArthur hadn't returned home, James would have done just that. Despite his frailty, Jenkins looked like the sort of man who could keep his mistress safely locked up if her life depended on it.

But the arrival of the equally frail Isaiah MacArthur threw a monkey wrench into the plan. He wouldn't sit by and let his daughter be locked in her bedroom, and he didn't look as if he were strong enough to hear the truth.

So James really only had one choice. If he shook the Alfa Romeo and lost Sally somewhere along the backroads on the way to Lake Judgment, she'd probably walk directly into trouble, popping up when he could least afford it. No, she was better off where he could keep an eye on her. If worse came to worst, he'd tie her up himself.

She opened the passenger door and slid into the seat beside him. "Hi there," she said with a bright smile. He could see the shimmer of tears in her sky blue eyes, and he told himself he wasn't a heel. "You sure you want to take this car rather than mine? It's not that I'm particularly worried about the Alfa, mind you. I've locked it, and if by any chance someone steals it, it's well insured. But it certainly goes faster than this old rust bucket."

James looked at her for a moment. Reaching over, he cupped her willful chin in his hand and wiped a stray tear away with his thumb. "You are one major pain in the butt, lady," he said. "Why can't you just do as you're told and stay put?"

"It's not in my job description." She'd become very still the moment he'd touched her, and he could feel the warmth flowing between them, see the startled expression in her eyes, the wariness. He'd been a fool to touch her. A fool not to let her go immediately. A fool to let his fingers linger on the warm, firm skin beneath her chin. "Why did you lie to me?"

He did release her then, turning away. "Because I knew you wouldn't take no for an answer. This would work a lot better as a one-man operation. You may think this is a game, but people like the Calderinis don't know how to play. Everything's life or death with them."

"Don't you think I realize that? If I thought it would all blow over, I'd concoct some lie for my father until Lucy decided to reappear. But I don't think she's going to get the chance to reappear on her own, and I can't sit back and leave her in danger."

"You're good at concocting lies," James said evenly, starting the VW and pulling onto the highway. "And we're taking this car. I can't afford to have mine stolen, even if you can."

"My lies don't seem to work too well with you."

"Don't let that get you down. I'm an old hand at seeing through lies. Most people would believe you when you told them that your father was a rigid pig who'd send your half sister to jail the moment he heard about his missing statue. Most people would believe you don't know why your sister's in trouble. I'm just not most people."

Sally was silent for a moment, digesting this. "What makes you think my father isn't a rigid pig?"

"Because I happened to pick him up at the airport last night and drive him home. We had a very illuminating time."

"You didn't tell him about Lucy?" she demanded, her panic obvious.

"I have eyes in my head, Ms. MacArthur. For all he's a tough old buzzard, he's also too old and frail to deal with the mess his children have gotten into. And Lucy's his child, or at least he certainly seems to consider her as such. He told me he's leaving her half his estate."

"Why in heaven's name were you discussing his estate?"

"He wanted to make sure I wasn't a fortune hunter."

"Didn't you tell him who you were?"

"No."

She was very wary. "Why not?"

"He was much better off thinking I was about to become fiancé number seven."

She laughed at that, a low, throaty chuckle, and James found he liked her laugh. Even if he wasn't sure he liked the cause of it. "You're a far cry from my fiancés," she said.

"That's what Isaiah told me. He suggested I skip the engagement and elope."

Her blue eyes were bright curious. "And what did you say to that?"

"I asked him if I looked like someone with a history of mental illness. He dropped the subject."

"He lied to me," Sally said, sliding down in the cramped seat and stretching her legs out in front of her. "He told me he had Jenkins drive him home."

"Lying must run in the family."

"I wouldn't call it lying. *Creativity* is a better word."

"Creativity is a crock. You're all a bunch of pathological liars and I'm a fool to become involved with you."

"Then why are you?" she asked, her voice calm and reasonable.

So reasonable that for a moment, James didn't know what to say. He had other ways of making money—he didn't need this aggravation. But he couldn't walk away from her and the convoluted mess she'd created. "Maybe because I know if you're left on your own, you might end up in the bottom of San Francisco Bay."

"The Calderinis—"

"The Calderinis don't tend to go in for cold-blooded murder. But they're in the midst of a major international expansion, and people get a little edgy in times like these."

"I don't see why. The Chinese..." Her voice trailed off uneasily.

"The Chinese?" James said in a silken tone. "What exactly do you know about the Chinese connection?"

"Is that something like the French connection?"

"Don't act innocent with me, you already know that I don't buy it. What do you know about the relationship between the Calderinis and the Chinese? And how do you know about it?"

"Vinnie said something?"

"Nope. Vinnie Calderini knows how to keep his mouth shut, and he certainly wouldn't blab anything to a space cadet like you. Why don't you tell me the truth for a change? If we're going to have any chance of getting your sister back, then you need to be straight with me."

She didn't like the notion; he could see it. She ducked her head, staring at the hands clasped in her lap. "I overheard him talking," she said in a very low voice.

"That's unlike Vinnie. He wouldn't have a conversation where he could be easily overheard."

"It wasn't easy. I had to hide in the bushes by his Lincoln while he talked with that so-called chauffeur that takes him everywhere. It started to rain and a spider bit me, and I had to use the bathroom and the damned people wouldn't leave." She sounded aggrieved at the very notion.

"Yeah, well, surveillance is like that. Boring and uncomfortable. Why were you crouched in the bushes, eavesdropping?"

"I was curious."

Diamond swore under his breath, something brief and explicit. "Why were you curious?"

"I didn't trust Vinnie. He seemed far too interested in my father's jade collection, far too interested in staying home and..." Her voice trailed off.

"And getting you in bed?" James supplied, keeping his irrational annoyance down.

She glanced up at him. "Actually, no. That was what made me suspicious. I usually have to spend the majority of the time fighting off my fiancés. With Vinnie, it was only a token effort. He didn't really want me. And while I don't have delusions that I'm the most seductive woman in the world, I still expect that if someone wants to marry me, he also wants to sleep with me. It's only reasonable."

"Only reasonable," James echoed. "So how come you don't sleep with them? Your half dozen fiancés?"

"Who says I don't?"

"You just did. You said you spend the majority of your engagements fighting off your fiancés. Why do they need to be fought off?"

"Maybe I'm a tease," she suggested, as if the notion interested her.

"Maybe."

"Or maybe I just want to make sure someone really, really loves me before I go to bed with him."

"Wouldn't they really really love you if they want to marry you?"

"I'm half heir to my father's fortune. It's quite considerable, you know, and Isaiah's not in very good shape. He's also quite old. Within ten years, I'll be a very wealthy woman, and people tend to underestimate my intelligence. A man might think he could marry me and be assured of a comfortable life for as long as he cared to hang around."

"Yeah, but he'd have to stick it out until Isaiah croaked. That would be years of wedded bliss without much remuneration."

She smiled then, a warm, self-deprecating grin that hit him hard below the belt. "I guess most of them have realized that. The prize isn't worth the game."

He glanced at her, at the sweep of midnight hair, the sky blue eyes, the soft, tempting mouth. "I wouldn't say that," he muttered beneath his breath. "So let's get back to the business at hand," he added abruptly, forestalling any reaction she might have had to that statement. "You were crouched in the bushes, listening to Vinnie talk with Alf."

"Alf? How did you know his name?"

"Alfredo Mitchell is one of Salvatore's right-hand men. He usually drives the old man around, but in the past few months, he's been low profile. He's a chauffeur, all right, but he's also an enforcer and one of the Calderinis' nastiest employees."

"I don't suppose when you say nasty that you mean he's rude?" Sally asked in a quavering voice.

"We're not talking rude, here. We're talking lethal. Did he go with Vinnie and your sister?"

"I imagine so."

"Then we're in deeper than I realized," James said. "So are you going to tell me the truth for once? Tell me what they were talking about. Or am I going to stop the car and let you hitchhike back to the Alfa?"

"You wouldn't do that."

"Try me."

She leaned back and James knew from the stubborn set of her mouth that she was going to embark on another string of lies. All of a sudden, he noticed the rearview mirror. Or to be more precise, the huge black car riding up on the almost nonexistent tail of the Beetle.

"Hell and damnation," he said, pushing down hard on the gas pedal. The VW made its usual chirping noise and jolted ahead, maybe pushing from fifty-two miles-an-hour to an even fifty-four.

Sally swiveled around in her seat. "We've got trouble?"

"We've got trouble," James affirmed. "Got your seat belt on?"

"Of course, but why...?" Her question was answered before it was formed. The big black Ford came up and gently kissed the bumper of the VW, sending it shooting forward on the rain-slick road.

"How the hell could they have made us so fast?" James demanded, more of himself than of her.

"You think that's Calderini behind us?"

"More likely a representative. Take off your seat belt."

"Are you out of your mind? Some huge tank is ramming into us, trying to kill us, and you want me to take off my seat belt? I know I'm annoying but this—"

"Take it off!" He'd unfastened his. "We're going to take a little detour, and you need to be ready to open the door, jump out and run like hell."

"Really?"

"Don't panic, just do everything I say and it'll be okay." He glanced over at her, considered putting a reassuring hand over hers, when the expression on her face stopped him.

"This is wonderful!" Sally breathed, excitement shimmering out of her.

"This isn't a game!" he snapped, reaching across for the glove compartment instead of her hand. "The people behind us are going to be shooting real bullets." He pulled out his gun and tucked it in his jacket.

"Bullets?" Sally said, undaunted. "God, Diamond, this is just great."

"When we get where we're going, I'm going to spank you," James muttered furiously, trying to coax more speed out of the poor, aging engine of his car. "Hold on tight." The black Ford hit once more, and with no more warning, James jerked the wheel to the right and the sturdy little car veered off the road and down over the bank toward a ravine at a murderous pace.

"Jump!" he shouted, opening his own door. Sally was looking utterly fearless and ridiculously happy as the car jolted down the side of the hill. "Jump, damn you." And without waiting to see whether she'd follow orders, he leaned over, opened her door and shoved her.

He was out his own door a second later, lying there in the wet grass and mud, the wind knocked out of him, as he listened for the sound of bullets, for Sally's scream of pain, for any number of sounds signaling disaster.

The only sound he heard was the crash and crunch of aging metal as his beloved car collided with several trees before taking one last, graceful dive into the ravine.

He didn't move. He couldn't. Even with his face in the mud and the gun digging into his stomach, he couldn't move, could only gasp for breath like a landed fish and hope to God Sally had survived.

In the distance, he heard the Ford roar away, and he could only hope his pursuers believed the two of them had gone over the cliff with the Beetle.

He heard the scrabble of sliding rocks, and for a moment, he wondered whether he'd made a mistake, whether someone was coming down the hill after them. And then he felt Sally's warm breath in his ear.

"Are you dead, shamus?" she asked. "Or just having a little nap?"

He lifted his head to glare at her. "Why couldn't you have broken a leg?" he demanded. "Even better, both legs? Something to keep you out of my hair for the next six weeks."

She laughed and the sound was a little shaky in the rainy afternoon. "I tried my best. I guess I'm just too flexible. How about you? Did you stab yourself with your gun?"

"They've gone, haven't they?"

"Of course, they have. Do you think I'd be fool enough to move until they left? They must think we went over the side with your poor car."

"My car!" James lifted his head in belated distress. "Is it...?"

"Gone. Looks like a recycled tin can down there on the rocks. Guess we're going to have to use the Alfa."

"Guess again. We're going to take you back to San Francisco and then I'll come out alone in a nice anonymous rental." He pulled himself into a sitting position, groaning loudly as he began to brush the twigs and dirt from his clothes.

"You guess again. I haven't gone through this just to be sent to my room like a good girl."

He turned on her, the strain of the past few minutes freeing his rage. "You're going to do exactly what I—" His words stopped abruptly. "You're hurt."

She managed an undaunted grin. "I told you I tried to break my leg for you. It's just a scrape. Take your hands off me, Diamond."

He ignored her as his fingers gently poked her bleeding shin. "It's not a scrape, it's a gash. Stop squirming, I want to make sure nothing's broken."

"I wouldn't have been able to scramble over here if it was."

"Don't count on it. I know someone who managed to climb seventy vertical feet and then walk three miles on a leg that was broken in three places. Stress and adrenaline can make you ignore pain."

She was pale in the lightly falling rain, but her eyes were bright and sassy. "That someone was you, wasn't it, Diamond? I don't know what you're being shy about. You're allowed to be macho."

"Give me strength," he muttered under his breath. "Why couldn't you have broken your jaw?"

"And smashed my porcelain beauty?" she countered cheerfully.

He looked at her then for a long, silent moment on the rainy hillside. "No, I suppose I wouldn't want that," he said finally, surging to his feet.

She struggled up after him. "Hey, I was only kidding, Diamond. A great beauty I'm not, and we both know it. We—" She let out a little shriek as he hoisted her over his shoulder like a sack of potatoes. "What the hell do you think you're doing?" she demanded.

"Getting us up the hillside the only way I know how."

"I can walk, damn it!"

"Maybe. But I can carry you faster."

"What are we in such a hurry for? I wasn't aware that salvation lay at the top of this hill."

"The sooner we get back on the highway, the sooner we can hitch a ride back to your car. We're not going to accomplish anything if we don't get moving."

"What if the black sedan comes back?"

"Then we're in deep—"

"I get the picture," Sally said. "Your shoulder is digging into my stomach."

"Trust me, lady, I'm in more discomfort than you are," James grunted. "Just stop wiggling, and we'll both be a lot happier."

"Why will I be happier?"

"Because I won't find it necessary to smack your butt."

"That's the second time you've threatened to spank me, Diamond," she said in a dangerous voice. "That sort of sexist behavior went out centuries ago."

"Can't have it both ways, lady. Either I'm a forties shamus or I'm a New Age kind of guy."

"How about a reasonable human being?"

"You go first," he suggested affably, puffing slightly as he reached the highway. He let her down, trying to ignore the feel of her body as it slid over his. Her leg buckled beneath her and he caught her, but a moment later, she'd pushed him away and was standing shakily on her own two feet. She glared at him, but the slight wobble in her stance wiped out any lingering acrimony.

He caught her arm, ignoring her faint struggle, supporting her. "Come on, lady, just relax and be a damsel in distress. We can fight after we get warm and dry."

She must have been feeling even worse than she looked. She leaned against him, and there was a faint catch in her voice. "How do you expect to manage that?"

"Simple," he said as the sound of a vehicle preceded its arrival. "We just flag down the next car."

Half an hour later, they were thoroughly soaked, the light drizzle having turned into a pouring rain. Twenty-seven vehicles had passed them, sedans and vans and semis and pickups, before one finally stopped. They climbed into the bed of a pickup that had to have held manure or goats or possibly both, and rode the endless miles back to Sally's car in miserable silence.

"We've got a problem, Diamond," Sally said as they watched the truck disappear down the rain-swept road.

"What's that?"

"My keys are in my purse."

He just stared at her. "And your purse...?"

"Is at the bottom of the ravine twenty miles back."

"Great. I don't suppose you keep an extra?"

"In the car. And the car is locked."

"Clever. Make yourself comfortable. This is going to take me a few minutes."

"Can you break into a car?"

"I could break into Fort Knox if I had to at this point. Shut up while I concentrate." He reached into his pocket and pulled out a crumpled pack of cigarettes. He could have used a shot of whiskey to ward off the chill that had seeped into his bones, but his flask had gone over the hillside with her purse.

"Do you really need those things?" Sally asked imprudently as she sank down daintily on the side of the road.

"Yes," he said flatly, concentrating on the locked door.

It took him longer than a few minutes, but eventually, sheer willpower prevailed. If it had taken much longer, he would have ripped the door off with his bare fingers.

"I'll drive," Sally said, rising from her perch in the dirt and starting past him with a noticeable limp.

He caught her arm and deftly steered her to the passenger side. "I'll drive," he corrected, moving back to the driver's side so that he could reach in and unlock her door.

To his numb rage she simply reached out and opened it. "I never lock the passenger side," she said evenly, climbing in.

"And you didn't bother to tell me that?" His voice was very dangerous. He wouldn't get more than ten years for justifiable homicide, would he?

"I forgot."

Diamond slid in beside her and held his hand out for the key. She fished it from under the seat, dropping it into his hand. He was about to let his absolute fury blast forth when she began to shiver, a slight, convulsive movement of her wet shoulders.

He subsided, starting the car with a roar and contenting himself by muttering under his breath. He was reaching into his pocket for another cigarette when Sally's voice forestalled him.

"I'd prefer if you wouldn't smoke in my car," she said faintly.

"If I don't smoke, I'm going to strangle you," James said evenly. "Take your pick."

"I'll choke either way."

"Choose cigarettes," he suggested affably.

She glared at him as he pulled onto the highway. "You know, Diamond, this isn't as much fun as I thought it was going to be. I'm cold and wet, I smell of manure and my leg hurts like hell."

"Welcome to the real world, Sally," he muttered. "Trust me, it's only going to get worse."

"It couldn't."

"It could. The best thing you could do is go back to San Francisco and let me deal with it." He glanced over at her, looking for signs of agreement. She wasn't used to this kind of rough stuff. He knew perfectly well she was going to take her little tail straight back home to Daddy, and he should be damned glad of it.

"Diamond," she said, her voice soft and sweet.

"Yes?"

"Not on your life. You don't get rid of me that easily."

Now why didn't he feel more annoyance? "I should have known," he said with an exaggerated sigh. "You're an albatross, kid."

"And I'm here for the duration. Face it, Diamond. You've got a partner."

"God help us both," James muttered. And wondered why he felt curiously lighthearted.

Chapter Seven

This wasn't going the way she had planned, Sally thought. Forty-five minutes later, the two of them were ensconced in a seedy establishment optimistically called the Sleep-Suite Motel, a hostelry that didn't consist of suites at all, but instead boasted five run-down cabins complete with rusty water, sagging twin beds covered with ripped chenille bedspreads and a black-and-white TV that seemed to get nothing but old episodes of *The Brady Bunch.* Sally had headed straight for the shower, a tin stall that provided a steady stream of flaking paint as well as tepid brown water, but she was beyond caring. The threadbare white towels were designed for midgets, but she still felt marginally more human by the time she stepped back into the room, clean underwear and a silk bathrobe wrapped securely around her still-damp body.

She was alone. She'd left Diamond waiting there, cooling his heels, determined to stake her claim to the shower first. She should have realized he'd decamp.

"Hell and damnation," she muttered, fighting back the absurd emotional weakness that had been plaguing her for the past few days. Lauren Bacall wouldn't cry. She'd simply hitch up her skirts and take off after Bogey if he dared dump her at some flea-bitten motel.

She limped over to the window, peering out into the pouring rain. It was already getting dark, assisted by the gloomy weather, and her gashed shin bone was throbbing. The Alfa was gone, of course, but then, she'd expected as much. She'd brought her suitcase in with her, but she had no money, credit cards or identification. So she was stuck here with a hunger the size of Pittsburgh and no way to feed it.

She sank down on one noisy-springed bed, sticking her legs out in front of her. He'd left the television on, probably to cover the sound of him absconding in her car, and the Bradys were now in the midst of a Christmas episode. Sally had always hated the Bradys, and right then, she wasn't in the mood for Christmas.

She looked around her for a telephone, coming up empty. Apparently the Sleep-Suite Motel wasn't equipped with such amenities; making a phone call to Jenksy an impossibility. It was just as well. Jenkins would be having his hands full lying to Isaiah, and Isaiah was damnably hard to lie to. Who should know that better than his own daughter, who'd spent most of her twenty-some years trying to con him?

She hadn't trusted Diamond any more than he'd trusted her, she reminded herself, sniffing loudly, so there was absolutely no reason why she should feel bereft, betrayed, shattered, despairing, miserable...

The door to the cabin opened, and James Diamond filled it, soaking wet, glowering at her. "You're going to be the death of me," he announced flatly, dumping a greasy paper bag at the foot of her bed. From that greasy paper bag emitted smells so wonderful that Sally almost did burst into tears.

"What is it?"

"Hot meatball sub with extra garlic. Take it or leave it."

"I'll take it," she said, attacking the bag with a blissful sigh. "What else did you get?"

"First-aid stuff and some clothes for me. There's a general store a few miles down the road that had what I needed." He dumped the other bag on the rickety table, pulling out some dark cloth. "I assume madame has finished with the bath?"

She didn't even mind the cynicism in his voice. She swallowed a huge bite of the meatball sandwich, then glanced up at him. "I was afraid you'd abandon me. I should have known you wouldn't."

"You shouldn't have known any such thing. I tried like hell to ditch you. I was twenty miles past the store when my damned conscience took over and I turned back. You're an albatross, lady, and I wish to God you'd never walked into my office that day."

She took all this with remarkable equanimity. "Why did you come back?"

"Guilty conscience?" he suggested.

"You don't strike me as the type to be bothered by something as mundane as a conscience," she pointed out, taking another big bite of the sandwich. "I don't think you suddenly remembered who was paying your salary or succumbed to an unexpected case of lust."

"Oh, yeah?" he drawled, pausing by the bathroom door, his expression giving nothing away. "Then what do you think caused me to be such a monumental sap and come back for you?"

"I think you discovered a belated sense of decency. Honor. You couldn't abandon me to the wolves, no matter how tempted you were. You couldn't just leave me here with no money or credit cards while you went off on an adventure."

Diamond had a dumbfounded expression on his face as he sank down on the other bed amidst the shriek of rusting springs. "Give me strength," he said in a voice weak enough to suggest he really needed it. "I'm not abandoning you to the wolves. If I take you with me, I'm transporting you directly into their den. And trust me, it'll be no adventure. People shoot real bullets, and the Calderini family seem to be very edgy nowadays. If you don't believe me, look at your shin. Look at the bruises all over you...." His voice trailed off, as his gaze rested directly on the four long bruises above her knee. "That didn't come from this afternoon," he remarked in a deceptively even tone of voice.

For some reason, she didn't want to tell him. She opened her mouth to spin him a tale that would at least temporarily distract him, and then shut it again.

"You've thought better of lying," he noted. "That's an improvement." He rose from his bed, went to the other paper bag and removed some first-aid supplies. He sat beside her, the bed creaking ominously, and began unscrewing the bottle of iodine. "I assume Calderini did that to you?"

"I bruise very easily," she began, uneasy about the sudden blackness in Diamond's already dark eyes. She pushed up the bright silk sleeve to expose similar bruises on her arm. "You inflicted these."

He regarded them stonily enough, showing none of the guilt she'd hoped for but hadn't really expected. "There's a slight difference. Calderini was trying to hurt you. I was trying to rescue you from the consequences of your short-sighted stupidity."

"It wasn't stupidity, it was—yeaooow!" she shrieked, as he dabbed iodine on her leg with what she considered to be sadistic enthusiasm.

"Trust me, it was stupidity," he growled, setting the iodine down and bandaging her shin with a huge gauze patch. "Got any other wounds you want me to attend to?"

"I don't care much for your bedside manner," she said in a lofty voice.

"Tough. I'm not thrilled about you saying I've got honor and decency." He rose, heading for the bathroom. "I assume I can trust you to stay put while I take a hot shower and get out of these clothes?"

"Assume anything you want," she said, turning her face to the Bradys with a set expression.

She waited until she heard the sound of the shower on those tin walls. She heard the thud and bang as Diamond tried to squeeze his tall body into that narrow metal space, and then she was up, throwing her things back into her suitcase. She was getting out of here and now. She wasn't sure where she was going, she wasn't sure how she was going to rescue Lucy, all she knew was that she had to leave.

The rain was coming down in earnest as she dashed outside, dived into the front seat of the car and reached for the keys.

They weren't there.

Of course. They were probably inside, in James Diamond's pants pocket. Which meant she had two choices. She could slink back inside, get back on her creaking bed and pretend she'd never tried to make a break for it. Or she could sneak inside the bathroom with its lockless door and hope Diamond would be too occupied behind that thin, plastic shower curtain to hear her. She certainly had no desire to confront all six foot whatever of James Diamond, soaking wet, naked and furious.

She dragged her suitcase back out of the car and up the broken steps to the cabin. He opened the door for her, reaching out to take the suitcase from her limp hand, and she no longer had any choices.

He wasn't naked, but there was far too much skin showing. He was dressed in a pair of black sweat pants and nothing else, and he was dripping wet from the shower. She didn't need to look at his face to know how furious he was, so she simply pushed past him and limped back to her bed. "You can't blame a girl for trying," she muttered, staring at the Brady Bunch.

He moved closer, blocking her view with his torso. It was a very impressive torso, she had to admit. Hard, well-muscled, tanned, with just enough dark hair to be enticing. She was willing to bet that Philip Marlowe hadn't looked that good without a shirt.

"Where did you think you were going?"

She forced herself to look up at him. Right now, he didn't look much like the hard-boiled detective of her dreams. He looked far too contemporary, normal and extremely male for her peace of mind. Philip Marlowe and Sam Spade were fantasies. The man standing in front of her was much too real. She could smell the faint scent of the soap the motel had grudgingly provided; the water on his warm skin.

She scooted backward on the bed, suddenly feeling very vulnerable. "I wasn't sure. It was clear to me that your heart isn't in this job, so I thought..."

He ran an exasperated hand through his thick, wet hair. "Do me a favor, Sally," he said wearily. "Don't think. I promise not to dump you, even if your life depends on it, if you promise not to take off. I'll trust you if you trust me."

"All right, Diamond. It's a deal. Though it seems to me we already agreed to this before."

"I expect we'll have to renegotiate almost every day," he said with a weary sigh, turning away and dropping onto the bed.

"I expect we will. You aren't going to smoke, are you?"

He'd already lit a cigarette. He glanced over at her, and with cool, deliberate calculation, he blew a stream of smoke directly at her. "Yup. You can sleep in the car if you don't like it."

"The car already smells like cigarettes. Do you know what you're doing to your lungs, Diamond? To the environment? To my lungs, for that matter?"

He glanced at her. Her silk bathrobe, now spotted with rainwater, was gaping open in the front, exposing far too much of her admittedly generous endowments. "Your lungs look just fine to me," he drawled, leaning back against the lumpy little pillow.

She ignored the comment just as she ignored her own flattered reaction to it. "Why are we sitting here? Aren't we going on to Lake Judgment?

"We are."

"When?"

"Tonight." He blew a smoke ring in her direction, damn him.

"Tonight?" she shrieked. "But we must be miles from there! It's dark and rainy and nasty outside and—"

"I'll be more than happy to leave you here with the Brady Bunch," he said in a silken voice.

Sally looked at the television screen and shuddered. "No, thank you. If you're going, I'm going too. But..."

"We're exactly nine miles from Lake Judgment. Eleven miles from Vinnie's so-called fishing cabin. It's only a little past five right now. I figure we'll warm up, dry off and head up there in another hour, hour and a half. That meet with your approval, your high-and-mightiness?"

"It sounds as if you've already made the decision. What did you mean by his 'so-called fishing cabin'? What else would it be?"

Diamond smiled obliquely. "You'll see."

"Don't you think you ought to warn me?"

"Nope. The less you know, the better."

"Diamond," she said, sitting up on her bed and pulling the silk kimono tightly around her, "you are the most irritating human being in the entire world."

He reached over and stubbed out his cigarette in the already dirty ashtray. "No, I'm not," he said, still stretched out on his bed. "You are." He shut his eyes, missing the full splendor of her glare.

"What do you think you're doing?" she demanded.

"Taking a nap. We're not going anywhere for at least another hour, and I, for one, am tired. Some fool woman woke me up at eight o'clock this morning, and I've had a busy day."

"You could at least put a shirt on."

He opened his eyes at that, a faint amusement making him suddenly very approachable. "Does all this naked flesh offend you, Miss MacArthur? Tough. My clothes are drying out in the bathroom, and even for your tender sensibilities, I won't put on a wet shirt."

"Don't be ridiculous! You could go around naked for all I care," she scoffed. "I just thought you might be cold."

"Sure you did. Look the other way if I disturb you. That's what I plan to do."

It took a moment for the import of what he was saying to sink in. "What do you mean by that?"

He moved so fast she was too befuddled to move. One moment, he was lying stretched out on his sagging bed, the next, he was sitting on hers, looming over her, too close.

Much too close. "I mean, lady, that you bother me. Disturb me. Irritate me. I don't know whether I want to throttle you or make love to you, but I do know that you are driving me absolutely crazy. Why you didn't think to pack a pair of baggy sweats is beyond me, or at least a bulky old bathrobe. Instead, you prance around in that slinky thing and expect me to ignore it. Well, I'm doing my damnedest. But I'd find life a lot easier if you'd either put more clothes on or slide under the covers. Or join me on my bed."

The last suggestion hung between them in the still night air. The Bradys were still in the background, fussing about something, but neither Diamond nor Sally was paying any attention. She wet her lips nervously, wishing she could still the sudden pounding of her heart. "I don't think that would be a good idea," she said in a husky voice.

"I don't, either. As long as we both agree, we should be all right." He still didn't move. She wondered whether it would be such a terrible mistake, after all. She wondered if his mouth would taste of cigarettes. Maybe she ought to kiss him, just a little, so she could find out. "Don't look at me like that," he warned her.

She licked her lips again. "Like what?"

He moved closer, so that his mouth hovered just over hers. "Like you're asking for trouble. I've told you before, I'm not your fantasy lover. I'm not Philip Marlowe, Sam Spade, Rhett Butler or Dirty Harry. I'm a man with too much history and too many problems to mess with a woman like you, and even if you're on the verge of forgetting it, I'm not."

He was so close. "I'm not forgetting it," she whispered. "You are." And she closed her eyes, waiting for him to bridge the last tiny bit of distance and kiss her.

The scream of the protesting springs wasn't any louder than the cry of her protesting heart as he moved away, quickly, without touching her. He dropped back down on his own bed and shut his eyes. Within moments, his breathing had regulated into the deep, even sound of sleep.

She stared at him in mute frustration, then glanced at the pack of cigarettes lying on the table beside him. For a brief, mad moment she could understand the temptation of them. She could picture herself looking like Veronica Lake, puffing away on one of them as she peered up at Bogart through her curtain of hair....

Shut up, Sally, she ordered herself, sliding down on the bed. *Get your head out of the movies for just a few minutes. Long enough to go to sleep like that damned man lying next to you, lying much too close, with much too much skin showing, and try to think about stuff like income taxes and Isaiah's ill health. Or whether Vinnie's realized that the Manchurian falcon isn't the real thing at all. Or whether James Diamond is as devastating to the senses in bed as well as out of it.*

JAMES WAITED UNTIL HE WAS certain she was asleep before he allowed himself to breathe normally. Despite what he'd said to Sally, he'd never been one for catnaps. He'd only had four hours of sleep the night before, but he was used to making do on even less, a holdover from his years in the police department. Stakeouts were incredibly boring, and the night hours were the worst. You couldn't allow yourself to sleep, you couldn't allow yourself to relax your vigilance even for a moment or you, or the person you were watching, could wind up dead.

He felt unnervingly like he used to when he was on a stakeout. Edgy, nerves crawling under his skin, a burning in the pit of his stomach, an achy, restless kind of feeling in his chest. Sort of like male PMS, his partner Kaz used to describe it.

James didn't like that feeling. It had been one of the reasons he'd left the force, along with a heavy-handed push from Internal Affairs. He thought he'd gotten rid of it, but it had come back, in slightly altered form, since Sally MacArthur had sashayed into his life.

He knew what it meant—he was old enough and experienced enough to recognize the signs and listen to his instincts. It meant that there was more trouble with the simple little story than Sally was admitting. It meant the Calderinis had become a great deal more dangerous in the past couple of years, and if he didn't handle things just right, it might all end in disaster.

It also meant one more thing. That restless little edge was more familiar. It meant he couldn't keep his damned mind off Sally MacArthur and her ripe body. He was near to being obsessed with her, and the more he told himself she was a pain, the more he wanted her.

It wasn't just her body, luscious though it was. Bodies could be had, ones just as nice, with an easier personality accompanying it. He'd never had a problem looking for female companionship, and if he preferred it with the minimum of attachments, most women were willing to accept him on those terms.

But there was something about Sally that drove him nuts. Something about the way she sassed him, chased him and lied to him, and thought she could get away with it. The way she wanted to rescue her sister, protect her father, watch over Jenkins and, hell, even protect him, was both exasperating and utterly enchanting. He never thought he'd be the sort to be enchanted by a female.

He climbed out of bed, the noise of *The Brady Bunch* covering the sound of the noisy springs. He moved over to the rickety chair, lit another cigarette and stretched his legs out in front of him.

Damn, he missed his car. He and the little Beetle had been together for longer than he cared to remember, and in one brief moment, it was gone. He should be used to life being like that—he'd seen enough people go in the line of duty to know how uncertain things are. He needed something a little newer, a little bigger, something with more convenience and less personality. He and his bank account had avoided that major purchase, but now it was out of his hands. Maybe Pacific Gas would have to wait another month while he replaced his car.

One thing troubled him, though. In the car were any number of things that would be hard to replace. The license for his gun. A couple of changes of clothing that he couldn't afford to lose. Sally MacArthur's purse, which probably came equipped with a fat wad of bank notes and a raft of plastic.

But the thing that he missed most, at that moment, was the flask in the bottom of the suitcase. The one he hadn't thought he needed but always packed just in case. The one that always left his office full and came back empty.

He would have bought another bottle at the store down the road, but his cash supply was damnably short. He was running low on cigarettes, too, and if he didn't watch it, he was going to end up a damned saint. Sober, cigaretteless and celibate. What a hell of a combination.

He glanced over at Sally MacArthur lying on that concave bed, his eyes lingering on the bruise on her thigh. He was going to get Calderini for that one. He wasn't quite sure how, but that little piece of cruelty wasn't going unavenged. He wasn't going to let a sleaze like Calderini mark his woman and get away with it....

His woman? *Whoa, Diamond, cool down.* Sally MacArthur is no more your woman than Madonna is. She's hired you, you'll drag her around after you, and once you get her sister, you dump her, picking up a fat check in the bargain.

James stubbed out the cigarette, headed into the bathroom and put on his still-damp clothes, shivering slightly in the too-cool motel room. When he came back, Sally was sitting up, blinking dazedly as she struggled out of the mists of sleep. She'd look like that every time she woke up, he couldn't help thinking. What would it be like to wake up with her?

"You got any money?" he demanded abruptly, wiping that particular thought out of his mind. "Besides in your purse? We know that's out of reach."

"No. Unless you can get me to a bank."

"Not tonight. We'll have to make do on my limited funds."

"What are we going to need money for?" She yawned, pushing her silky, black hair away from her face.

"You'll see. By the way, my fees have gone up."

She looked up, startled. "You're already charging me five hundred dollars a day."

"Plus expenses. I figure the loss of my car is a legitimate expense. Those were Calderini's men who drove us off the road. I'll expect you to cover my losses."

She slid her legs over the side of the bed, the silk robe sliding up, exposing most of her gorgeous thighs. "Sure, Diamond. I think I can come up with the seventy-five dollars she was worth."

"I figure replacement value. She was a classic car."

"She was a classic piece of garbage. Don't worry, Diamond. You get my sister back safely and you can have a brand-new Ferrari."

"I'll settle for an Alfa." He lit another cigarette, lounging in the door of the bathroom. "Are you coming with me or staying behind?"

She stood up, a little wobbly, then smiled with deceptive sweetness. "I'm coming with you, Diamond. I figure you're gonna need me for backup."

He blew the smoke out his nostrils, looking like an enraged dragon. "The day I need you for backup is the day I move into a nursing home."

"Diamond," she murmured, moving past him, brushing up against him, her skin smelling like flowers, "I hope you have Medicare."

Chapter Eight

"Why are people out hunting at this hour of the night? In this weather?" Sally demanded, peering through the inky, rain-swept darkness as they drove up the winding road toward Lake Judgment. She could see the shadowy figures wandering around, in groups of two or three, nasty-looking guns over their shoulders, dressed in ill-fitting camouflage hunting gear. "I didn't realize it was hunting season."

"Around here, it's always hunting season," Diamond muttered, taking a sharp right onto a dirt road. One that had obviously seen a surprising amount of traffic, considering how far off the beaten track they were. "You need to follow my lead and keep your mouth shut. For once, just trust me." He pulled up to a dark cabin. There were even more hunters strolling around, and Sally noticed with interest that some of them were wearing sunglasses in the rainy darkness. And they all wore the same shoes. Not hunting boots or even comfortable running shoes. They all wore highly polished dress shoes.

"Those aren't hunters, are they?" she said.

"Not of animals, they aren't. They're Calderini's men."

"Then we're here. At Vinnie's fishing cabin?" She peered through the darkness. "They need all these people to guard Lucy?"

"I don't think Lucy's got anything to do with it. This place usually comes equipped with this much security."

"A fishing cabin?"

"It's not what it appears to be. Come on, princess. Do as I say and maybe we'll get lucky."

"But what is it?" Sally demanded, following him out of the car. "Listen, Diamond, I'll do a lot better if I know what I'm walking into..."

He put his hand under her elbow, his long fingers tightening slightly in warning. "You're walking into a log cabin, darling," he murmured. "Isn't it obvious?"

One of the hunters was stationed at the door, and he laughed as he overheard Diamond's words. "A surprise for the little lady?" he inquired cheerfully, opening the door for them.

"The answer to her dreams," Diamond replied, drawing a reluctant Sally into a room that looked just as it ought to, complete with rough-hewn table, a fire burning in a stone fireplace and mounted heads on the log walls.

"Where are we going?" Sally demanded again.

"Be quiet. We have to look like we know what we're doing or they're not going to let us in there."

"In where? If this is some weird sort of sex club, Diamond, I'm going to—"

"You're the one with the weird sex fantasies, not me," he growled back, halting her as the cupboard on the opposite wall began to open. Noise and heat and light spilled forth from beyond it, and it took Sally a moment to realize just what she was witnessing.

Diamond half assisted, half shoved her through the door, past the elegantly dressed couple who were just leaving, and the door closed behind them, sealing them in.

"It's a gambling casino," Sally gasped.

"Exactly. The Calderinis wouldn't waste their time with something as mundane as a fishing cabin. Word on the street has it that this place has been going strong for more than ten years."

"If I'd known Vinnie wanted to bring me here, I wouldn't have been so skittish," Sally murmured, looking around her with unabashed fascination.

"You like to gamble?" Diamond's disapproval was obvious.

"Not much. But I was afraid he had other, more personal matters on his mind, and the thought of a secluded weekend with Vinnie the Viper wasn't exactly to my taste. If I'd known it was simply a business trip..."

"An illegal business trip. This isn't Nevada, you know."

"Why do they bother? I mean, why would someone want to go gamble illegally when Lake Tahoe isn't that far away?"

"Because the odds are better, the stakes are higher and the risk is part of the attraction. If gamblers liked to play it safe, they wouldn't be gambling in the first place."

She glanced up at him, caught by his bitter tone of voice. "Do you like to gamble, Diamond?"

"Too much. I drink too much, smoke too much, and I'm a hell of a lot better off if I keep away from all games of chance. Once I start I can't stop."

"What about women?"

He stared at her, his bitterness vanishing in sudden confusion. "What do you mean?"

"I mean, do your addictions extend to women? You've managed to leave me alone, but do you tend to..."

"Tend to what?" He looked back over the oblivious crowd. There had to be at least two hundred people in the huge, noisy room, and the smell of smoke and whiskey and excitement was overpowering in such an enclosed space.

"Tend to sleep with any female who'll hold still long enough?" she said in a torrent of words.

He turned back to her. "I've been able to resist you so far, haven't I? Trust me, lady, if I can resist you, I can resist anyone."

He couldn't be meaning that the way it sounded, she told herself. "But, Diamond—"

"We're in trouble," he said. "Follow me." And without another word, he began snaking through the intent crowd of brightly dressed people, heading toward the opposite end of the room. Sally followed, resisting the impulse to look back over her shoulder to make sure no one was following them. She didn't need to check—the prickling feeling in the back of her neck told her someone was on their trail, and it wasn't a friendly sort.

Suddenly Diamond disappeared, swallowed up in the crowd. She panicked, dodging to the left, but a small, hard hand clamped down on her shoulder, and a voice breathed a garlicky threat in her ear. "Keep on walking, Miss MacArthur, and you won't be hurt. Make a fuss, and you'll be very, very sorry."

The voice was vaguely familiar, but she couldn't quite place it, and the steely strength in that small hand didn't allow her to turn around and look. She had no choice but to nod, allowing that hand to propel her forward through the excited, oblivious crowd.

She was hoping, counting on coming face-to-face with Vinnie. Despite everything that had happened in the past few weeks, despite her miserable failure with Vinnie's formidable father, she still had no doubt that she'd be able to get Vinnie to accede to her wishes. Despite his lineage, despite his leanings toward chicanery and organized crime, he was still a basically decent Yale Law School dropout who, she suspected, had an honest fondness for her sister. If she could just get him alone...

But the room beyond the casino was empty, with nothing but a desk and two chairs. The hand on her shoulder gave her a harsh little shove, and when she turned, she almost wished she didn't recognize the man who'd brought her here.

It was a lucky thing she'd had so much practice with tall tales. She immediately plastered a bright, cheerful smile on her face, pressing a theatrical hand to her heart. "Goodness, you scared me! You're Vinnie's chauffeur, aren't you? Thank heavens! I've been trying to get in touch with him for days now. I really need to see him as soon as possible. He's here, isn't he?" She racked her brain for the man's name, but for a moment, all she could think of was Smurf. Or Garfield. Some cartoony kind of name.

The man didn't even blink. "You brought a friend along to help you find your way?"

Her smile didn't waver. "Yes, and now he's abandoned me, probably for some bimbo in a tight dress." Alf, that was his name! Like the furry alien. "Maybe you could help me find him, Alf. But first, I need to see Vinnie."

"How'd you know my name?"

Sally's smile wavered. "You're Vinnie's driver. I remember you...."

"I was using a different name then. Your buddy Diamond must have tipped you to my real name. And he's not off with a bimbo. Tony the Cannon spotted the two of you, and they're having a little argument out in the back. Him and a couple of the boys."

Sally's smile vanished completely. On the one hand, this sort of discussion was like something straight out of a Bogart movie. On the other hand, if Diamond was in trouble, being hurt, then this was getting a little too real for comfort. "I want to see him," she said, suddenly urgent.

"I thought you wanted to see Vinnie first. Actually, we both know you're looking for your sister, and she ain't here. Neither is Vinnie, for that matter. They left three days ago."

"Left for where?"

Alf shook his head. "If either Vinnie or your sister wanted to get in touch with you, I think they'd know how to find you. You've been real lucky so far, Miss MacArthur. Luckier than your friend Diamond. The men who gave his car a nudge down the hillside tend to be a little overenthusiastic. And they're the ones who are working him over."

"They're not going to hurt him?" she asked in horror.

"Honey, they've already hurt him by this time. A lot. Better you should ask whether they're going to kill him. And I don't think so. At least, not this time."

"Take me to him!" There was no pleading. There was pure, old San Francisco patrician demand in her voice. "Take me to him or I'll start screaming the place down."

"This room is soundproof," Alf pointed out. "But I'll take you to see him. Maybe it'll teach you a lesson as well. Don't stick your nose where it don't belong. And don't mess with the Calderinis."

"I'd much prefer not to mess with the Calderinis at this point. I simply want my sister back."

"She don't want to come."

"That's for her to say."

"No way. That's for Vinnie to say, and he says she stays. 'Smatter of fact, maybe I'd better do a little checking. If the boys get a little too rough with Diamond, we may end up with some explaining to do. And you know a little too much.''

To Sally's amazement, Alf left the room, closing the door behind him. She waited for the telltale noise of a lock, but there was nothing but the muffled noise from the casino beyond. She dived for the door, yanking on it, but it held fast. She began kicking at it, but the sound was no more than a muffled thump. Staring around her in frantic haste, she started toward the desk chair, thinking she might try crashing that against the door, when she noticed the business card on the floor.

''Desert Glory,'' it read. A spa for physical and spiritual fitness in Glory, California. Without thinking, she shoved the card into her pocket just as the door opened again.

Alf reentered, looking a tiny bit ruffled. Someone had managed to connect with his jaw, and he was nursing his knuckles as if they'd run into something. Something like Diamond. ''He's a tough son of a bitch, I'll say that for him,'' Alf muttered. ''I'm taking you out to the car. They'll pour him into it when they're finished with him.''

''They're not finished yet?'' She tried to control her mounting panic.

''I told you, he's a tough guy. If he'd just learn to take a fall, he'd end up with a lot less grief. Damned fool had the nerve to take a lunge at me.'' He held up his abraded knuckles, staring at them disconsolately. ''Come along with me—we'll go out the back. And watch yourself.''

The last thing Sally considered herself to be was a physical coward. But for some reason, the notion of sharing whatever Diamond was going through was unappealing, so she shut her mouth, following Alf's short, burly form through the utility tunnels that ran behind the rambling complex.

She stared around her in fascination. "This is amazing," she said, struggling to keep up with him. "It just looks like a log cabin on the outside."

"It's supposed to," Alf said in a bored voice, not bothering to look behind him. "The Calderinis know what they're doing."

"But don't the police guess?"

Alf snorted in genuine amusement. "The police fall into two categories—those who are paid not to notice, and those who can't get enough on us to make a bust. The first group of police make sure the second group stay that way, too. It works out well, and it gives our poor, underpaid men in blue a well needed second source of income."

"This is disgusting," Sally said, her spirits rising. Maybe not so much Philip Marlowe as Serpico, but still quite nice as fantasies go.

Someone had moved her car. The back utility lot was filled with panel trucks and anonymous-looking sedans, but even in the darkness, Sally could tell that neither Vinnie's Bentley nor his red Mercedes was anywhere in sight. She had no choice but to take Alf's word for it. He was waiting for her by the driver's side of her car, and in the distance, she could see a group of dark figures huddled around something, could hear the sound of thumps and grunts of pain.

"Is that Diamond?" she asked, starting toward the men in sudden urgency, but Alf's meaty hand clamped down once more, propelling her back against the car.

"You just stay here. Don't want to interfere while the boys are working. They know how to judge these things just right, but if you distract them, they might make a few mistakes. Just climb in the car and wait.'' He opened the driver's door.

''Diamond has the key,'' she said helplessly, sliding in.

''That's okay. He won't be in any shape to drive. You just wait. I'll see if I can't hurry them up a bit. They tend to be perfectionists, take a lot of pride in their work. But I think we'd all agree that the sooner you two get back to San Francisco, the happier everyone will be.''

''Yes,'' she said, since that seemed to be the called for response.

''You aren't going to make the mistake of keeping on with this?'' Alf demanded, suddenly suspicious.

''Of course not,'' she lied.

''Trust me, Diamond isn't going to be in any shape to do much more than moan for the next two weeks. You take him home and take good care of him, Miss MacArthur. And remind him he's lucky that we didn't decide to teach him an even bigger lesson.''

''I'm sure he'll feel very lucky,'' she muttered. ''But I'm taking him to a hospital first.''

''I wouldn't do that if I were you. And I'm sure Diamond will tell you the same thing. Lessons like these are supposed to be private.'' He glanced over his shoulder to the men heading toward the Alfa. They were dragging something between them, and Sally knew with a sick feeling that it was Diamond.

They dumped him into the passenger seat, but even with the brightness of the interior light, she couldn't see how badly he was hurt. She could see the brightness of fresh blood and hear his groan of pain, and she found tears filling her eyes.

One of the men tossed the key toward her before slamming the door, plunging them into darkness. The key fell somewhere around her legs, and as she searched around for it, she heard Diamond's rough breathing change slightly.

"Get the hell out of here," he wheezed, pain making his voice breathy. "Before they change their minds."

"Thank God." She sobbed as her shaking fingers connected with the spare key. "I thought they'd killed you."

"Not a chance. Get moving!"

It took her a moment to get the key into the slot, and the car stalled when she first tried to start it. A moment later, they were off, the back of the car fishtailing as she sped out of the parking lot.

Sally glanced behind her for the telltale signs of pursuit, but the road was black behind her as she tore down the muddy dirt road, skidding slightly on the slick surface. Diamond's body thudded against the side of the car as she swerved to regain control.

His pain-wracked cursing was so poetically graphic that at least some of Sally's panic began to abate. "You can't be dying," she said, easing off the gas pedal a fraction. "You couldn't be so inventive if you were dying."

"Well, I feel like it," he gasped back. "Where are we going?"

"I'm going to find an emergency room—"

"You're going to do no such thing. Calderini's boys aren't as good as they think they are—I've gone through worse beatings than this one and been doing sit-ups the next day. We just need to find a drug store, a liquor store and a motel. Preferably as soon as possible."

"If you insist. I still think you ought to have a doctor look at you. You might have a broken rib, a concussion, a—"

"The rib's only cracked, if that, and they didn't connect with my thick skull," he wheezed. "It'll be a simple job of taping—"

"Your rib's cracked?" she screeched, swerving on the road again."

"For Pete's sake, drive in a straight line!" Diamond gasped, clutching his side as he tried to pull himself upright. "A cracked rib isn't going to kill me—I've had enough so that I know what they feel like."

"But it could poke into your lung, your heart, you could bleed to death—"

"Stop babbling. I thought we already figured out that I don't have a heart, and if it came anywhere near my lungs, it would probably figure I've done them enough damage with my smoking. Speaking of which, I don't suppose you'd light me a cigarette? I really need one." He was trying for a plaintive tone, and it came out reasonably well, given the obvious pain he was in, but Sally refused to be moved.

"A cigarette's the worst thing for you now. You're right, we need to get you taken care of, and if you refuse to see a doctor, we'll have to do it ourselves. What do you want from the drug store?"

"An elastic bandage, ibuprofen, ice pack, morphine if they have it."

"I doubt they'll hand over morphine," she said dryly.

"That's why we go to the liquor store. You get the biggest bottle of mid-priced Scotch we can afford. I need something for anesthesia." He glanced over at her. "They didn't hurt you, did they?"

She wished she could see his face in the darkness. "No. But they told me Vinnie and Lucy weren't there."

"They weren't," Diamond said on a little gasp of pain. "They left three days ago for some place in the desert."

"Then that's simple enough. As soon as you're feeling better, we'll head for the desert."

"Lady, 'the desert' is an awfully vague destination. We can't just drive across it and expect to find them."

"No. But I have a clue."

"God help me, a clue," he echoed in an aggrieved tone of voice. "Now we're beginning to sound like a Charlie Chan mystery."

"I sort of like the idea of Nancy Drew."

"I sort of like the idea of getting someplace where I can lie down," he snapped. "You can play out your fantasies while I get quietly drunk."

Sally grew very quiet at that. She could sense from the unevenness of his breathing that he was in unbearable pain, and she wished she had the force of will to override him and take him to a hospital.

But she found she had to trust him. Trust him to know his own body and the limits he could endure. And there would be a lot of uncomfortable questions, there was no doubt about that. Doctors probably didn't have to report beatings the way they were required to report gunshot wounds, but she and Diamond wouldn't be able to leave the hospital with a few Band-Aids and a handful of painkillers.

No, Diamond was right, they could take care of it themselves. If, in the light of whatever motel they ended up in, he looked even worse than she suspected, she could always call an ambulance. He wasn't going to die on her. He wouldn't dare.

The muddy track turned into pavement and from pavement into highway as the rain beat down steadily on the Alfa. The interior of the car was silent, broken only by each painful rasp of James Diamond's breathing. Sally clenched the steering wheel, afraid to floor the gas pedal but just as frightened of getting lost, when the dim lights of a town speared through the darkness.

It wasn't much of a town. There was no drug store, no liquor store. Just a gas station with a mom-and-pop convenience store added on to the back. It seemed more equipped with hunting gear than the necessities of life.

Fortunately, the hunters of the area also appreciated a strong drink at the end of the day, so the liquor department was reasonably well stocked. Sally thought of Diamond, huddled down in the front of the Alfa, and bought the largest bottle of Chivas the meager contents of his wallet could afford. Which looked like something you'd get on an airplane.

By the time the toothless grandmother behind the hand-cranked cash register had totalled up her purchases, Diamond's wallet contained two parking tickets, an expired credit card, and one dollar. The paper bag contained an elastic bandage, the minibottle of Scotch, a bag of taco chips and three cans of diet Coke that cost just slightly more than the Chivas.

The Beddy-Bye Motor Hotel wasn't an improvement over the Sleep-Suite. These cabins came equipped with insect wildlife, the black-and-white television couldn't even offer forth the Bradys. The light bulbs were all twenty-five watters, and the bed was a double. A very small double. It looked even smaller with James Diamond collapsed across it.

Sally shut the door behind her, leaning against it and staring into the shadowy gloom of the motel room. It was going to be a very long night.

Chapter Nine

James had felt better in his life. As a matter of fact, despite his macho assertion, he'd seldom felt worse. His rib hurt like hell, not to mention his face, his stomach, his fists and just about every square inch of his flesh. The last thing he wanted was for Sally MacArthur to see him in this battered, weakened condition. The last thing he wanted was for her to put her hands on him. Particularly when he was in too rough shape to do anything about it.

Maybe if he didn't move he'd fall asleep. Maybe she'd let him be and when he woke up tomorrow morning, he'd be feeling normal again. Scratch that. If he didn't get his rib taped, his cuts washed and cleaned, ice on his wrist and medication in his system, he was going to be feeling even worse than he felt right now, even if that seemed an outright impossibility.

"What do you want first?" Sally asked from halfway across the room. "First aid, ibuprofen or whiskey?"

"Whiskey," he managed to say on a wheeze of pain as he struggled to sit upright. A small hand planted itself in the middle of his aching chest, pushing him back downward again.

"Don't move," Sally said, peering at him through the murky light. "You look like death warmed over. I'll get you your drink while you try to get your jacket off. I'm afraid it's in rather poor shape. Do you want ice and water?''

''I want the bottle,'' he growled, holding out one hand. For a moment, his mind didn't register when she placed something the size of a perfume bottle in his aching hand. ''What the hell is this?''

''Your bottle of Scotch. Chivas Regal, as a matter of fact. I thought you deserved the best after what you went through.''

''I deserve a quart of this stuff. How many bottles did you buy?''

''Just this one,'' she said cheerfully, pulling a can of something out of the bag and opening it. ''That was all we had money for.''

''I'm going to strangle you,'' he said, hurting too much to even struggle to his feet.

''You can't scare me, Diamond. You're in rough shape and we both know it. I figured drinking too much on top of everything else wasn't going to do you any good.''

''I figured getting drunk on top of everything else was going to do me a hell of a lot of good.'' He tried to break the seal on the miniature bottle, but his fingers were too numb and swollen to comply and he dropped the ridiculous thimble, listening to it roll under the bed with only faint regret.

''Let's get you cleaned up,'' Sally said, setting her drink down on the rickety little table. ''Then you'll feel better.''

''Unlikely. I don't suppose that's beer you're drinking,'' he said morosely, staring at the ceiling.

''Are you always this obsessed with drinking?'' She sat down on the bed, and the shift of the mattress beneath her weight made his chest scream in agony.

"Not always," he said between clenched teeth. "Listen, you can sing me temperance songs all night long if you just go out and get me a normal-sized bottle."

"Can't do it." Her hands were fiendishly gentle as they pushed the torn jacket from his bruised shoulders. "I spent all the money."

"All *my* money?" She'd managed to get the jacket off and dumped it on the floor. Now she was at work on the buttons of his shirt. He didn't know why she bothered—it was ripped up the back and not worth saving. But he let her work on it, for some reason enjoying her ministrations.

"Don't worry, Diamond, we'll put it down to expenses. Including your bottle of Chivas. Now stop bitching for a moment while I get this shirt off." There was a sudden, swift silence in the seedy motel room. "God, Diamond, what did they do to you?" she asked in a quiet little voice.

"You know what they did to me. They beat the hell out of me. Something about teaching me to keep my nose out of their business. It probably looks worse than it feels. Though I'm not sure if that's possible."

"James," Sally said, still in that very quiet voice.

"Yes."

"I'm afraid I'm going to faint." And without another word, she slumped backward on the bed, out cold.

With a grunt, he pulled himself from the bed, limping over to the desilvering mirror that hung at an obvious angle to the sagging double bed. No one could accuse him of being a fantasy hero at this point, that much was certain. His face was battered and bloody, with one eye almost swollen shut. The dark stain across his torso was spreading, and in a few hours, it would probably be a bright purple.

But he was right when he told Sally it looked worse than it felt. He'd been beaten up enough to know what was dangerous and what wasn't. He hurt like hell, but within a couple of days, he was barely going to notice. The cracked rib might twinge a bit, but apart from that, he was going to be more than ready to meet up with Tony the Cannon again. Not to mention the sadistic Alf. As a matter of fact, he was looking forward to it.

The slight movement on the bed signaled Sally's return to consciousness. She sat up, blinking, her face pale.

"It's lucky I didn't get shot," he said, his customary drawl sounding slightly muffled through his battered mouth. "You probably would have puked."

Her head snapped up, color brightening her pale cheeks again, her blue eyes losing their wan look. "You must think I'm a wimp."

"Hell, no. I think you're a civilian. That's why you should have stayed home, safe in that nice big house, and let me take care of things."

"Who would have driven you out of there if I hadn't been with you?" she countered with a trace of her old fire.

"Who's to say they would have recognized me if I'd had a chance to go in there alone?"

She pushed her sheaf of silky, black hair away from her face, and he noticed her hand was trembling. "We're wasting our time with what ifs. Don't you want me to tape that rib?"

"Can you do it without fainting?"

"If you can keep your mouth shut," she said sweetly. "Get on the bed."

He was about to come back with a suggestive response, and then wisely thought better of it. For one thing, she was about to tape his rib, and she'd be in the perfect position to inflict a great deal of pain if he riled her. For another, unless she was going to make do with the floor, they'd be sharing that very narrow double bed, and even in his current battered condition, he was going to have a hard time keeping his mind off her very tempting presence. The less said the better.

He shrugged out of his tattered shirt and moved gingerly to the bed, sinking down with a muffled groan of pain. "Ever taped cracked ribs before?"

"Not in this lifetime." She sat beside him with surprising delicacy as she unwrapped the elastic bandage. "Any special tricks to it?"

"Make it tight."

Her face was very close to his as she began wrapping his torso. She was concentrating, biting down on her lower lip as she wound the bandage around him, and he could smell that flowery scent that always seemed to cling to her. He wished he could lower his arms around her, pull her down onto the bed with him. But even if that wasn't a professionally disastrous idea, it was a physical impossibility. He could hear the faint catch in her breath, hear his own rattled breathing as her silky hair brushed against his stomach.

When she finally fastened the end with those tiny silver clips and pulled back, her face was even more flushed than it had been. "How does that feel?"

"Like hell," he groused.

"I can rewrap—"

"Hands off," he snapped. "You did an okay job. It's just going to hurt for a few days."

Sally nodded, accepting the thanks he hadn't really given. "Lie down and let me take care of the rest of you."

Didn't he wish? Again, he kept his mouth shut, stretching out carefully on one side of the bed.

Her hands were surprisingly gentle as she bathed the cuts on his face. At least the Beddy-Bye Motel had an ice machine, and she must have used every threadbare towel in the place, fashioning ice packs for his wrist and his jaw. She even scrambled under the bed to find the miniature bottle of Scotch, holding it out to him as a peace offering.

He was still half tempted to fling it back at her. But her words still rankled—he *was* more upset about the lack of whiskey than the state of his abused body. If the booze mattered that much, it was more than time to give it up.

"You drink it," he said. "You're probably going to have a harder time sleeping than I am." He closed his eyes, trying to forget how much he wanted a drink.

"You're not going to sleep like that?" she demanded in a scandalized voice. "With no shirt on?"

"I'd prefer to take off my pants, too, but I figured I ought to spare you such temptation. Are you coming to bed?"

"With you?"

"Honey, I don't see anyplace else to sleep around here. I wouldn't choose the floor if I were you—I saw something moving down there a little while ago."

"I'm not going to sleep with you."

"That's your choice. I'm certainly not in any shape to ravish you, even if I were tempted, which I'm not." The lie came out quite easily. He didn't expect her to believe that he wasn't tempted, but he felt he ought to at least pretend not to be. "I'm going to have a cigarette and then I'm going to sleep. Preferably through the night. And while I'd prefer to have this bed to myself, I'm enough of a gentleman to be willing to share it, even with a harridan like you."

"Harridan? What kind of word is that for an ex-cop to use?"

"I went to Berkeley," he muttered drowsily, reaching on the bedside table for his cigarettes.

"I forgot."

He opened his eyes again. "Why did you know? Was that part of your little checkup?"

"I like to know who I'm hiring."

James's cursing was genial and obscene. "I don't suppose you know where I put my cigarettes?"

"In the car. I'll make a deal with you, Diamond. I'll share the bed with you if you don't smoke."

He tried to sit up, but it hurt too damned much. He had to content himself with glaring at her. "Lady, I'm doing you a favor by sharing this bed. Don't push me."

For a moment, she didn't move. A second later, he heard the door slam and he wondered whether he'd pushed her too far. Whether she was going to abandon him in this run-down motel with nothing but a thimbleful of Scotch. *Stop thinking about the Scotch, damn it!*

A moment later, the door opened again and something landed in the center of his taped chest. Something cold and wet and hard. "Here are your damned cigarettes," she said, crossing the room and turning on the television set. Nothing came on but black-and-white fuzz.

He fumbled with the cigarettes, but his hands were too numb and stiff to manage. She must have been watching because he heard her exasperated sigh and a moment later, she'd grabbed the cigarettes out of his hands and put one in her mouth, lighting it with a certain amount of savoir faire that made her look just a bit too much like a forties movie heroine. She spoiled it with her coughing fit, but when she placed the cigarette between his lips, he could just picture Lauren Bacall and Humphrey Bogart.

He took a deep drag, trying not to cough himself. "I don't know how you can smoke those disgusting things," she remarked. "They taste like an ashtray."

"Reasonable enough." He took another deep drag, regretfully, and then handed it back to her. "That's enough. You can stub it out."

"I'll drown it in the toilet."

"Whatever makes you happy." He shut his eyes again, listening to her move around the motel room. His body ached, and the ibuprofen was burning a hole in his stomach even as it smoothed away the sharp edges of the pain. It was just as well he hadn't washed it down with his customary half a bottle of Scotch.

He didn't know when he fell into a pain-filled sleep. He didn't know what time Sally finally gave in and crawled into bed beside him. He felt the scratchy weight of the blanket draped over him, felt the warmth of a smaller body beside him. For a moment, he wondered how she managed to find that much space to put between them in such a small bed. And then he fell back to sleep again, curiously content.

IT TOOK SALLY A LONG TIME to get up the nerve to get in bed with James Diamond. She felt like a fool for hesitating. As he'd put it so succinctly, he wasn't in any shape to make a pass at her, even if he was so inclined. She still wasn't quite sure whether he was so inclined or not.

On the one hand, she occasionally caught an expression in his dark blue eyes that convinced her that he wasn't the slightest bit immune to her dubious charms. On the other hand, he hadn't done a thing about it, and most of their conversations seemed to degenerate into arguments.

She wasn't about to delude herself in the matter. She knew perfectly well that she was more attracted to James

Diamond than she had been to her six fiancés. Put together. She'd always managed to get involved with men who left her essentially untouched. No one threatened her sense of self, her firm belief that life was hers to make what she wanted of it.

Diamond was different. Diamond wasn't a man she could twist around her little finger and then abandon when he made too many demands. Diamond wasn't a charming companion, an easy friend, a handsome partner for silly social gatherings.

Diamond was a man. And if Diamond were to make demands of her, chances are she'd agree, and willingly. If she didn't run away.

But he hadn't made any demands. He hadn't touched her, kissed her, flirted with her, charmed her. He'd threatened her, pushed her, cursed her and possibly saved her life a number of times. If she had any sense at all, she'd realize that the man lying half-naked in the bed wasn't the kind of man she should be attracted to. He wasn't Sam Spade or Philip Marlowe. He was James Diamond, a slightly broken-down ex-cop who probably found her completely unappealing. Maybe.

The room was chilly. She left the light on in the bathroom, a little nervous of the crawly creatures Diamond had mentioned. Diamond had shifted in his sleep, taking up a good two-thirds of the bed, and he shivered slightly. She kicked off her shoes and climbed onto the bed, still dressed in her black pants and turtleneck. The pants were a bit too tight, the turtleneck shirt constricting even if it was made of silk. She knew she'd be a lot more comfortable in her bathrobe. Still, she needed as much protection from James Diamond's exposed flesh as she could muster. He might be in too much pain to experience temptation. She wasn't.

The bed had a concave dip in the middle. She perched herself on the edge, feeling her body slip toward his as if she were steel being drawn to a magnet. She clutched the edge of the bedsprings, holding herself in place, and let out a weary sigh. How a man who smoked cigarettes could smell enticing in the dark of night was a mystery to her. But he did. He was warm and male and near, and she wanted to cross that concave dip and wrap her arms and legs around him. She could just imagine his scream of pain if she did any such thing.

She pulled the blanket up around them, wishing there was more to keep them warm, more than simple body heat. He was warm beside her, an absolute furnace, and for a moment, she allowed her paranoia to run wild. His rib had punctured a lung, he was bleeding internally and infection had set in, spiking a monumental fever, and tomorrow, she'd be in bed with a corpse.

She reached out a hand to touch his forehead, one of the few parts of his face that wasn't battered and bruised. Warm, but not too warm. His cheek was cool from the ice pack, his mouth soft and—

His hand shot out and caught her wrist. "What are you doing, Sally?" His voice was low and sleep dazed.

"I wanted to see whether you had a fever. You felt warm...." She tugged at her hand, but his grip was surprisingly strong.

"I don't. I always run a few degrees warmer than other people. For crying out loud, will you just lie down and go back to sleep?"

"I will if you let me go."

He didn't seem to be aware of the fact that he was still holding on to her. "As a matter of fact, you feel cold."

"I am cold. This place only has one thin blanket, and I don't happen to come equipped with an inner furnace."

She should never have admitted it. A moment later, he'd pulled her across the narrow gap that separated them, tucking her against his bandaged chest.

"Don't be ridiculous, Diamond," she muttered, struggling, both against his enveloping arms and her own baser instincts. "You've been hurt, you're in pain, you—"

"I'd be in a hell of a lot better shape if you didn't wiggle so. Stop talking and go to sleep."

His shoulder was warm. Hot, even. Well muscled and smooth, and his arms were strong. How long had it been since she'd slept in a man's arms? Had she ever?

Certainly she hadn't with her six fiancés. She hadn't slept with, made love with or had sex with any of them. She hadn't made love with very many men in this life, and the ones she'd chosen had all been ultimately bad choices. Was she making another bad choice after years of being careful?

She wasn't making love with Diamond, she reminded herself. She was simply sleeping with him. There was a great deal of difference between the two. And yet, when she thought back to the three very different men she'd been involved with before she got into the habit of getting engaged, she knew that sharing this bed with James Diamond was a very great deal more intimate than sharing her body with her overeager boyfriend when she was eighteen, or her lawyer's clerk when she was twenty-one, or Teddy Van Lessing when she was twenty-two.

She ought to run. She'd be safer on the floor with the cockroaches. Safer in the car, risking pneumonia in the cold night air, than lying in the arms of a man she could fall in love with.

She was going to run. In just a few minutes. After she got warm. After she allowed herself a taste of what it could be like. After she flirted with danger, emotional disaster, for a brief moment.

Diamond wouldn't know. He was already asleep again, his arms clasped loosely around her, his breathing steady and even. He wouldn't know the torment she was going through, the temptation and despair. He wouldn't know that she wanted to rip off the rest of the clothes and crawl right inside his skin. He wouldn't know that she wanted to find out if there was any truth to fantasies, to desires that never seemed to be fulfilled. She wanted to know if he was the one, even if she knew he couldn't be.

Just a few more minutes and she'd do what she had to do. Pull away from him, at least to her own side of the bed, or maybe out of the bed all together. Just a few more minutes.

THE LIGHT FILTERING in the uncurtained window was gray, wet and sullen. Sally's eyes fluttered open, and she lay very still, wondering how she could feel so glorious, so brightly optimistic on such a gloomy day.

And then she turned her head to look at the face on the pillow next to hers, the body entwined with hers. One of his long legs was between hers, and his hand was under her loose silk turtleneck, cupping her breast through the thin lace bra.

She went rigid with shock, but her sudden tension failed to waken Diamond. He slept on, peacefully enough, and she noticed he looked even worse in the light of day. More battered and bruised than before. And oddly, curiously dear.

She ought to pull away in outrage, slap his face and declaim "how dare you!" like a proper Victorian virgin. Except that she was neither Victorian nor a virgin, and that had never been her particular fantasy. What would Lauren Bacall do in a situation like this?

She reached out the one hand that wasn't trapped beneath their bodies and she touched his face very gently, a light benediction on his battle scars. His breathing was regular, even, the sleep of exhaustion, she thought, drawing her hand down his arm. And then she placed it over his, over the strong, long-fingered hand that cupped her breast, and she pressed just slightly.

His fingers flexed, automatically. He shifted, murmured something in sleep, and his thigh moved up to the juncture of her own thighs, pressing, arousing. Phrases like "don't wake the sleeping tiger" flitted through her mind. And then her mind went blank when he moved over her, his mouth settling on her unsuspecting one.

Chapter Ten

For a first kiss it was a revelation. A deeply disturbing one. If only she hadn't spent the night wrapped up next to him, absorbing his heat. If only she wasn't half-asleep herself, vulnerable, oddly innocent. If only she wasn't half in love with the man. Maybe three quarters of the way in love.

His mouth was warm, wet on hers, kissing her with a leisureliness that was both insulting and highly erotic. His one hand continued to knead her breast, his other reached up to cup her face, to hold her still for his long, measured assault on her defenseless mouth.

She would have been able to resist an attempt to overwhelm her. Men had tried it often enough, and she had simply shoved them away. She would have been able to resist a polite brushing of his lips against hers. That was usually all she allowed. But she couldn't resist the slow, sensuous nibbling of her lips, the way he drew her lower lip into his mouth and sucked lightly, the way his tongue moved against hers, the way his fingers stroked her breast into pebbled hardness, feeding the fire that was burning in the pit of her stomach.

She slanted her head just slightly, wanting to kiss him back, and she moved her arms around him, her hands greedy on the smooth warm skin of his back as she melted against him, increasing the pressure....

He let out a muffled shriek of pain, releasing her as if she were radioactive waste and rolling onto his back. His curses, punctuated by groans of pain, filled the dawn-lit room. Sally lay on her back, not touching him, trying to control her rapid breathing, her pounding heart, her sweating palms and the twisting ache in the pit of her stomach. She listened to him curse as she fought her own frustration and felt a certain savage satisfaction. She was hurting as much as he was, in a far different way.

She slipped out of the bed, tugging her shirt back down, shifting her clothes back around her and heading for the bathroom. Her reflection in the mirror was a total shock.

She looked wanton. Her black hair was a tousled witch's mass around her pale face. Her lips were swollen, damp. Her eyes were glazed with passion and anger. She looked like a woman interrupted in the act of making love. Which, she supposed, she was.

When she returned to the room, Diamond was sitting up in the bed, a thunderous expression on his face. At least, she assumed it was thunderous. With the bruising, it was hard to tell. He'd pulled his tattered shirt back on and was trying to button it. For a moment, she was tempted to go over and help him, and then she dismissed the notion. For one thing, he was sure to bat her hands away. For another, she didn't trust getting that close to him right now. She was still feeling edgy, unsettled, warm and uneasy. She wasn't about to define her problem, but she had enough sense to know that proximity to James Diamond made it worse.

"How are you feeling?" she asked in a brisk, bright voice, delving into the paper bag and coming up with two lukewarm cans of diet Coke and the bag of taco chips.

"No, don't answer that. I'm not crazy about obscenities first thing in the morning. Obviously, you feel like three-week-old garbage. You need some breakfast." She popped open one can and held it out to him.

He glared at her, the effect increased by the truly startling black eye. "You've got to be kidding."

"It's caffeine, Diamond. Don't be picky. Maybe once we hit the road, we can afford to share a cup of coffee from McDonald's. In the meantime, you need something to help you wake up."

"Did you drink that Scotch?" he growled.

For a moment, she was shocked into silence. "You're not serious," she finally managed to say.

He stared at her for a moment. "No, I don't suppose I am," he muttered. "Hand me the damned soda." He drained half of it in one gulp, shuddering, and lit a cigarette.

She opened a soda for herself, ripped open the bag of taco chips and perched on the one rickety chair the motel room boasted. Not for the life of her would she risk getting near that bed again. "So what's next?" she asked.

"Do you always have to be so damned perky in the morning?" he responded.

"Do you have to smoke in the morning?" she countered sweetly.

His answering growl was warning enough. "The way I see it, we have only one obvious choice. We drive back down to San Francisco, where I get new clothes, a new car and a life of my own. You go home, tell your father the truth and wait for your sister to return home."

"That's the obvious choice, is it?"

"It is."

"And you can seriously sit there, in the shape you're in, and say that my sister isn't in any danger?"

"Why would she be in danger? Vinnie has the statue, and he has her. He hasn't made any effort to send her home yet. Presumably, they're both very happy."

"For now," Sally muttered gloomily.

"Why do I have the horrible feeling you're not telling me everything?" he inquired of his cigarette. "Maybe it's the innocent expression in your eyes. Maybe it's the way I've caught you in lies before. Maybe it's just instinct, but my instincts have saved my hide any number of times and I've learned to listen to them."

"They didn't save your hide last night."

"No, they didn't. You want to tell me why the Calderini boys would be so upset that we showed up?"

"They don't want to lose the falcon or Lucy."

"Why not? I mean, they're not going to lose the falcon unless they want to. You and I aren't much of a threat to that kind of muscle. And I can't see why anyone would want to hold on to your sister if she wanted to leave. What's the point? Vinnie's not a white slaver. Unless she's some sort of hostage," he added slowly, stubbing out his cigarette and staring at Sally. "Is that it?"

She tried to look limpid. Since she wasn't quite sure what limpid looked like, it was a trial and a waste. Diamond wasn't buying it. "Why should she be a hostage? They have the falcon."

For a moment, he didn't move. Then he scooted back on the bed somewhat gingerly, nodding. "So that's it. They don't have the real falcon, do they?"

Sally went from limpid to outraged innocence. "Why in the world would you think that?"

He nodded, more to himself. "That's it. Where's the real one?"

"I don't know what you're talking about."

"The real one, Sally. Stop playing games with me. If the Calderinis discover they've got a phony statue, they're going to be very upset. And they have your sister to get upset with."

Sally gave up. "Don't you think I haven't realized that? Why do you supposed I'm so determined to get her back?"

"Where's the real falcon?"

"I don't know what you're talking about."

She didn't realize he could move so swiftly, given his general condition. He was up off the bed with a fluid grace unmarred by his grunt of pain, towering over her in tightly controlled rage. He caught her chin in his hand, forcing her to look up at him, and she knew without question that she wasn't going to get away with any more prevarication. "Where's the real falcon?" he said again, the words terse and sharp.

"I don't know."

"Explain." He hadn't let go of her chin, but his long fingers were cool against her warm skin, almost caressing.

"When I found out that Vinnie was after me just because he wanted the falcon, I had a copy made. I hid the original in my closet and put the real one in the safe, and then I took off for Europe. I didn't realize he was so determined to get the falcon that he'd go after Lucy. I figured he might have someone break into the place, but I never thought he'd take Lucy, too."

"So where's the real falcon?"

"I don't know!" Sally cried. "When they took the copy, I put the real one back in the safe. A couple of days later, that one was gone, too. Maybe Vinnie came back. I don't know. I can't believe he'd take the real one without saying anything."

"So, you think Vinnie only has the phony. Do you think he knows?"

"I'm afraid he might suspect. Otherwise, everyone wouldn't be so unfriendly when I've tried to get in touch with Lucy."

"Hey, they're an unfriendly bunch." Diamond released her chin, moving back toward the bed and his unfinished can of soda. "Besides, you haven't exactly been discreet. If they didn't suspect something before, your desperate attempts to get in touch with your sister would have to arouse their suspicions."

"Are you blaming me?"

"Damned right. Didn't you realize you can't play games with people like the Calderinis? They don't come equipped with a sense of humor."

It took all of Sally's considerable self-possession to keep from losing her temper. On the one hand, she was still feeling shaken, edgy, and the sight of his bruised, bandaged, strong back beneath the tattered shirt wasn't doing much to calm her. On the other hand, she didn't think it would be a good idea to goad him further. Goad him into putting his hands on her again. Despite his hostility, she had the feeling that he wouldn't want to stop any more than she did.

"All right," she said calmly enough. "We're not getting anywhere arguing about it. So I blew it. We need to worry about where we go from here."

"I told you where we go from here. Back to San Francisco. And then, if you ask me real nice, I might head back out on my own and start looking for your sister. If the Calderinis discover they've got the wrong falcon, we're going to have some very angry gentlemen. Particularly since the Chinese contingent are expected in this country sometime within the week."

"The Chinese contingent?"

"You remember. The people you overheard Vinnie discussing with Alf," he said.

"Oh," Sally said, having conveniently forgotten that. "If they're coming within the week, then I don't think we have time to go back to San Francisco, get you a new car and then get back up here. Besides, what do you need a new car for? We can use this one."

"*We* aren't going to use anything. I told you, you're going back home. We don't have any choice—we're broke and your purse is gone."

"I keep extra credit cards in the glove compartment."

"And besides— What did you say?"

"I said, I keep extra credit cards in the glove compartment. Plus bank cards. All we have to do is find the right kind of machine and we can have cash coming out the ears." She looked up at him, expecting praise, or at least a pat on the head.

"Why didn't you tell me that yesterday?"

"I forgot. Listen, Diamond, we were forced off the road, I gashed my shin, hitchhiked in a manure truck, then had the dubious pleasure of having someone beat the hell out of you. I'm not used to physical violence, and I find it just a little distracting."

"'Distracting,'" he echoed faintly. "What's your credit limit?"

"I don't think that I have one."

He shook his head, sinking down on the bed again. "Sally..." he began.

She moved swiftly, no longer afraid to touch him. She sank down on the floor beside him, taking his battered hands in hers and looking up at him beseechingly. No longer limpid or innocent or like a wounded puppy dog. For once, all her playacting had vanished. "Don't send me back, Diamond. I can't go back and wait to hear. I have to come with you, don't you understand that? It's my fault Lucy got into this mess. It's my fault they have the phony falcon. I *have* to go with you. I have to."

He stared down at her. His gaze dropped to the hands clutching his, and seemingly without volition his long thumbs stroked the backs of her hands. "I'm not sure I can protect you."

"I can protect myself."

"Sure, you've given me ample proof of that," he scoffed.

"Diamond, please. Don't send me back."

He was going to kiss her again. He was going to pull her into his arms, up across the bed, and she'd go willingly, gladly. All he had to do was give her a little tug. All he had to do was touch his bruised mouth to hers. All he had to do...

He dropped her hands, rising and pushing past her. "It's your funeral," he said in a carefully noncommittal voice. "If you don't mind the heat, you may as well hang around. You're right—getting a new car will be a major pain. I'd be more inclined to do it after I've got your sister safely back and you're feeling generous."

She didn't believe him for a moment. She wasn't sure why he wasn't sending her back, but it wasn't because he thought he could get more money out of her. Worried as he might be about her safety, he didn't want her to go any more than she wanted to.

"Thank you, Diamond," she said, hiding her sudden burst of happiness. "I promise to behave myself."

He snorted as he pulled on his jacket, grimacing with pain. "That'll be the day. Get your shoes on and let's get out of here. I'm ready to show you how easily I can be bought."

"How easily is that?" She rose, slipping on her sneakers and grabbing her can of diet Coke.

"A decent-sized breakfast ought to do it."

"Cheap," she scoffed. She saw the tiny bottle of Chivas lying on its side next to the bed. "I would have thought it would require at least half a gallon of good Scotch."

"That's if you want me to be nice," he said, his eyes following the direction of her gaze. "You gonna pick up the bottle or leave it as a tip for the chambermaid?"

"Do you think they have chambermaids here?"

"Not likely. If they do, they've probably already had more Scotch than is good for them."

"Do you want me to bring the bottle?"

A wry grin curved the corner of his mouth. "What is this, a morality test? Leave the damned bottle."

"All right," she said, hiding her rush of relief as she followed him out of the door.

"You can buy me a half gallon later," he said over his shoulder.

She stopped short, staring after him. And then, for lack of anything better to do, she stuck her tongue out at his retreating back before following him out into the early-morning air.

A HUGE BREAKFAST ACTUALLY did go a great ways toward improving his mood, James thought a few hours later. A new change of clothes, a carton of cigarettes and Sally being uncharacteristically docile also helped. Particularly since he knew Sally's docility wasn't the sort to last for very long.

He was being a fool and a half for letting her come with him, he knew that. He was counting on the Calderinis' old-world deference to womanhood to protect her to some extent, but even that had its limits. Once the Calderinis found they had the wrong falcon they were going to be infuriated, and James didn't relish either of them being in the way.

But sister Lucy couldn't be thrown to the wolves, either. Sometime during the past twenty-four hours, his last reservations about the case had vanished. Maybe it was when the Calderinis had trashed his car and nearly killed him and Sally for no better reason than they might be inconvenienced. Maybe it was when he'd felt Tony the Cannon's pointed boot in his ribs. Maybe it was when he'd felt Sally MacArthur's soft mouth under his.

Whatever the reason, it was no longer a case he was pursuing with half-hearted reluctance. It was personal. And it was a cause. He wasn't going to back down when things got a little inconvenient or dangerous. He was going to get Lucy extricated from Vinnie's clutches, and if he managed to find the real falcon at the same time, so much the better. In any case, he was going to do the job he was hired to do.

And he wasn't going to go to bed with Sally MacArthur. No matter how tempted he was.

Lord, that woman was exhausting! Her sheer babbling energy was enough to make him want to run for cover. To stop her mouth at all costs. Unfortunately, he kept thinking of the most effective way of stopping that mouth. With his.

He lit a cigarette, glancing over at her as she drove down the highway and tacitly ignoring her glare of disapproval. "I hate to be picky," he drawled, "but where are you going?"

"I'm not sure. I thought we might head toward the mountains."

"Why?"

"We have a vacation home up near Mount Sara. It's about four hours from here. I thought they might have gone there."

James shifted in the seat with a muffled groan that was becoming more reflexive than necessary. "What makes you think that? The word was they'd headed to some place in the desert."

"That's what they want us to think. Anyway, maybe I've been overreacting. Maybe they really did want some time alone together. Obviously, the little fishing cabin at Lake Judgment isn't the place for privacy. Maybe Lucy told him about our place at Mount Sara."

"It's worth a try," he said finally. "Four hours, you say? We could make it by midafternoon. If there's no sign of them, we head back to San Francisco."

"Diamond, you promised...!"

"I didn't say I was going to leave you there. I have some people to talk to, to see if I can get a line on where in the desert Vinnie and your sister might have gone to. Assuming they're not in the mountains."

"Couldn't you just phone them?"

He snorted in amusement. "Not likely. The kind of people I need to see don't have regular addresses or telephones. They like to deliver their information face-to-face and to be paid for it. I'm afraid I can't call in with a credit card."

"Oh." Her hands were gripping the steering wheel. Good hands, he thought, not for the first time. Long fingers, short, buffed nails, no rings. More capable hands than he would have expected of her. He hated long fingernails and too much jewelry on a woman. At least, on a woman who mattered. He liked women who looked like they could accomplish things with their hands, not just use them to model jewelry. He wondered if her hands were as capable as they looked. If they were downright inventive.

"Oh," he echoed, trying to distract himself from the direction his thoughts kept heading. He should never have slept with her. That was half the problem. Once you share a mattress with a woman, breath the same air in your sleep, then you've got ties. Commitments. And he wasn't interested in either. He didn't have time for either.

"If you think you're going to dump me, Diamond, you better just disabuse yourself of that notion," she warned him, some of her old energy reemerging.

"I can't do that—I need your car."

"You could always steal it."

"Good idea. But there's no guarantee you wouldn't call the cops on me. And there are any number of people on the SFPD who'd love the chance to pick me up."

"Made a few enemies on the job, Diamond?" she inquired sweetly.

"A few. Must be my charm."

"Why'd you quit the force?" she asked, her clear, blue eyes concentrating on the horizon. It was a warm, clear, fall day, the rains of the day before having thankfully vanished.

"I didn't quit. I was encouraged to seek my professional fulfillment elsewhere."

"You were fired?"

"More like a mutual agreement. My partner had died, and I'd always been a pain in the butt to anyone in authority. I liked to do things my own way, and the police department is a bureaucracy just like every part of city government."

Sally smacked the steering wheel. "That's my problem," she said. "I've been wrong about you, Diamond. You're not Philip Marlowe or Sam Spade at all."

He had a sudden, horrified suspicion of what was coming next. "Don't say it, Sally," he warned her. "There's no telling what I'll do. . . ."

But there was no stopping her. "You're Dirty Harry," she said triumphantly. "Come on, Diamond, growl it just once."

"I don't growl things," he growled. "And I don't know what the hell you're talking about."

"Just once, Diamond. . . ."

"Listen, Sally, we've come to a temporary truce. Don't push it."

"Or what?" she asked too damned cheerfully.

He shut his eyes and offered up a silent request for patience. "Or I might tie you up and gag you and dump you in the back seat," he snapped. "Now just be quiet and drive us to Mount Sara. I intend to sleep most of the way there."

"As long as you don't smoke."

"I can't smoke in my sleep," he murmured.

There was silence in the car, broken only by the hum of tires and the unusual stillness of the woman next to him. He was mortally tired—last night, he'd hurt too much and been too distracted by the warm, sweet-smelling body curled next to him to sleep that well. He couldn't turn off his awareness of her last night, and he couldn't do it now. He sighed, glancing over at her.

To his horror, he saw that her eyes were filled with unshed tears. He didn't know what it was about her. He'd seen women cry all his life, far too many women cry. He'd inured himself to tears, knowing that either the woman crying was just trying to manipulate the situation, or else the situation was too bad for him to do anything about it.

But Sally's tears were different. They were like a punch in the gut, and he found himself thinking he'd do anything, *anything* to make them disappear, make her smile and babble again.

"Diamond," she said, her voice faintly husky as she glanced over at him.

He closed his eyes quickly so she wouldn't realize he'd been watching her. "Yeah?" he grumbled.

"You are going to find her, aren't you? You're not going to let them hurt her?"

He never made promises. When backed against a wall, he usually managed with a gruff, "I'll do my best" and figured that would have to suffice.

He turned his head and opened his eyes. "I'll find her, kid," he said. "I promise you."

And the smile she gave him was of such a dazzling brilliance, filled with such trust, that it took a full one hundred and twenty seconds to realize what a fool he'd been to promise what he might not be able to deliver.

Chapter Eleven

"You're lost, aren't you?"

Sally plastered her most innocent expression across her face. It was a wasted effort—it was quarter past nine on a dark autumn evening and Diamond wouldn't be able to see well enough to appreciate the nuances of her reaction. "What makes you say that?"

"Because we left at eleven for a place that you assured me was only four hours away. And you, lady, drive too damned fast. So I can only guess that you took a wrong turn somewhere along the way." He pushed in the cigarette lighter and Sally gave it an impotent glare, rolling down her window in exaggerated disapproval.

"Well, I didn't."

"Didn't what?"

"Didn't take one wrong turn. I took several."

"I'm not spending another night in a sleazy hotel with you," he warned.

"There are a number of men who'd consider it a great treat to share a sleazy motel room with me," she said with undaunted cheer.

"I'm not one of them. Where the hell are we?"

"Twenty-seven miles away."

"Oh yeah? Pardon me for sounding skeptical, but..."

"Look at the road sign, Diamond. I made so many wrong turns, I finally ended up where I belonged."

"Only six hours later," he groused.

"Well, maybe if I'd had a navigator instead of someone snoring beside me..."

"I don't snore," Diamond said.

"You do. Both last night and all day long. I hate to think how you'd be if you had any Scotch. You'd probably be comatose."

"Don't count on it. If Isaiah keeps a well-stocked bar in your summer house, you're going to have a chance to find out."

Sally bit her lip. "James..." she said hesitantly. "I don't like people who drink too much."

The silence in the car was oppressive, broken only by the rush of warm night air outside the windows. "Then I guess I'm going to have to live with the fact that you don't like me," he said finally. "Let's leave it at that."

But Sally had never left anything alone in her life. "But why? It can't make you feel good. It makes people stupid and sloppy and sick the next day."

"It dulls the pain."

"What pain? What's hurting so badly that you have to ruin your life—"

"Hey, Carrie Nation, I'm not ruining my life, okay? I like to drink, okay? I'm not hurting anyone but myself, and I figure it's my business."

"You hurt the people who care about you."

He took a deep drag of his cigarette and the tip glowed in the darkness. "Like I said, I'm not hurting anyone but myself."

"Diamond, people care about you...."

"Listen, Sally, my partner's dead, and his family just find me an upsetting reminder of all they've lost. My own family's been gone a long time, my ex-wife is happily remarried, and the guys I used to work with are just as closed up as I am."

"What about women?"

"What about women?" he countered, hostility thick in his voice.

"Surely there must be someone..."

"I keep away from women who expect anything of me. My relationships are casual, friendly, expecting nothing but a damned good time in bed. I avoid entanglements, women who fall in love, who dream dreams, who think I'm something I can never be. I avoid women like you."

It was a direct hit, one she couldn't duck. All she could do was sit there and absorb the blow. "Fair enough," she said, her voice deceptively even. "But what about you?"

"What about me?"

"Don't you think you deserve better? Don't you think you're worth more than drinking yourself into an early grave? Don't you think—"

"Give me a break, lady!" Diamond shot back. "Have you seen me rolling around on the floor? Drooling and staggering? I like Scotch. There are times when I like a lot of Scotch. There are times when I like too much Scotch. But I'm not drinking myself into an early grave, and I can stop anytime I want to."

"Then stop now."

"Have I mentioned that I am going to strangle you?"

"Several times. Please don't drink, Diamond. For me."

"Lady, that's the one thing calculated to get me completely wasted."

"Diamond..."

"Do you think we could discuss something other than my drinking habits?" he said in a bored tone of voice.

"Like why the Calderinis want the Manchurian falcon. What are they planning to do with it?"

Clearly the subject matter was closed. For now. Sally had no intention of letting it stay off-limits indefinitely, but she was willing to compromise. "I gather they're planning to give it to the Chinese when they have their meeting. At least, that's what it sounded like when I eavesdropped on Vinnie and Alf."

"When and where is the meeting?"

"I don't remember. It was more than six weeks ago when I left for Europe. I thought everything was behind me."

"The Calderinis shouldn't be underestimated. If they're planning to give it the Chinese then they mustn't have had their meeting yet."

"Why do you say that?"

"Because the Chinese would know it wasn't the real falcon, and they'd be after us like fleas on a dog. We've probably got a few more days until they find out they've got a ringer on their hands. But how did they know your father had the falcon in the first place? Was it ever exhibited? Photographed? He said it was the pride of his collection—I would have thought he'd keep it under tighter security."

"There's a little problem with the falcon."

"What's that?"

"It's not really his. He somehow got his hands on it after the war. As far as I know, its existence is a secret."

"Not much of a secret, if he told me the first time he met me."

"That's different."

"Why?" Diamond demanded, tossing his cigarette out the cracked window.

"He liked you."

"So he said."

"He approves of you."

"I'm thrilled."

"He wants you to marry me."

"I'm— What the hell makes you say that? You didn't even know I'd met him."

"Well, if he'd talked to me, I know he would have said so," she said, trying not to sound defensive. "I know Isaiah very well. I know who he approves of and who he doesn't. He's hated every one of my fiancés."

"Is that why you got engaged to them? Some sort of rebellion against Daddy?"

She considered it for a moment. "Actually, no. It always grieved me that he didn't like the men I chose. It didn't surprise me, just grieved me. I tended to pick men I could handle. Isaiah wanted someone who could handle me. That's why I know he approves of you."

The stunned silences lasted only a moment. "Handle you? Are you nuts? You are driving me out of my mind. If I don't find your sister and the falcon in the next couple of days, you can simply drop me at the nearest mental hospital."

Sally laughed, a deep throated chuckle. "You're tougher than that, Diamond. I imagine if it came to a full-scale battle between the two of us, you'd always come out on top." A moment later, the import of what she said came through and Sally choked.

Diamond slid down in the seat. "Oh, not always on top. It gets boring that way."

"You know what I mean."

"I don't understand why you're blushing. You charge through life like a maniac, but all I have to do is mention sex and you suddenly become shy. You brought it up."

"I did not. I just made an unfortunate slip. And I wish you wouldn't do that!"

"Do what?" he asked lazily.

"Make suggestive remarks when you know perfectly well you don't mean it. You have no intention of going to bed with me, so you shouldn't tease me about it."

"I have no intention of doing so," he agreed. "However, you know what the road to hell is paved with."

"Diamond, making love to me is not hell."

"I wouldn't know."

"Diamond...!"

"You still haven't answered my question. How did the Calderinis know about the falcon if it's existence is a secret?"

"I haven't the faintest idea. Maybe the Chinese kept track of it for all these years."

"Don't you care? It might prove to be important. Whoever took the real falcon had to know of its existence. Maybe that's the person who tipped off the Calderinis in the first place. Maybe if we find out who told them we can find out who has it now."

"It doesn't matter. If we get close enough to the Calderinis to find out who told them, then we'll be close enough to get Lucy away."

"Just because we're close enough doesn't mean we'll be able to do it."

"Are you always this pessimistic?" she asked, irritated.

"Naah, sometimes I'm positively morose. Are we ever going to get to Mount Sara?"

Sally jerked the wheel, throwing him against the side of the car as she gunned the engine. They started up a narrow, winding road as fast she could make it, the bumps and ruts making Diamond curse in ill-concealed pain. At the end of the track, she slammed on the brakes, her passenger hurtling forward, restrained only by the seat belt she'd insisted he wear.

"Yes," she said sweetly.

"Yes, what?"

"Yes, we're going to get to Mount Sara. We're here."

Diamond looked up, past the windshield to the silhouette of the gabled and dormered old house. "We're here," he echoed. "And they're not."

Sally's temper vanished abruptly as she stared at the house, a woebegone expression on her face. "No, they're not," she said in a quiet voice. "I hadn't thought that far ahead. What do we do next?"

"We're not going any farther tonight. My ribs couldn't take it. Besides, I didn't really expect to find them here. Did you?"

"Then why did we come here?"

Diamond shrugged. "I was humoring you before we headed back to San Francisco. This was only supposed to take four hours, remember? I don't suppose this place comes equipped with a telephone?"

"It does if it hasn't been turned off for the season. Why? I thought your stool pigeons didn't accept phone calls?"

"Such a sweet tongue," he chided. "There are a few people I can try. Why don't you see if you can rustle up something to eat while I see what I can find out?"

"Women's work?"

"Hey, it's your house. And believe me, you wouldn't want to try my cooking."

"I believe you."

It was a warm night. The air smelled of pine pitch and fresh air and dry leaves, the warm, nostalgic smell that reminded Sally of long summer nights when everything was so much simpler. For a moment, she simply stood by the car and breathed in the earthy aroma, feeling an accustomed tightening in her stomach. Diamond had moved ahead, walking with a bit more ease then he had that morning, and for a moment, she watched him.

When had she thought she was three quarters in love with him? It seemed ages ago. That last twenty-five percent had fallen, and she couldn't imagine why. He was everything she'd been wary of. A cynic, a loner, someone who probably didn't even know how to care. He smoked too much, drank too much, and he lived a life-style that was as foreign as it was romantic. Her fantasy world was dissolving into a reality that she could no longer manage. She wanted James Diamond. She wanted the reality of him. And she didn't even know what that reality was.

The house was cool and faintly musty smelling when she unlocked the front door, dumping their suitcases inside. But the power and water were still on, and moments after Diamond disappeared, she could hear the dialing of the telephone.

She wanted to listen in. She wanted something to eat even more. By the time Diamond appeared in the huge, old-fashioned kitchen, she had canned soup boiling on the stove, blackened toast on the table and a pot of coffee perking cheerfully.

"You aren't much more of a cook than I am," Diamond observed as he sat down at the table.

"Your rib seems much better," she observed in return. "Mind if I punch you in it?"

"I don't think it's cracked, just bruised." He took a sip of soup. "Ever hear of a place called Desert Glory Health Spa?"

She reached into her pocket and tossed the business card onto the table. "You mean this place?"

Diamond set his spoon down with great deliberation. "Where did you get that?"

"On the floor of the office at Lake Judgment." She didn't like the sheer, frustrated rage in his eyes. "Why, do you think it's important?"

"I'm betting that's where your sister is. If you'd had the sense to show me this—"

"You weren't in any condition to listen to me. Besides, I told you I had a clue, and you told me to stop acting like Nancy Drew."

"You were the one who said you wanted to be Nancy Drew."

"Whatever. How was I to know it was important? You don't seem to take my suggestions very seriously."

"We're here, aren't we? Stuck in the middle of nowhere, with your sister somewhere in the desert, surrounded by gangsters who might just possibly want to do her a great deal of harm. Particularly if they decide she's been playing them for fools."

"They won't."

"What makes you so sure of that?" Diamond reached for his pack of cigarettes.

"I don't suppose I can tell you not to smoke in my house?" she asked plaintively.

"I don't suppose you can. What makes you think that the Calderinis won't suspect her of double-crossing them?"

"Because she's even more scatterbrained than I am. She couldn't keep a secret if her life depended on it, and by now, Vinnie would know that."

"*More* scatterbrained than you?"

"A real ditz," Sally verified. "Don't grin like that, Diamond, you look like the Cheshire Cat. I know I don't seem like the epitome of calm reason, but compared to my sister, I'm very sensible."

"Unbelievable," he said, blowing smoke in her direction. "Where's your father's Scotch?"

It was suddenly too much. She hadn't had much more sleep the night before than Diamond had had, and the long drive with its multitude of wrong turns hadn't improved her state of mind. He sat there so cool, so superior, smoking his blasted cancer weeds and demanding whiskey, and even with his bruised face and swollen knuckles, he still was almost wickedly handsome. The battered face only made him more enticing.

They'd replaced his ripped suit with jeans and a cotton sweater, and the casual clothes made him look less like something out of her silly fantasies and more like a real man. Sally wanted to jump on him and shake him out of his sardonic mood. She wanted... She no longer knew what she wanted, except to have her sister home safe.

She pushed away from the table, knocking her chair over as she went. "Find it yourself," she snapped.

"What's happened to that chirpy Nancy Drew attitude?" he drawled. "Did you finally discover I'm not the man of your dreams?"

"Maybe my worst nightmare."

"Wrong movie. I'd never pass for Stallone. Too wiry."

"There are times, Diamond, when I think I hate you," she announced with deceptive calm. "I'm going upstairs to bed. You can find a room for yourself—feel free to take any of them. You can fill the room with smoke, drink yourself into a stupor and be as unpleasant as you want. I'll see you tomorrow."

"Sally..."

"Don't apologize, Diamond," she said in a voice high-pitched with strain. "It's too late."

"I wasn't going to apologize. I simply wanted to now if you have an alarm clock. If I drink myself into a stupor, I probably won't wake up before noon."

He had that damnable smile on his face, as if he found her temper amusing. "You know, Diamond, I have had quite enough," she said pleasantly. And she tipped the kitchen table over on him, splashing him with soup and burned toast and hot coffee.

She ran then, half hoping he'd follow her. She didn't know what she expected from him, maybe just that he'd put his hands on her and things would take their natural course.

But he didn't follow her, and by the time she reached the second floor, reaction began to set in.

What was happening to her? She tried to treat life as a party, a wonderful feast for her enjoyment. Long ago, she'd learned what pain and loneliness was like, what abandonment and rejection did to one's soul when her feckless mother had left for greener pastures. She'd sworn it would never happen to her again; she'd never care about someone who could twist her around inside.

So why had she fallen for someone like James Diamond when she'd been so careful for so long?

It was too late, she thought as she moved down the second-floor hallway toward the door at the back. She couldn't withdraw into her shell like a cheerful tortoise and pretend that it never happened.

And she sure as hell couldn't make a cynic like Diamond fall in love with her. So she had one choice and one choice alone. To pretend it never happened.

After all, he didn't have to know she'd fallen in love with him. She certainly hadn't given any indication of it—she'd done her best to argue with him night and day. And even though she had kissed him back with enthusiasm, that was acceptable, since he'd been the one initiating the kiss in the first place. It was only polite to kiss back, wasn't it?

The door to the attic creaked loudly in the silent house as she opened it. The musty air was stronger there, staler than in the rest of the house, and she supposed she should be feeling uneasy, stepping into the darkness.

She shut the door behind her and leaned against it, reveling in the sense of safety and peace as it washed over her. It was an unseasonably warm night for autumn in the mountains, and the moon was almost full, shining in the casement windows at the far end of the attic.

She fumbled in the darkness for the table she always kept beside the door. The candelabrum was there, and the matches, and in a moment, she'd managed to create a decent amount of light.

The old iron bed was where it belonged, angled beneath one of the casement windows. The old feather bed was there, the piles of antique quilts that no one knew she'd stolen from the rest of the house, the four pillows and the bookcase full of her favorite books. *The Secret Garden, A Little Princess,* Nancy Drew mysteries from the thirties. Historical romances published in the early seventies, teeming with sex, Jane Austen novels full of proper courtships. Fantasies, all of them, a world in which nothing could hurt her.

She climbed up onto the high bed and opened the window, letting in the warm night breeze. She could see the Alfa parked below, the moonlight gilding its dark green paint. For a moment, she wondered where Diamond was, and then she put the thought out of her mind. She didn't need to be thinking about Diamond or Philip Marlowe or Rhett Butler. She simply needed a few moments of peace, without thinking about anything or anyone at all. Later, when she'd regained some of her usual amour propre, she could deal with things. Things like Diamond. And the ache inside her. And why the hot water still worked and the phone was still running and the air in the rest of the house barely smelled musty. For now, all she wanted to do was breathe in the warm night air and dream of happy endings.

Even though she knew, in the best of hard-boiled detective novels the endings were always bittersweet and the boy didn't get the girl. For now, she could pretend this was Jane Austen, not Raymond Chandler. And that she was going to live happily ever after. At least for one night.

Chapter Twelve

The house settled down around her. Diamond must have located the shower—Sally could hear the screech of ancient pipes through the attic. And then stillness once more, with only the sound of the soft breeze through the ancient pines, the creak of the bed springs and the ancient stirrings of the old house to break the silence.

In the end, it didn't take that long for him to find her. She was kneeling on the high bed, resting her arms on the sill of the open window, when she heard the door open behind her. She didn't turn; all her attention was focused on the moon.

"When I was young," she said in a dreamy voice, "I used to run away from Lucy and Isaiah and Jenkins. I'd hide up here with bags of cookies and bottles of pop, and piles and piles of books. I'd spend hours up here, listening to them call my name, lost in my own special world. Isaiah says I'm still lost in my own special world."

She heard the creak of the old wood floors as he crossed the attic, but she still kept her back to him. Afraid to look at him. Afraid to let him look at her, to let him read all the longing that consumed her soul.

"What did you think about?" His voice was low, husky from cigarettes, and dangerously beguiling.

She shrugged, pushing her hair back away from her face. "What every lonely adolescent dreams of. A hero to rescue me from my solitude. A white knight to carry me off. Most hot, summer nights, I'd lie here alone and wish I had someone to share this bed with me beneath the moonlight." She smiled wryly into the darkness. "Someone to show me the things I read about in books. Someone to take care of me."

He was closer, standing at the edge of the bed. "That's bad politics. Women shouldn't want to be taken care of anymore. They should want equal partners."

"When you're seventeen, you don't worry about politics. You think with your heart."

"Seventeen-year-old boys think with their glands."

"I remember," she said.

"I don't take care of anyone."

"I know," she said, resting her chin on her arms. "But there's nothing wrong with being taken care of. As long as you can take care of the other person in return. Everyone needs a little comfort every now and then."

"I'm not someone to provide comfort."

"I know," she said again.

"How old are you? Twenty-seven? Twenty-eight?"

"Twenty-eight."

"Then I'm ten years older than you. That's too much of an age difference."

"I know," she said, turning from the window to look at him.

The candles beside the bed had guttered down, and the empty attic was lit only with moonlight. He was standing too close, and his body radiated tension. He was wearing his jeans and nothing else. She could see the droplets of water across his bare shoulders. He hadn't replaced his elastic bandage, and the bruising across his torso didn't look quite as bad in the moonlight. He still looked battered, tough and very handsome. And very very dear.

"I didn't think you'd be able to find me," she said, her own voice as rough as his.

"I'm a private investigator, remember? It's my job to find missing people." He didn't move. He didn't walk away, as she half expected. He didn't come closer, close enough to touch her, as she half hoped.

"Yes," she said, suddenly patient, suddenly sure.

"I'm going to find your sister—"

"I don't want to talk about my sister."

He was so good at shielding his emotions. "Then I might as well go back to bed."

"Yes," she said, patient as she'd never been before.

"Yes," he said, moving toward her, sliding his hand behind her neck, underneath her hair and pulling her up to him. He held her there for a moment, and in the darkness, his eyes glittered down into hers as his mouth hovered over her parted lips. "This is a mistake," he murmured.

"I know."

His lips brushed hers, gently, soft against her. Softer, sweeter than she would have thought. And then harder, pressing, opening his mouth against her, using his lips, his tongue, his teeth as his other hand snaked around her waist and pulled her up tight against him, her full breasts pressed against his naked, bruised chest.

For a moment, she was afraid to reach out and touch him, afraid to do more than let him kiss her with an intensity that was as devastating as it was practiced. Once she lifted her hands and touched him, she'd be lost. Vulnerable, open to him, with no more defenses or holding back.

He lifted his head and looked down at her in the moonlight. "Put your arms around me, Sally," he said evenly. And her last hesitation was lost.

His skin was smooth, hot beneath her fingers. She could feel bone and muscle beneath his flesh, feel strength and power. She shivered lightly in the night breeze, and then he kissed her again, a full, deep kiss that ended any doubts. This was the man she loved. For some reason, he wanted her, at least for that night. She would take what she could get.

He eased her back down on the high bed, against the welter of quilts, following her down with a fluid grace belied by the bruise on his ribs. Stretching out beside her, he began unfastening the row of tiny buttons on her silk blouse, his face in shadows, unreadable. Pushing the fragile material out of the way, he covered her breast with one large hand and she realized he planned to take her without speaking a word.

She didn't expect declarations of love from him. She wouldn't have believed them. But she needed something more than this dedicated silence, this attention to business that had him unfastening her jeans with far too much expertise.

She put her hands over his, stalling him. "Wait," she begged, her breath coming in short rasps.

"Change your mind?" It was a challenge, pure and simple. He wanted an excuse to stop, to leave her. Before he got as enmeshed as she was.

"I just wanted..." she began. "I wanted..."

He wasn't going to make it easy for her. "What did you want?"

"Don't...don't frighten me," she said, putting her hand over his as she had that morning, unwilling to let him leave.

He froze. "You're forgetting something. Philip Marlowe isn't a sensitive New Age kind of guy."

"But you're not Philip Marlowe."

"Remember that."

She wouldn't have thought he'd be so deft, sliding her clothes off her without fumbling, pushing them onto the floor. She was shivering slightly, but the moonlit night was still warm and she knew it had to be nerves. And then he pulled her into his arms, wrapping his body around her, and the nerves, the doubts vanished. It had been long, too long since she'd even wanted this. The need she felt for him was so tense, so rare, that she thought she might explode from it.

He was almost frighteningly efficient about it. He seemed to know just what to do, just where to touch her, how hard, how soft, to elicit the response he wanted. She hadn't known her breasts were so sensitive, but beneath his hands, his mouth, her reactions were astonishingly strong. She lay beside him on the bed, squirming, whimpering, straining to get closer to him as he quickly, cleverly brought her to the edge of explosion, all without letting her touch him.

Just when she thought she'd go mad from frustration, from being so close and yet so far, he pulled her beneath him, spreading her trembling legs with his big hands and filling her with a thrust that belied the distant control he was exerting. She could feel the iron tension running through his body and feel the sweat on his hot skin, and she knew that he was not nearly as removed, as proficient as he would have her believe. He was holding back even as he filled her body, holding back his heart, his soul, his emotions even as he was giving her a kind of pleasure she'd never felt.

She wanted to keep that response from him. She wanted to argue, to force him to break through that control, but the words wouldn't come, her hands could only clutch his sweat-slick shoulder, her body could only move with his, reaching for him, clenching around him in a sudden shower of stars.

She remembered being almost surprised that he followed her, his body going rigid in her arms, his eyes closed tight, his mouth clamped shut as he gave her the one thing he couldn't withhold.

She wanted to cry. She wanted to scream at him, shove him away from her. He'd given her the most profound physical experience of her life, and he'd done it like a scientist, an observer, hardly involved in the act at all until the climax. And she knew that despite everything, after tonight, she'd never be able to break free. No matter how much he wanted her to.

She waited for him to pull away. To roll over and fall asleep, to get up and leave her. To somehow pull his defenses even more tightly around him, leaving her out in the cold.

She could feel his fingers on her temples, pushing her hair away from her face. She could feel the dampness and realized she must have been crying, after all. She waited, patiently, knowing he was going to leave her.

"Sally," he said, his voice husky. "Open your eyes."

She didn't want to. She had her own secrets now, her own love and distrust that she didn't want him to see. But she couldn't resist his quiet request. She couldn't resist anything he asked of her.

His face was in shadows, looming over hers. "Don't look at me like that," he said.

"Like what?"

"Like I just kicked your dog. You came. I felt it. You can't pretend—"

"Do we have to have this conversation?" she demanded, thoroughly embarrassed, pushing at him. She'd never realized quite how big he was until she was trying to shove his almost-two-hundred-pound frame off her much smaller one.

"Yes. Don't tell me you're going to be one of those women who hates any man once she goes to bed with him."

"You've run into that before?"

"A few times."

She stared up at him, willing her expression to be stony. "Then maybe it's your technique."

She waited for him to leave. She knew perfectly well she'd said the one thing calculated to drive any man away. And she wanted to. She wanted him to leave her alone so that she could pull her tattered defenses back around her and somehow deal with the rest of her life.

But he didn't move. To her amazement, he stroked the sides of her face with his thumbs, and his voice was very gentle. "What's wrong, Sally? You didn't want me to tell you I loved you, did you?"

She couldn't tell him. Couldn't tell him that she'd never felt so alone in her life. Couldn't tell him that she didn't want him to say he loved her. She simply wanted him to love her. So she remained silent, trapped beneath him, mute and miserable.

He kissed her then, a gentle brushing of his mouth against hers, a gentle teasing of her passivity into a burgeoning response. He kept on kissing her, coaxing her into participation, until her arms came up around him, and her last conscious thought was that even if it was all a performance designed for her pleasure, there was no denying her pleasure was something she'd never felt before. And right then, she'd rather have misery with James Diamond than a comfortable life without him.

JAMES WAITED UNTIL she slept. The breeze from the open window was cooler now, and he pulled one of the old quilts up around her bare shoulders. She murmured something, sighed and snuggled deeper into the feather bed, and for the moment, her face was smooth, untroubled, even happy.

He sat up carefully. He knew how to move without making a sound, he knew how to leave a bed without disturbing the woman sleeping next to him. He was adept at that particular feat. He didn't like to sleep with the women he made love with. Hell, he'd hated the fact that he'd slept with Sally in the motel, even though that time he'd kept his pants on. That was probably behind his current mess. If he'd just stayed out of bed with her in that motel, he never would have been tempted to make love to her tonight.

He gave a quiet snort, contemptuous of his weak rationalizations. Hell, he'd wanted to make love to Sally MacArthur since the moment she'd showed up at his office. She'd been arguing with Frankie, and he'd assumed she was one of his girls and had immediately started considering whether he could break an ironclad rule and pay for it just once.

It would have been better if she were a hooker. James didn't have many scruples, but one hard-and-fast rule was never sleep with a client. It just made things too messy, particularly when you handed them the bill.

And he kept away from women like Sally, trouble through and through. But this time, he hadn't kept far enough away.

And he couldn't even blame it on booze. He hadn't had a drink in more than two days, and he was thinking of making it longer. He'd found her father's Scotch with no trouble at all, even poured himself a generous glass. He'd poured that generous glass down the old iron sink and headed upstairs in search of his client.

He didn't know why he went looking for her. Maybe to do something as asinine as tell her he wasn't going to drink and see if she'd give him a pat on the head. Maybe to fight with her enough to goad him into going back downstairs to the bottle. Or maybe to do exactly what he'd ended up doing.

Well, he'd done it. Twice, as a matter of fact, and he could have gone for a third if she hadn't looked exhausted. He'd managed to keep himself fairly uninvolved the first time around. It had been sheer cussedness on his part. She'd spent the past few days being so damned perky, he'd wanted to see what she looked like in his arms, dazed with pleasure.

And she was amazingly responsive. No defenses at all once her clothes were stripped away. She had burned in his arms like a torch, and it had taken all his wavering control not to ignite with her.

But the second time, his control had gone. He tried to tell himself he just wanted to pleasure her, but somehow, his own needs became overpowering. Particularly when she pushed him over onto his back and began kissing him, dancing her mouth across his bruised torso with feather-light kisses.

He hadn't realized she'd be so good with her hands. Outside of bed, she was slightly, endearingly clumsy. In bed, she was a gazelle—graceful, sleek, magical. This time, he didn't make love to her. This time, they were in it together and he couldn't choke back his cry of pleasure when he came with her. And he knew he'd called her name.

He looked down at her, sleeping so peacefully now, the tears dried on her pale cheeks, her silky black hair tangled around her. He needed to move away, back to his own bed, back to his own life.

She'd gotten what she'd wanted all along. She'd slept with her vision of Philip Marlowe. She'd gotten Sam Spade into bed—no, she'd gotten Sam Spade to seduce her on the childhood bed where she had her first erotic day-dreams. And James had played right into it because he couldn't help himself. Because she made him vulnerable the way no one, man or woman, had managed to in years and years.

But he wasn't Philip Marlowe or anyone remotely like him. And he wasn't here to fulfill her fantasies or be her fantasy lover. This was a one-night stand, and he'd tell her that first thing in the morning.

In the meantime, he was going to find his own bed and forget about her luscious body curled up in that quilt. He was going to forget the way her arms and legs wrapped around him and the soft little noises she made, which were the same and yet different from the noises other women made. Damn, he'd hear those noises in his sleep for a long, long time.

All he had to do was slide out of bed. He wouldn't wake her; he knew that perfectly well. All he had to do was get away now, fast, before he got any more entangled with her.

His hand moved, almost of its own volition, and pushed the strand of hair away from her mouth. In her sleep, she moved against him, pushing her face against his hand like a contented kitten, and murmured something unintelligi-ble. It sounded hideously close to "love," but he couldn't ask her to repeat it. He could only hope it was his imagination. And not wishful thinking.

It took him almost till dawn to climb out of that bed. There was something so peaceful about the way she slept, at odds with her constant chatty energy during the day. And he didn't move far, only to the sagging director's chair beside the bed.

He sat there, his jeans pulled up but not fastened, and watched her while she slept. Knowing that if he wanted anything like a normal life in the future this would be the last time he could watch her while she slept. It was back to a business relationship when the sun rose. Back to the search for her sister. Back to reality.

Whether he liked it or not.

JAMES AWOKE WITH A START, one of those jerky little movements that come when you're fool enough to try to fall asleep in a chair. The day was colder again, and the air coming in through the open casement window was chilly.

The bed was empty, the pile of quilts on the floor. He could hear the noise of the water pipes—she must be off taking a shower. He looked down his lap. She'd thrown one of the quilts over him. Had tucked it around him, in fact.

He stared at it, running a wondering hand over the faded patchwork design. It had been decades since someone had tucked him in. It gave him a peculiar feeling—uneasy, oddly sentimental.

He yanked the quilt off and stood up, stretching angrily. He wasn't the kind of man who liked or needed to be tucked in. Why the hell didn't she realize that? Why the hell didn't he realize that?

He passed the first bathroom as he padded down the hallway. He could hear her humming over the noise of the shower, and he felt that old companion, guilt, begin to eat at his gut. She was expecting things from him, he just knew it, and he was going to have to tell her that she couldn't.

He washed up in the downstairs bathroom, throwing on a fresh T-shirt and brushing his teeth. He looked marginally more human in the mirror—the black eye was beginning to turn yellow, and the scrapes on his face were starting to heal. He still looked like someone who'd gone ten rounds with King Kong. He also knew that his slightly swollen lips hadn't come from anybody's fist.

He could smell coffee when he stepped out into the hall. Real coffee, not instant, the sweetest smell in the world. He'd wait to tell her. He'd even put up with sappy glances and good-morning smooches for a decent cup of coffee. Or three or four. Maybe he could even justify a brief return to the creaking iron bed....

Down boy, he ordered himself. There was no justification whatsoever. Last night was last night; this morning was a whole new day. Squaring his shoulders, he marched down the hallway to the huge, old kitchen, then halted in dumbfounded amazement.

"Good morning, handsome," the woman at the kitchen table greeted him saucily, waving her cup of coffee at him. "Want a mug?"

She had Sally's china blue eyes, except Sally's were warmer, happier. She had Sally's mouth, except that he didn't want to kiss this one. She had ash blond hair, and even though he knew she was years younger, she looked to be in her early thirties, older in worldly wisdom if not in years.

"Hello," he said evenly, not giving anything away.

"Sally still in bed? You must have been showing her a hell of a good time—she's usually up with the rooster. I didn't know she knew how to cut loose. I guess there's hope for everyone."

He didn't like this woman. Sibling rivalry was nothing new to a man with two brothers he never even sent Christmas cards to, but he didn't like her. He could hear the steady thud of Sally's footsteps as she came down the stairs at her usual breakneck pace, and to stall for time he headed for the coffeepot, pouring himself and Sally each a mug.

"How long have you been here?"

The woman grinned. "Long enough, handsome. I recognized Sally's car when I came back last night, and I was all set to have a cozy little gossip with her when I heard the bedsprings. So I figured she wasn't alone. What I didn't figure was that her taste would make such a rapid improvement. You're a hell of a lot more man than the usual wimps she hangs around with. Don't tell me it's true love?"

The door to the kitchen slammed open and Sally stood there, shock making her skin whiter than usual, except for the two bright red spots on her cheekbones.

James took a sip of his scalding coffee, stalling for time, telling himself it didn't matter if she was still so damned beautiful he wanted to carry her back upstairs. Last night wasn't going to change anything.

"As you can see," he drawled, "our troubles are over. Sister Lucy's come home to roost."

Sally closed her eyes for a moment, then opened them, shaking her head. "Not quite, Diamond," she said wryly. "What we have before us is the proverbial bad penny."

"Is that any way to put it, darling?" the woman protested in a silky voice.

Sally ignored her. "Diamond," she said flatly, "meet my mother."

Chapter Thirteen

"You might at least sound more welcoming, darling," Sally's mother said in a cheerful drawl. "It's been almost a year since you've seen me. How about a hug?"

"It's been two and a half years since I've seen you," Sally said, mustering her last vestiges of calm. As if this morning wasn't going to be traumatic enough, facing Diamond, she had to contend with her mother's astonishing reappearance. Trust Marietta to show up at the worst possible time. Never when she was needed. "And I learned years ago that hugging you messed up your hair and makeup. I'll blow you a kiss." Her salute was just faintly mocking, and Marietta nodded, accepting the mockery.

For a moment, Sally thought she detected the faint shimmer of hurt in her mother's blue eyes. She dismissed the very notion, just as she had long ago dismissed the vain hope that her mother ever cared more for her child than she did for her own pleasures. She'd always wanted to see pain and hurt in her mother's eyes, some sign of love and caring. They'd always been blank, and she'd learned to accept that.

Diamond was standing beside the counter, a mug of coffee in one big hand. He had that wary expression on his face that she'd been expecting, and she sighed inwardly. He looked too damned handsome in the morning light, and not a bit like a hard-boiled detective in a black T-shirt and jeans. She wanted to cross the room, put her arms around his lean waist and rest her head against his chest. She wanted him to hold her, just for a moment, and make the bad dreams go away.

But that was a mistake she wasn't about to make. "Got some coffee for me?" she asked instead, as casually as if they'd spent the night on different planets.

She'd surprised him, she could see that. Score one for her. Marietta nearly blew it with her arch intervention. "Is that any way for young lovers to greet each other in the morning?" she cooed.

"It's been a long time since you were a young lover, Marietta," Sally said flatly. "It's the way we do things nowadays." She took the mug from Diamond's hand, careful not to touch him. Touching him would set off all sorts of impossible longings, and it was taking every ounce of her concentration to be calm and matter-of-fact. "Thanks," she said, dismissing him, feeling once again his start of surprise.

She moved to the table, sinking down opposite her mother. "So, what brings you here, Ma?" she asked, her voice ironic. "You always hated this place when you were married to Isaiah. What makes you show up here at this particular time? And how did you get a key?"

"Darling, I don't need keys if I want to go someplace. And besides, Isaiah has been very generous, you know that. Unlike you, he doesn't bear grudges. He doesn't expect me to be anyone other than who I am."

"I've heard this before. Why are you here?" Once again, Sally might have imagined the hurt expression in Marietta's eyes.

"Just passing through, darling. I stopped by to see you all in San Francisco and only Isaiah was home. He had no idea where you and Lucy were."

"So you came looking for us?"

"Hardly. I haven't changed that much. I decided I needed some peace and quiet. Some fresh air away from the bustle of the city. It was sheer good luck that you happened to turn up. Where, by the way, is your sister?" It was tossed off almost casually, an afterthought, but Sally wasn't fooled. For some reason, Marietta was just as concerned about Lucy as she was.

"Didn't you hear Diamond when he saw you? He thought you were Lucy. We haven't the faintest idea where she is."

Marietta flashed Diamond her most magnificent smile, the one calculated to make strong men weep. He didn't look teary eyed, but then, he was made of sterner stuff than that. "Darling man," Marietta cooed. "Mind you, I was very young when I had my children—"

"You've also had four bouts of cosmetic surgery," Sally interjected with a daughter's ruthlessness.

"You're behind the times. I'm up to six. It's amazing the things a plastic surgeon can do nowadays." Marietta took a delaying sip of her coffee. "So you're looking for Lucy? Why?"

"Who says we're looking for Lucy?"

"Your gentleman friend. Diamond, you called him. What a delicious name. How did you two lovebirds meet?"

Diamond had understandably had enough of this. He took the third chair at the table, swung it around and straddled it with a casual grace. "Sally and I are old friends," he said. "She's the only one who gets away with calling me Diamond. I prefer James."

Marietta once more tried that high-voltage smile. Diamond blinked in the light for a moment, but resisted. "And I'm Marietta. Heavens, I don't even know what my current last name is. I suppose I'm still Von Troppenburg, but I won't be for long. So you've known my daughter a long time? Are you one of her fiancés? I had word that she was going to marry a gangster."

"How'd you hear that?" Sally demanded.

"Oh, I have my sources," Marietta said, waving an airy hand. "So that doesn't explain who you are, James."

"What makes you think I'm not the gangster?"

Marietta nodded, according him the hit. "I'm assuming you're not. You don't look like a gangster."

"Neither did Vinnie," said Sally. "Besides, how do you know what a gangster looks like?"

"Darling, I've lived a long and adventurous life, despite my extremely youthful good looks." She cast a roguish smile at Diamond. "So, you dumped the gangster and moved on to a private detective. You always were one for extremes."

Sally set her mug down on the table, her eyes meeting Diamond's for one pregnant moment, devoid of any memory of the night before. "How did you know he was a private detective?" she asked carefully.

Marietta didn't even flinch. "Why, you said so, darling."

"No, I didn't."

"Of course, you did. How else would I know?"

"She didn't," Diamond said, his voice deep and raspy.

Marietta simply smiled. "I say she did. You two are both still suffering from the afterglow of your energetic night. Though I must say the two of you don't seem to be glowing."

"Answer my question, Marietta. How did you know what Diamond does for a living?"

Marietta shrugged. "I suppose I have to be honest?"

"If you possibly can."

"I went through his wallet. He'd left it in one of the upstairs bedrooms, and you know how insatiably curious I am." She made a tiny moue. "There, I admit it. I am without honor."

Sally stared at her, immune to the masterful performance. She didn't believe her. Oh, Marietta would certainly go through any wallet that happened to be lying around, and she wasn't above filching spare cash if she happened to need it. But the answer was just a little too easy, and too hard to prove otherwise. "You'll never change," Sally said.

"Lord, I hope you're wrong. How fatally boring to be predictable. I am never predictable."

"Yes, you are. You're never there when you're needed, and you're always around when you're not wanted," Sally said flatly.

This time, there was no mistaking the hurt in Marietta's eyes. "That's a terrible thing to say." Her voice was choked.

"Well, I guess that makes me a terrible daughter. It runs in the family." Sally drained her coffee and pushed back from the table. "This is a waste of time. I'm going to get my things together. Diamond and I are taking off. I don't suppose you want us to drop you anywhere?"

Marietta's pathetic grief vanished instantly. "I have my own car. Where are you going, darling? Off to see Lucy?"

"Nope. We're just going on a round of endless sex in strange places. I think we're going to try for Yosemite next."

Marietta beamed at her. "There's hope for you yet, darling."

Sally looked pointedly at Diamond, who'd been taking this all in without saying a word. "Are you coming?"

"In a minute," he said. "I need another cup of coffee."

The last thing in the world Sally wanted to do was to leave James Diamond alone with Marietta. He was tough, all right, but Marietta had powers unknown to mortal man. She could have him eating out of her hand in a matter of minutes. She could have him...she could have him...

Sally shook herself, disgusted at her paranoia. "I'll meet you in front in ten minutes. See you around, Marietta."

"No goodbye kiss?"

"I thought we settled that." She blew her another mocking kiss. She hadn't touched her mother in seven years, not since Marietta had taken off with the lawyer's clerk Sally had been in love with, and she wasn't about to start now. Not when Marietta was so obviously lying to her.

Besides, Sally was more like her mother than Marietta suspected. Closing the door behind her, Sally moved swiftly, silently through the house, heading with unerring instinct to the master bedroom, where Marietta had set up shop.

Marietta didn't come equipped with anything as organized or mundane as a wallet. Her Gucci purse was stuffed with store receipts, uncashed checks, parking tickets, makeup and airplane ticket stubs. Sally moved fast, pawing through things, looking for some sort of clue to her mother's reappearance. As far as she could tell, her mother had flown in from the Riviera, having spent time in Germany, Italy, and Ireland since the last time she had emptied out her purse.

Within moments, Sally gave up. There was no way of finding out anything about Marietta that she didn't want found out. If she had some hidden agenda, if she knew anything about Lucy's whereabouts, she'd divulge that information on her terms alone. It would do no good to ask, to beg, to plead. Marietta was a law unto herself, and all the longing of a little girl for a real mother wouldn't change the way life was.

Diamond was waiting on the front porch, smoking a cigarette. He had that unreadable expression on his face, the one that hid so many secrets, and Sally was feeling just a bit too fragile to try to work her way past those secrets. She concentrated on the symptoms instead, starting an argument.

"Is that your first cigarette of the day?"

"It is."

"Why are you smoking outside? Don't tell me you finally decided that other people have lungs, too?" she demanded.

"Marietta's allergic to cigarette smoke."

Sally had always heard the term "seeing red," and she assumed it had to do with bulls and bullfights. Now she knew it was something far more basic, a bright red color at the back of the eyes when rage exploded. She had two choices—to start screaming, which would benefit no one, particularly herself, or to take deep, calming breaths.

It took her to the count of thirteen before she finally had her temper back under control. "Marietta smokes unfiltered Gauloises when she's in Europe," Sally said flatly. "It's part of her image."

She started toward the Alfa, not bothering to look back to see if Diamond was following her.

He climbed into the passenger seat, dumping their meager luggage in back. "You really hate her, don't you?" he asked, tossing his half-finished cigarette out the window.

Sally started the car with a vengeance. "No, I don't. I still love her. And that's the problem." She gunned the engine, starting down the driveway with a spurt of gravel, not daring to look back.

She knew exactly what she'd see if she was fool enough to turn around. Marietta would be on the front porch, a faint, sad expression on her face, one she'd perfected years ago, one hand fluttering in a sad farewell. Sally had fallen for it too many times.

Diamond had the extreme good sense to be quiet for the first half hour. When he did speak, his choice of subject matter was not auspicious. "Exactly where are we going?"

"I don't know," Sally snapped back.

"That's a first."

"Don't mess with me, Diamond. I'm not in a good mood."

"Neither am I. Why don't you pull over and let me drive? I have to have a better sense of direction than you have."

"Everyone has a better sense of direction than I have," she admitted. "But a sense of direction doesn't do much good if you don't know what direction you want in the first place."

"Pull over."

She didn't want to. But she couldn't keep driving aimlessly. She knew perfectly well once she stopped the car, they were going to have the conversation she'd been dreading, and she wasn't quite sure if she was up to dealing with it.

It had all seemed so very simple a few short hours ago. She had woken up in that rumpled bed, feeling better than she ever had in her life. Her body felt as rumpled as the quilts, slightly tender, warm and sated. She'd opened her eyes and had seen Diamond sitting there, sound asleep in the chair, and a rush of tenderness had swept over her.

He hadn't been able to hold back the second time. She'd determined that. And the results had been even more blindingly glorious than before, so overwhelming that she still trembled a little at the thought.

She lay in bed and watched him for a while, cozy and comfortable as she considered her options. He was going to run; she knew it. He was going to push her away, repudiate everything that had gone on the night before. He was going to be cool, distant and professional, and if she brought up the subject he'd inform her that it was a mistake or a one-night stand, or a mutually enjoyable interlude that wouldn't be repeated. She knew him too well.

She could take that kind of dismissal. She could curl up inside and weep. She could respond with angry pride. She could die a little and then move on.

Or she could fight for him. She already had a fair idea of what he was going to do next—she could forestall him, strike the first blow and keep him off balance.

Because she wasn't going to let him get away. She'd known yesterday that she was in love with him. She knew this morning that that love was worth fighting for. Even if the object of her passion was her enemy, she was going to win him over. No more self-pity, no more flight, no more fear and loathing. She'd made up her mind, and when Sally MacArthur's mind was made up, it was a formidable thing.

If only Marietta hadn't shown up when she did, Sally could have dealt the opening salvo. She'd climbed out of bed, tiptoed past the sleeping Diamond, and then, on a whim, had gone back and tucked a quilt around him. It was cold in the room and she wanted more than anything to crawl into his lap and pull that quilt around them both.

But that's what he'd expect and be prepared to reject. The only thing she could do was the opposite of what he thought she'd do. Keep him so off balance, he wouldn't realize he was in love with her until it was too late to do anything about it.

She stopped the Alfa on the side of the road, putting it in neutral. Diamond reached over and turned it off, and Sally allowed herself a long-suffering sigh. Apparently, the confrontation wasn't going to wait any longer.

"I'm in a bad mood, Diamond," she warned him as he pulled the key out of the ignition. "My mother affects me that way."

He was momentarily distracted. "Don't you think you were a little hard on her?"

"Yes, I was a little hard on her. Harder than she deserves? I don't think so. Would you like my opinion on your marriage, Diamond?" she inquired sweetly.

"It's ancient history."

"So is my relationship with my mother. She may have fooled you, but she'll never, ever fool me again."

He reached for a cigarette. "You'd be a lot happier if you didn't feel the need to pass judgment on her. She's human just like the rest of us, with human faults and failings."

"A little too human, if you ask me," Sally said, stifling her pang of guilt.

"Look, I don't want to talk about your mother."

"Fine. Neither do I. As a matter of fact, I have no interest in discussing anything but what our next step in finding Lucy is."

"We've got something else to discuss first."

Sally sighed again. "I know what you're going to say, Diamond. And I agree with you completely."

"Last night we— What?" He stared at her in amazement.

"A mistake," she said airily. "Hormones running amok, fun and all that, but unwise on both our parts. We won't let it happen again, will we?"

For the first time since they'd met she'd been able to stun him into silence. He just looked at her, his mouth open in voiceless protest, and a sudden spark of mischief overwhelmed her. She couldn't resist it, not this once.

She put a hand on his knee, plastering a solicitous expression on her face. "Oh, no, Diamond, don't tell me I misunderstood! Please, please don't say that you were going to suggest otherwise! That you might have..." she allowed herself a distressed, dramatic pause "...have fallen in love with me."

"Good God, no!" he said with unflattering haste.

"And you don't want to embark on a *relationship,* do you?" She put heavy emphasis on the word, waiting with a certain naughty satisfaction for his horrified shudder.

But this time, he surprised her. "No," he said in an even voice. "I'm not the type for relationships."

"Well," she said brightly, "neither am I. At least, not the kind you're talking about. I like to get engaged, and clearly you're not candidate number seven. You're much too distracting. So let's leave it at that, shall we?"

"No."

"Come on, Diamond." Her control was beginning to fray just a bit at the edges. "We don't need any postmortems, do we?"

"I just wanted to say I'm sorry."

Oh, God, she thought. "For what?" she said. "Not for last night, I hope. There's nothing to apologize for. We were carried away for a moment, but both of us are much too sensible. Besides, there's no need to make a federal case out of it. I'm sure you've had your share of brief flings, as have I. You simply learn to enjoy them in passing."

She was pushing it, she realized. He'd accept a certain amount of sang froid about the whole thing, but professing a great deal of experience was an easily disproven issue. He'd felt her fall apart in his arms, dealt patiently with a shyness that wouldn't have existed if she'd been through it all too often.

"Sally..." He reached out a hand to touch her, and she jerked out of the way. If he put his hands on her, her control would shatter. She'd fling herself on him, begging him to love her, and all her hard work would have been for nothing.

"Don't, James. Please." Her voice had a telltale rawness, one she couldn't hide, but she kept the cool smile plastered on her face.

For a moment, he didn't move. "All right," he said finally. "We'll leave it at that." He reached for the door handle. "For now."

She watched him walk around the front of the car. She hadn't noticed his walk before. A sexy, slouchy kind of stroll that made her think of Richard Gere at his to-hell-with-you best. She watched him, and wondered whether she'd fooled him at all with her cool renunciation. Maybe the best she could hope for was that he didn't know what to think.

The passenger seat was still warm from his body. She wriggled into it surreptitiously, drinking in the warmth through her pores, then caught him watching her curiously.

"Got an itch?" he inquired, and she suspected he was deliberately goading her.

She refused to rise to the bait. "Just tired," she said. "Do you mind telling me where we're going? Time might be running out for Lucy while we sit here and bicker."

"If Lucy's anything like the rest of the women in her family, I suspect she can take care of herself. I almost feel sorry for the Calderinis."

"What do you mean by that crack? Marietta and I have nothing in common!" Sally was immediately incensed.

"No," Diamond said, turning the car and heading in the opposite direction. "I don't suppose you do. Other than porcelain skin, blue eyes and better looks than are good for you. Of course, she's too skinny and too old, but you both are hell on wheels at lying, and the performance you just put on had to equal hers at the table this morning."

Sally was speechless. Diamond smiled with devastating sweetness. "None of which matters," he continued. "You can just keep spinning your little fantasies, and I'll do my best to see through them. At least now I can see where you got your talent from."

"Damn you, I'm not like my mother. She doesn't love anyone but herself."

"And who do you love, Sally?"

She wasn't going to let it slip. He was goading her on purpose, maybe because his ego couldn't handle that she wasn't pining with love for him. The fact that she was didn't matter—she'd go through torture before she admitted that fact to him.

"My sister and my father and Jenksy," she said flatly. "That's not very many people, and I can't afford to lose one of them while we sit around and talk absurdities. For the last time, Diamond, where the hell are we going?''

''Isn't it obvious, Sally?'' he replied, tapping his long fingers on the leather-covered steering wheel. ''We're bound for Glory.''

Chapter Fourteen

Sally just stared at him. "Glory?" she echoed.

"Glory, California. The Desert Glory Health Spa. Unless you've got a better idea."

"Aren't we grasping at straws?" she demanded.

"That's what following clues is, lady. People rarely send you engraved invitations when they're hiding out. Besides, it's a little more concrete than that. I made a couple of phone calls before I came upstairs and seduced you." James put it that way on purpose, waiting for her reaction.

He saw her hands clenched together for a moment, but she let the provocation ride over her. "I thought your informants didn't have office hours."

"I still know how to find things out when I need it. Desert Glory's a health spa, all right. Guess who owns it? I mean, after you wade through three different dummy corporations to find out who actually pulls the strings."

"The Calderinis?"

"Obviously. And you can imagine what goes on there along with mud baths and saunas."

"Gambling. But aren't they right near the Nevada border? Why would anybody bother?"

"I told you before—the danger adds spice to the games. Besides, you don't have to pay income tax on money you make on these games, and there's no limit." He pushed in the cigarette lighter. "Your sister is probably going through their seven-day beauty make-over right now, while Vinnie waits for the Bho Tsos to arrive."

"The Bozos?" she echoed in astonishment. "Who the hell are the Bozos? Some clown contingent of the Calderini family? Do they run tickle concessions as a sideline?"

"Bho Tsos," James said wearily, spelling the name. "A very ancient Chinese crime family. They're the ones who want the Manchurian falcon, not the Calderinis. Vinnie's just trying to provide it for them as a gesture of good faith. Probably also as a demonstration of his ability to get things done."

"Vinnie's not very capable," Sally muttered. "I don't think he was cut out for organized crime."

"He was born to it."

"So what? I was born to money and social activities, and I always get bored. What I'd really like to do is work for a living."

She still had the power to surprise him. "Then why don't you?" he countered with little sympathy.

There was something about her rueful smile that always got to him. "I've tried. Everybody keeps firing me. I can't even hold a volunteer job for very long. I tend to destroy office machinery. I don't know why, but photocopiers just fall apart at my fingertips. Faxes explode, computers collapse, even telephones experience core meltdown."

"Yeah, I saw what you did to my office in a few short minutes. Broke the window, the coffeepot and the overhead light."

"I did not break the light!" she protested.

"It hasn't worked since you touched it."

"You might consider changing the light bulb!"

"I don't suppose—" James stopped himself, reaching for his cigarettes instead. She had the power to infuriate him faster than anyone he'd ever known. Even his ex-wife hadn't driven him so nuts. Scratch that. His ex-wife hadn't bothered him in the slightest. He hadn't cared enough to be annoyed.

Not that he cared about Sally MacArthur, he had to remind himself. In fact, he needed to remember that he was relieved that she saw things as clearly as he did. That she grasped the futility of any possible relationship between two such disparate human beings. It was typical of the boneheaded way he'd been going about things recently, that instead of gratitude, he felt out and out annoyance that she was taking the events of the night before with such a cavalier attitude. He'd expected at least a few tears. Possibly an attempt at changing his mind, or at least at making him feel like the world's worst heel.

Instead, he felt as though he was the one who'd been seduced and abandoned. She was sitting next to him, a smug little smile on her slightly swollen lips, and the very memory of what she'd done with that mouth last night made him have to shift his position in the bucket seat.

God, he had to get away from her. They were as different as night and day, and even if either of them wanted to pursue their off-kilter attraction, it would be doomed to failure.

He needed to remember who he was and what sort of woman he did best with. The older, comfortable types who didn't expect much but a good meal beforehand and a good time afterward. Women who'd lost their innocence, their illusions years ago, and were glad of it.

Sally MacArthur was still a virgin of the soul. And he had the hideous, terrifying suspicion that despite her cool avowals, she just might fancy herself in love with him. After all, he fulfilled her favorite fantasies, and he knew better than anyone how well she responded in bed.

She wasn't used to having a man, that much was clear. And most women who didn't sleep around usually had to talk themselves into being in love with their bed partner, at least for as long as the relationship lasted. Then it turned quite abruptly to undying hatred when the man couldn't live up to her impossible expectations. It was a good thing he knew he was beaten before he even tried. Or he might find himself trying to be the man she wanted.

He needed to reunite Sally with her long-lost sister and get the hell away from her, back to the sleazy corridors and mean streets where he felt at home. He didn't belong out in the daylight, in fresh air and sunshine. He didn't belong with a twenty-eight-year-old debutante with a crush on him. And he certainly didn't belong in a life in which he hadn't had a decent drink in three days and was considering cutting back on his cigarettes. She was unmanning him, damn it, and the sooner he got away from her, the better. Because if he waited too long, he wouldn't be able to leave.

James pushed the lighter in for another cigarette; Sally reached over and yanked it out. "My mother may not be allergic to cigarette smoke, but I am," she said pointedly.

"You've been breathing in my secondhand smoke for days now, and I haven't even heard a sniffle." He pushed the lighter in again.

She yanked it out. "If you don't have any consideration for your own lungs, at least think about mine."

He pushed the lighter in. "You'll survive. I've given up Scotch for you, lady. The cigarettes stay."

She stared at him in amazement, and he recognized that telltale fatuous gaze in her blue blue eyes. "You've given up drinking for me?" she echoed in a soft voice.

"Don't get all gooey on me. I figured I couldn't stand the arguments, and you're bad enough when I don't have a headache. If I had to deal with you and a hangover at the same time, I'd probably either slit your throat or mine."

"James..."

"The moment I dump you, I'm getting the biggest, most expensive bottle of Scotch I can buy to celebrate," he warned her.

It didn't do any good. She still looked like a kid who'd won the prize at the local fair, all shiny eyed and smiling. He never should have said anything, James thought morosely. Maybe the best thing he could do was stop at the next store and buy a bottle, just to convince her that she couldn't believe a word he said.

Problem was, he really didn't want the bottle. And the cigarettes were starting to taste funky, too. The lady was going to reform him and then go on her merry way, and he'd have no happy vices to fall back on.

"There's a simple solution to that," Sally said in a cheerful voice.

"Oh, yeah? What's that?" he grumbled, eyeing the road, forgetting about his need for a cigarette for the time being.

"I simply won't let you dump me."

"That's supposed to cheer me up?" he countered. "An albatross around my neck?" He reached for the lighter one more time.

She put her hand out to stop him, and instead, he grabbed her wrist, forcibly pulling her back. Her cheerful expression vanished, but what lay behind it was even more unsettling. "Are you going to hurt me, Diamond?"

He didn't release her. "I don't hurt women," he said.

"Then let me go."

Of course, he had to. He felt foolish, driving down the highway, his hand wrapped around her slender wrist like a manacle.

He dropped her hand and reached for the cigarette lighter. She was faster than he was, yanking it out of the socket and throwing it out her open window.

He slammed the car to a halt, nearly hurtling her toward the windshield. "What the hell do you think you're doing?" he demanded, enraged.

"Throwing out my cigarette lighter. I don't have any use for the thing, and since my car is for nonsmokers, I don't see any reason to keep it."

"You ever think about forest fires?"

"Not in the middle of the rainy spell."

"I can stop at the next gas station and get matches."

"Go right ahead," Sally said affably. "At least I won't be an enabler."

"Oh, God, psychobabble garbage on top of everything else," James moaned. "What in heaven's name did I do to deserve a pest like you?"

"Just lucky, I guess," Sally said with unimpaired good cheer, keeping her hands folded in her lap.

She hadn't touched him since this morning. He'd been waiting for it, expecting it, bracing himself for it, but she'd kept her hands to herself. No soft caresses, no gentle touches, no accidental brushing of her hand against him.

He couldn't stand it any longer.

Reaching out, he caught her stubborn chin in his hand, turning her face to his. "You think you're pretty funny, don't you?" he grumbled, knowing that his fingers were caressing the smooth line of her jaw, unable to stop them.

He expected her eyes to be bright with triumph. Instead, they were vulnerable, something she was doing her best to hide. "We'll play this any way you want to, Diamond," she said in a quiet little voice.

He couldn't resist. He knew it was absolute madness on his part, but he couldn't stop himself. He leaned forward, across the seat, and kissed her, just a light feathering of his lips across hers, a momentary clinging of his mouth to hers. And then he pulled back, releasing her, and started the car once more.

"Get in the way of me and my cigarettes again," he warned in his calmest voice, "and I'll take up cigars."

James didn't dare glance at her again as he pulled back onto the highway. If he did, he might pull off at the nearest exit and head straight for a motel. The only way he was going to survive was to keep his hands off her. He'd managed for a full three hours since waking up—maybe next time, he could stretch it to six hours. But he didn't know how he was going to make it through the upcoming night.

GLORY, CALIFORNIA, was a small tourist town in the midst of the California desert. Up until the end of the self-absorbed seventies, it had been nothing but a gas station and a mom-and-pop store for the outlying residents. With the advent of the Desert Glory Health Spa, business had boomed. The town was filled with trendy little shops—New Age bookstores, basket shops, health-food restaurants and the like. Sally glanced around her as they drove through, shuddering at the vestiges of California yuppiedom. It was just after five in the afternoon, and Diamond had driven like a demon through the day, stopping long enough for a take-out meal packaged in polystyrene containers.

She'd lectured him for a solid half hour until he turned on the radio full blast. Since he'd found an oldies station with a preference for rhythm and blues, she could hardly complain, and she'd sat back and counted his cigarettes, all the time listening to her body remember the previous night.

She was going to have to do something about birth control, she realized, and probably sooner rather than later. Even if Diamond seemed determined to keep his distance, he still couldn't stop himself from kissing her. She'd kept to her side of the car, curled up and sleepy, but she'd been completely aware of the number of times he'd glanced over at her, his gaze drawn as if he couldn't help himself. She might be sleeping alone tonight. But she doubted it.

The Desert Glory Health Spa was an oasised paradise in the midst of the desert. *The water bills alone must be astronomical,* Sally thought as Diamond pulled up under the canopied front entrance. Maybe self-absorbed health fanatics could support an operation like this. But it was far more likely the Calderini gambling money underwrote the whole thing.

"How are we going to handle this?" she said, finally breaking the silence that had filled the car, and noting with disapproval that Diamond was lighting his fifth cigarette of the afternoon. "Don't tell me to stay in the car, either, because you should know by now, I'm not going to do any such thing. And are you sure we should just be driving up bold as brass? I mean, think about what happened at Lake Judgment. You may enjoy pain, but I don't find any great pleasure in patching you up."

He glanced at her and she was startled to see the alert brightness in his eyes, the faint twist of a smile at his mobile mouth. "Now I would have thought that right now there'd be nothing you'd like better than having someone beat the hell out of me again."

"Now that you mention it..."

"Forget it. And no, you're not going to wait in the car. You're getting your big chance, kid. We're going in undercover."

Her irritation with him vanished as visions of television cop shows danced in her head. "Undercover?" she echoed in delight.

"Yup. Like Philip Marlowe in *The Big Sleep,* when he first goes to the antique bookstore."

"You mean you're going to pretend to be gay?" she asked, amused at the notion.

"Don't be so literal. We're a married couple. Two professionals looking to improve our life-style. We're here for the Fast-Track Weekend Package. That should be more than enough time to find out where your sister is."

"If it isn't?"

He glanced over at her, and Sally could feel the heat in his eyes. "It will be."

She followed him into the fern-encrusted lobby like a dutiful wife, glancing around her with ill-disguised curiosity. Lucy was there—she knew it with a sixth sense that seldom appeared but was always infallible. She tugged at Diamond's sleeve, but he ignored her, and she realized with amazement that he was someone else entirely. His walk, the set of his shoulders, even his clothes looked different. He looked anonymous, like the thousands of young urban professionals who cluttered the streets of San Francisco at lunch time, moving from bank or law office or stock brokerage to the latest trendy restaurant.

There was no way she could even come close. She stumbled, clumsy, and he reached out and caught her arm, apparently aware of her even as he seemed to ignore her.

The woman behind the vast, teak desk looked like every California blonde who'd ever intimidated Sally. She looked like a Barbie doll—giant smile, perfect teeth, mile-long legs and rippling muscles. She rose as they approached, and Sally watched with ill-disguised fury as the woman took in Diamond's attributes with obvious appreciation, then glanced over and dismissed his dowdy little "wife" as someone of no account.

"Mr. and Mrs. Chandler?" she greeted them, her voice as breathless and phony as the rest of her.

"Please. Raymond and Velma," Diamond said with an easy smirk that reminded Sally of Tom Cruise. And then the names registered. Raymond Chandler, creator of the magnificent Philip Marlowe. And Velma, one of Chandler's quintessential good/bad girls. Sally was going to marry this man if it was the last thing she ever did.

"I see you're here for the Fast-Track Weekend. You look like you're in superb shape. I can't imagine you need any toning," the woman purred.

"Everyone can do with a little refresher," Diamond murmured, eating this up. Reaching behind him, he pulled Sally forward, his arm around her waist in a gesture that was meant to look affectionate. It felt like a stranglehold. "And this is my wife. I'm sure you can do something for her."

"Of course. I recommend the modified fasting and intensive conditioning program. We can at least make a good start at getting rid of those extra twenty pounds she's carrying around."

Only the pressure of Diamond's arm kept Sally from lunging at the smug creature. "I don't need to lose twenty pounds," Sally said between clenched teeth.

"You're right, thirty would be better. After all, you can't be too thin or too rich, isn't that right?" The blonde let out a high-pitched trill of laughter, and Diamond joined in, a well-bred neigh of a laugh that was perfectly in character. His fingers digging into Sally's waist prompted Sally's own less-than-enthusiastic chuckle.

"I wouldn't want her too skinny," Diamond said in an unctuous voice.

"I wouldn't worry about that, Ray," the Barbie-clone murmured, reaching out and touching his arm with a confiding gesture. "It'll take a lot more than Desert Glory's Fast-Track Weekend to do that." She moved back to the desk, every muscle rippling beneath her skintight black unitard. "Let's see—the two of you are down for one bedroom. Are you certain you wouldn't be happier with two singles? It's always difficult in cases like these, where one partner fasts and the other doesn't."

Diamond patted Sally's clenched fist. "Velma and I couldn't stand to be parted. We haven't been married that long, have we, darling?" There was a devilish light of merriment in his eyes as he looked down at her.

"Not nearly long enough, darling," she responded, reaching her arm around his neck, yanking him down and kissing him hungrily.

She was calling his bluff. His response astonished her. Instead of holding still for her half-playful assault, he simply hauled her into his arms and kissed her back, plastering her body against his aroused one.

The hell with Barbie, Sally thought dizzily, wondering whether she could get away with wrapping her legs around his waist. When he finally broke the kiss, Diamond's expression was dazed. Hers was probably comatose. "One room, one bed," he murmured, still staring down at her.

Barbie sniffed. "Certainly. Though we do recommend that our clients refrain from as much...marital contact as possible during their stay with us. They need to concentrate on their own fitness, be totally centered on strength and wellness. Not, if you'll pardon the expression, on sex. You do understand?''

The woman struck Sally as someone already fixated on sex, particularly with her ersatz husband. ''What are you going to do, run a bed check every few hours?'' she inquired sweetly.

Barbie managed a strained smile. ''As I said, it's just a recommendation. What you do in the privacy of your room is, of course, your business. However, we do have certain rules here at the spa.'' She waited while they disentangled themselves.

''Such as?''

Barbie held out a golden basket. ''No drugs, prescription or otherwise. No alcohol. Drop any pills in here. They'll be returned to you when you leave. Also your car keys.''

''Why?'' For a moment, the jovial yuppie attitude slipped, and Diamond sounded like his old, suspicious self.

''Why, so the valet can park it,'' Barbie replied, pushing a button on the desk. She waited while Diamond dropped the keys and his bottle of ibuprofen into the basket, and then she rattled it slightly. ''One more thing, Ray.''

''Yes?''

''We need your cigarettes.''

Sally quickly turned her laughter into a choking sound. Diamond glared at her before turning his attention to Barbie. ''Why?''

''Isn't it obvious? We maintain a smoke-free environment—we're very careful about that. And if you're serious about toning and strengthening your body, you must know that cigarettes are the worst thing you can do. Your body is a temple. Smoking is blasphemy.''

''Oh, God,'' Diamond murmured. ''Two of you.''

"The cigarettes, Ray?" Barbie was sounding more like a drill sergeant at this point. Diamond glared at her.

"And if I refuse?"

"Then I'm afraid we'll have to cancel your weekend. Regretfully, of course." She smiled at him, wetting her pink lips with her pink tongue. "And I was looking forward to putting you through your paces."

I bet you were, sister, Sally thought, tempted to walk out. And then she remembered why they were there. And who else was there, somewhere in the rambling building.

She reached over, plucked the crumpled pack of cigarettes from Diamond's pocket and dropped it into the basket. "He's been wanting to quit," she said in a dulcet voice.

Barbie even managed a trace of warmth for her. "Then that's settled. I've rung for someone to show you to your rooms. You'll need a chance to settle in before you get started on your program. Dinner's served from six-thirty on. Your diet sheets will already be in place."

"Will you be at dinner?" Diamond inquired.

"Oh, you can count on it," Barbie said. "I'm going to take you on as my personal project."

"I'm looking forward to it," Diamond murmured.

"I wouldn't miss it," Sally said with a growl.

"We're going to have lots of fun surprises for you two," Barbie promised them.

And the first trickles of uneasiness danced down Sally's spine.

Chapter Fifteen

"God, I hate good taste," Diamond muttered when the door finally closed on their suite.

"So I noticed. This is a far cry from your office," Sally said, glancing around her. Much as she wanted to irritate him, she found herself in reluctant agreement with him. The place was so tasteful, it was gaudy, from the southwestern decor, the huge king-size bed, the thick carpeting and the gold fixtures in the bathroom. Everything was very new, very expensive, very soulless, and Sally started to feel nostalgic for the Sleep-Suite Motel, insect livestock, *The Brady Bunch* and all.

"At least there's one good point—no television," Diamond said, dropping down onto the bed.

"I happen to like television."

"That's probably responsible for what ails you." He reached into his pocket, an automatic gesture, seeking cigarettes.

"Nothing ails me."

"There are times, lady, when your grasp of reality is not that strong. I imagine that comes from too many episodes of *Magnum, P.I.*"

"Wrong. It comes from too many old movies. Speaking of which, Raymond Chandler, thank you."

Diamond actually looked embarrassed. "It was spur of the moment. I couldn't think of anything else."

"All my life I've wanted to be called Velma," Sally said with a blissful sigh.

"Now your life is complete." He reached again for the cigarettes, then pulled his hand away in disgust.

"Any particular reason why you insisted on sharing a room?" she asked. "Apart from your insatiable lust for my body." The lightly ironic tone she aimed for failed completely. Probably because of the stormy expression in Diamond's dark eyes.

"Don't let that Barbie doll fool you, kid. This is Calderini turf beneath the fern-bar decor. You saw what they did to me at Lake Judgment. They would be only too happy to carry that one step further if they had the opportunity. We're safer sticking together. We just need to find out whether your sister's here or not, and then we're gone. I don't know—"

"She's here."

He sat up. "You saw her?"

"No. I just know she's here. Instinct, a sixth sense, whatever you want to call it. She's here."

"I like you better as Velma than Shirley MacLaine," he drawled.

"She's here, Diamond. And I'm not leaving until she goes with me."

"If you say so." He came off the bed in one restless move, pacing around the spacious room. He stopped by the tiny refrigerator. "At least there's a bar."

"I thought you'd given up drinking."

"That was before I had to give up cigarettes. I can't do both. If I'm going to make it through the night with clear lungs I'm going to have to make do with Scotch."

"Don't, Diamond. Please."

"Temperance songs, Sally?"

She moved toward him, putting one hand on his arm. "Please, Diamond," she said again.

He shook it off. "My drinking is my own business, lady. All the pleases in the world aren't going to stop me."

She stepped back, admitting defeat. After all, there was a difference between a heavy drinker and an alcoholic. She'd certainly seen him drink a great deal, but he never seemed to show it. And he was probably right. The only person who could make him stop was himself. "All right, get me a diet Coke while you're at it," she said, dropping into the tasteful chair by the full-length windows.

For a long moment, he didn't move, and she could see the battle he was waging within himself, recognize it by the tension in his shoulders, the grim set of his mouth. "Diet Coke isn't a bad idea," he said finally. "Maybe I'll have the Scotch later." And he opened the refrigerator door.

She'd heard enough of his spectacular cursing in the past that his current performance shouldn't have surprised her. The lack of cigarettes must have prompted new inventiveness, however, for the variety and color of his swearing startled even her.

"What's wrong?" she asked when he finally stopped ranting.

"We've got tomato juice, carrot juice, celery juice, and salt-free mineral water. Period."

"No diet Coke?" Sally asked, suddenly galvanized.

"No diet Coke."

She didn't waste time cursing. She headed straight for the phone, regretting the fact that she didn't know Barbie's real name and couldn't very well ask for her by appearance. A few moments later, she hung up, staring at Diamond with a tragic expression.

"It's worse than we thought, James."

"Don't tell me. . . ." he begged.

"No alcohol, no artificial sweeteners," she said. "And no caffeine." Her voice broke slightly on the last.

"No caffeine? As in no coffee?"

Sally swallowed. "That's what the man said." For the first time, she realized how very dangerous Diamond could be. The expression on his face was cold, ruthless, frightening.

"We're finding your sister tonight," he said in a tight voice. "I can do without alcohol. I can even do without the cigarettes. But when they take away my coffee, they're in real trouble. What time is it?"

"Six-fifteen."

"We're going in to dinner promptly at six-thirty. We'll see what our hostess has in mind for us, and then I want you to distract her while I case the joint."

"I think you'd have an easier time distracting her," Sally pointed out with a certain amount of asperity.

Diamond's smile wiped the bleak rage from his face. "You noticed that, did you? Jealous?"

"Of a Barbie doll? Don't be ridiculous. Besides, there's absolutely nothing to be jealous of. I wouldn't make the mistake of assuming there was anything between us, apart from an ill-advised night of sex." She shrugged. "I have no claim on you. If you want to see if you can seduce my sister's whereabouts from Barbie, go right ahead."

His quiet chuckle made Sally want to smack him. "I don't think I've ever managed to seduce anything out of anybody, much as the idea appeals to me. Besides, I doubt Barbie knows anything about your sister. This place is highly segregated—the spa part is completely legit."

"I wouldn't underestimate her if I were you, Diamond. She looks like one tough cookie. God, I'm hungry." Sally quickly shifted gears. "I hope their food is better than their choice of beverages. At least, they'll have fresh fruits and vegetables. After three days on the road with you, experiencing the joys of fast-food and sleazy diners, I feel like I'm about to get scurvy."

"I think scurvy's the disease where your tongue swells up and you can't talk," Diamond said. "If only fate would be so kind."

"Come on, Diamond. Let's go strap on the feed bags," Sally said, holding out her arm in a reluctant truce.

He took it, and once again she saw the light in his eyes, the one that told her he was enjoying himself, the lies, the danger, the subterfuge. "Something tells me we aren't due for steak and potatoes."

"Even a lettuce leaf would look good to me now."

Barbie had given them a brief tour on the way to their room, and Diamond, with his excellent sense of direction, led Sally to the dining room, pulling her back from the several wrong turns she would have made.

The place was packed with a disparate group of people. There were healthy, glowing yuppie couples, plump, determined looking matrons, older, birdlike people who looked as though they ate twigs and branches to survive and might very well burst into warbles at the drop of a hat. These healthy souls were being waited on by people who looked like gym instructors. Sleek, tanned, blond and gorgeous, they moved through the room on perfectly coordinated muscles, carrying trays that looked ominously light.

All those people and waiters were congregated on the main floor of the room. On the right side of the dining area, on a raised platform, sat a very different group of people. The women wore spangles, and each one had a larger bra size than all the health nuts in the rest of the room put together. They were all blond, young and not very bright looking. Sally doubted there was a wedding ring among the lot. The men were older, balding, plump and powerful looking. Their waiters wore tuxedos, and Sally was willing to bet their vegetable-juice cocktails came spiked with a large amount of vodka.

"Ray and Velma?" The toothy jock who served as the spa-side maître d' greeted them. "Glad to have you here. We've got your menu already set up. Just walk this way." He headed toward a small table in the corner of the room, and his gait was a combination mince and swagger.

"I'd like to see you walk that way," Sally muttered to Diamond in an undertone.

"Hell, I'd like to see *you,*" he countered.

The waiter who brought their dinners could have been a clone of the maître d', or Barbie's identical, male twin. He flashed a thousand large, white teeth at them as he presented their plates with a flourish. Sally looked at them both and smirked.

Diamond had a plate piled high with boneless chicken breasts, wild rice, fresh asparagus, avocado slices and a huge golden corn muffin. She had a plate with three curly slices of carrot, five green beans arranged like a star, two symmetrical pieces of brown wafer, and pile of something that looked like fish food.

"At least I get an appetizer," she said cheerfully.

She didn't like Diamond's smug expression. "No, you don't," he said, digging into his overloaded plate with gusto.

"What do you mean by that?"

"Look at the menu card, kid. That's the sum total of your dinner."

She stared down at the meager plate in dismay bordering on despair. "No!" she said in real anguish.

"Yes."

"You've got to give me some of yours," she said urgently. "This isn't enough to keep a bird alive. I haven't eaten a thing since you insisted we stop at that disgusting fast-food place, and I'm starving. Starving, do you hear?"

"Sorry. But you know the rules are very strict and you've been put on a modified fast. You want to lose those twenty pounds, don't you?"

"I want to lose you, and fast," she snarled. "I don't need to lose twenty pounds. Ten, maybe..." she admitted with belated honesty, thinking of her beaded dress.

"Well, much as I hate to admit it," Diamond said, chewing thoughtfully on a tender-looking piece of chicken, "I happen to think you're just right."

Her temper vanished in sudden astonishment. "You do?"

"I'd go even further than that," he said, his voice low and his gaze warm. "I think you're perfect."

"Perfect? Me?" Her voice rose in a little squeak of surprise.

He leaned back. "Your body, that is," he drawled. "Your behavior leaves a lot to be desired."

"Go to hell," she said amiably, reaching across the table for an asparagus spear.

He slapped her hand and she dropped the asparagus, scowling at him. "Much as I would love to see how you eat asparagus, I think you'd better behave yourself. Here comes our hostess."

The Barbie clone was weaving her way through the tables, a toothy smile on her face. She'd changed from the spandex she'd been wearing to something even tighter, and her tanned, freckled chest was obviously supposed to be a come-on. Sally wondered whether Diamond had been teasing her. Whether he could really prefer her soft curves to all that toned, rippling muscle. Illogical as it seemed, she believed him. Maybe just because she wanted to.

"You haven't eaten anything, Velma," Barbie cooed. She sank down into one of the empty chairs. "Aren't you hungry? I can have your plate taken if you've decided to go, if you'll pardon the expression, whole hog."

Lucy, Sally thought. *If I attack this woman, I'll ruin all chances of finding Lucy.* She plastered a sickly sweet smile on her face and picked up one crisp carrot curl. "It just looked so beautiful, I hated to wreck the arrangement."

"Our chef prides himself on the presentation. And what about you, Ray? Are you enjoying your dinner?"

Diamond, the pig, had eaten every single morsel on his plate, leaving absolutely nothing for her. Sally started in on the green beans, crunching disconsolately.

Their waiter came up, placing a meaty hand on Barbie's shoulder. "Hey, Barbie," he said. "The boss wants to see you, pronto."

"Duty calls. I'll be right back." She wove her way through the tables with muscular grace, as Diamond and Sally met each other's gaze.

"Don't laugh," she warned him. "If you start, I won't be able to stop."

"Barbie," Diamond said, shaking his head. "Who'd have believed it? I wonder what the boss wanted to talk to her about. And who the boss is?"

"You think they know we're here?"

"Most likely. It doesn't do to underestimate your adversary. The Calderinis do very well for themselves, and they didn't get to their position of power without being on top of things. You finished?"

Sally looked down at her empty plate. There was a tiny flake of fish food left and she scarfed it up with a weary sigh. "I'd say so. They're not giving us dessert, are they?"

"Don't count on it." He rose and pulled her chair out for her, the two of them moving through the crowded room.

The hall was deserted when they stepped outside the dining room. The other inmates had learned to stretch their meager rations. "God, I'm hungry," Sally moaned piteously. "All right, Diamond, what do we do next?"

"Here." He pulled one of the white damask napkins from out of his suit jacket and handed it to her with a flourish.

She took it, opening it with shaking hands to discover the slightly crumbling corn muffin. "Diamond," she said, "I love you." And she shoved the whole thing into her mouth.

"That's what they all say," he drawled. "If I'd known your price was corn muffins, I would have done something about it days ago."

She swallowed convulsively. "Diamond," she said, her voice low and husky, as she lifted her hands to his chest.

He caught them before they could travel upward. "Don't do it."

"Don't do what?"

"Don't look at me like that, don't touch me, don't kiss me." His fingers tightened reflexively around hers. "If you do, I'm going to carry you back to that disgustingly tasteful bedroom and we're not going to leave until tomorrow morning. We need to find your sister."

She didn't move. "I know that," she said, her fingers caught in his, her heart caught in his.

"There you are!" Barbie breezed by. "I have to check in some new guests, and then we can get you started on your program, Velma. Just a few moderate aerobics, a few laps, just so we can judge how out of shape you really are. Nothing too overwhelming."

The corn muffin hadn't gone far in assuaging Sally's hunger. Diamond's touch had only fanned the flames higher. "Fine," she said with a tight smile.

"After I get Velma started, we can go over your program, Ray," Barbie added over her shoulder as she continued down the hallway at a breakneck pace. "I'll come to your room."

"Over my dead body," Sally muttered.

Diamond had moved away, out of temptation's reach, releasing her hands. "I guess whatever the boss wanted didn't have anything to do with us."

"I guess not," Sally said.

"We have a choice. We follow Barbie and see what she's doing. Or we go back to the room."

Back to the room, Sally's heart cried. "Follow Barbie," her mouth said.

"Good girl. Maybe Vinnie and Lucy have just arrived." He started down the hallway.

"Nope. They're already here," Sally insisted, following him. "And we're going to find her."

They'd just reached the front lobby when Diamond's arm shot out across Sally's chest, blocking her progress. "Well, I'll be damned," he muttered, backing her behind a convenient potted plant.

"Probably." She tried to crane her neck around his larger, obstructing body. "What is it?"

"Bozos," he said flatly, letting her peek.

It was a very large contingent of Chinese. A dozen or so businessmen dressed in silk suits, all looking very disgruntled. They were accompanied by a similar number of women, but unlike their American counterparts, these gentlemen had clearly brought their wives, not their mistresses. The women were regal, elegant and of a certain age not usually associated with chorus girls or bimbos. There must have been two dozen in all, and they were all glaring at the unintimidated Barbie.

"I'm sorry," she said, very loudly, as if speaking to a convention of the hearing impaired. "But this is a smoke-free resort. If any of you smoke, you'll have to leave your cigarettes and lighters here."

No one moved. *High noon at the health spa,* Sally thought irreverently. The future of East-West criminal relations lay in Barbie's hands, and she was about to blow it.

Then one man, a bit older, a bit shorter than the rest, said something in Chinese. With sullen grace, they all moved forward, dumping gold and silver cigarette cases into the little basket.

It was overflowing by the time the last Bozo dropped her emerald-encrusted case on top of the others. She looked like the Dragon Lady, taller than the others, and frankly contemptuous. She ran her dark eyes over Barbie's sturdy frame, said something in a musical Chinese voice that was clearly a great insult, and then stepped back as the other women nodded and laughed.

"These will be returned to you when you leave," Barbie continued at a shout. "In the meantime, you'll be shown to your rooms while we set up a diet and exercise program for you all."

The small man shook his head. "No diet, no exercise. We're here for business, not Western foolishness."

Barbie blinked her huge black eyes that were completely devoid of intelligence. "I'll have to discuss this with my boss...."

"Do that. In the meantime, show us to our rooms and send champagne to each of my people. Dom Perignon '73."

"We don't have champagne," Barbie shouted helplessly. "This is a health spa, not a resort. I think you've made a mistake—"

"I think *you* have made the mistake," the man said in a quiet, stern voice that made the exuberant Barbie turn pale beneath her perfect tan. He clicked his fingers at his assembled entourage and started for the door.

"Mr. Li!" An urgent new voice entered the fray as someone appeared from a doorway at the opposite end of the room. "Forgive my failure to be here to greet you. Welcome to Desert Glory." An elegantly dressed young man, suavely handsome and urbane, moved across the room. Vincenzo Calderini, Vinnie the Viper, smooth and charming as always. Sally slunk backward, hiding behind the potted plant, hoping he wouldn't glance toward the darkened hallway.

Mr. Li was not appeased. "Your employee apparently knew nothing of our arrival."

"She was only just informed, and she was given no details. That's the beauty of Desert Glory, Mr. Li. We keep everything separate. The fewer people who grasp the entire concept, the safer we are. Isn't that right, Barbie?"

Barbie blinked. "Yes, sir," she said automatically, obviously not knowing what he was talking about.

"If you and your people would follow me, I'll do my best to see that you're made comfortable. We've reserved the best rooms, the finest chefs have been flown in . . ."

The elegant woman said something in a low hiss. Mr. Li grimaced. "My wife wishes to know about our cigarettes."

Vinnie looked sorrowful. "I'm afraid Barbie's right about that. We really can't allow smoking. This is ostensibly a health spa, and cigarette smoke is too difficult to disguise. I thought that was made clear when this meeting was set up."

Mr. Li simply nodded, neither agreeing nor disagreeing, and Vincenzo charged onward. "I understand your displeasure. Even my father has to do without his customary cigars when we hold meetings out here, but the inconvenience is more than compensated by the safety and security of our surroundings. We have the finest in athletic equipment, running tracks, exercise machines—"

"We are not here to exercise. We are here for the falcon."

"Of course. And to sign an agreement."

Mr. Li's contempt was obvious. "And to sign an agreement. Assuming your required gesture of good faith is intact. Where is the falcon?"

Vinnie smiled, that easy smile that meant his back was against the wall. "When my father arrives. At our meeting, tomorrow. In the meantime, let me show you what the finest in American hospitality can mean."

For a moment, Mr Li didn't move. One of the other gentlemen murmured something, something the Dragon Lady didn't like. She overrode him, her clear strong voice echoing in the cavernous room, and Mr. Li nodded. "You have until tomorrow, Mr. Calderini."

Vinnie smiled his most engaging smile. "I knew you'd be reasonable. This way." He gestured toward the far hallway.

Barbie scurried after them, a worried expression on her face. It wasn't until the sound of footsteps died away that Diamond turned to face Sally.

"Vinnie the Viper?"

"In the flesh. But I wonder where Lucy is," she said, trying not to let her worry overwhelm her. Vinnie looked normal, not like a man in the midst of domestic turmoil. Lucy must still be safe.

"That's what we have to find out. And the sooner, the better. One thing's obvious—he knows he doesn't have the right falcon. If he did, he'd hand it over. The Bho Tsos are already in bad moods, and the longer they go without their cigarettes, the madder they're going to be. Speaking of which..." He started across the deserted reception room, heading straight for the overflowing basket of confiscated cigarette cases.

"Diamond!" Sally said, aghast. "How low can you sink?"

"Pretty low," he admitted, opening the jeweled case. "But not low enough to smoke Chinese cigarettes." In disgust, he dropped the case back into the basket, glancing back toward her with a rueful shrug. And then his expression froze.

"What are you looking like that for?" she asked, irritated.

He glanced away from her toward the front door. It was only a few feet away from him, and outside, under the lights, someone had left a car idling.

It was then that she heard the heavy breathing behind her, and knew their time had suddenly run out. Someone was behind her, someone who meant her no good. Diamond was obviously going to make a run for it, leaving her to get out of this mess any way she could, and she wondered whether she could reach the car when he did and get the hell out of there with him.

But she couldn't leave Lucy behind. She didn't turn around to face the threat behind her. She didn't have to. "Get out of here, Diamond," she said across the room in a clear, calm voice.

He was poised to run. Suddenly the tension drained his body. "I can't, Sally."

"Smart move," said the person behind Sally, one she'd heard before, maybe in a nightmare. "You might have gotten away, but I would have been plenty irritated. And I might have taken it out on the little lady, and then everyone would be mad at me. Turn around, Miss MacArthur."

Sally turned. "Hullo, Alf."

The man chuckled evilly. The gun in his hand was much larger than the one Diamond kept in his shoulder holster, and he looked like a man who knew how to use it. "I thought we'd be seeing you sooner or later. Your friend didn't learn his lesson too well. Guess we'll have to repeat it. Maybe a little harder this time."

"You hurt him," Sally said in a fierce voice, "and I'll...I'll..."

Diamond came up behind her, sliding his arm around her waist. "Don't mess with her, Alf. She's dangerous."

"Yeah, sure. I think you two need a place to cool off. Vinnie's busy right now—I can't tell him you two showed up. Maybe we'll just put you in storage for the time being."

Diamond's hand was moving behind her back. Sally had the truly horrid suspicion that he was reaching for his gun, and she wished she could simply warn him not to. But Alf was watching them too closely, and then it happened so fast, she couldn't even scream.

Diamond shoved her hard, away from him, crashing her against the wall. There was a blinding flash of light, a muffled pop as her head banged against the bleached oak trim. Once more, she heard Diamond's spectacular cursing, and then everything went dark as a welter of pain closed around her head.

Chapter Sixteen

James was a tangled mass of fury and panic. Not three feet away from him lay Sally's still body, and while he thought he could hear fairly regular breathing, he wasn't sure how badly she was hurt. The room Alf and his buddies had dumped them into was some sort of storage room, and Alf wasn't the type to turn on the overhead light once he locked someone in.

He'd certainly done a thorough job of tying James up. No matter how he struggled, he was bound fast to the straight-backed chair. All he could do was sit there and tell himself Sally was breathing as he worked in vain at ropes that held him.

He didn't know whether the low moan that emitted from her was any improvement. "Sally," he hissed in the darkness. "Are you all right? Sally?"

Nothing but silence answered him, and the dim shape on the floor didn't move. "Sally," he tried again, his voice more insistent, bordering on panic. "Are you okay? Speak to me, Sally."

And then miraculously, out of the darkness came a small, grouchy voice. "No, I am not okay. Did you shoot me?"

Relief washed over him. "Of course not."

"Well, don't tell me you haven't been tempted." She still wasn't moving, but her faint voice was growing infinitesimally stronger. "What the hell happened to me?"

"Alf."

"Alf?" she echoed. "The last thing I remember was you shoving me against the wall while you played shoot-out with the boys." He could hear her moving slightly, possibly rolling over.

"Yeah, well, you were momentarily stunned. You started to get up, and then Alf knocked you out."

"But I don't understand why. I would have thought he'd be much too busy dealing with you to bother with any trouble I might cause."

"That's the way he dealt with me. The moment he had his hands on you, there wasn't a thing I could do."

She considered that in silence for a moment, then he could hear her moving again, struggling to change her position on the floor. "You mean you gave up? Rather than let him hurt me?"

"Something like that." James hated to admit it. He knew she was going to take an admission like that and run with it, jump to all sorts of conclusions. And she was going to be right about every conclusion she jumped to.

But she made no comment. Instead, she asked another question. "Why didn't you run for it when you saw Alf come up behind me? You could have made it. I can't imagine he would have done me that much harm."

"Maybe not. The Calderinis aren't known for their brutality, but this deal with the Bho Tsos is a major step for them. People tend to act impulsively when their livelihood is threatened, and I couldn't count on Alf's restraint."

"Hmm," said Sally, sounding unimpressed. "But wouldn't it have been better to take the chance? That way, you would have been free to rescue me and Lucy."

"Or free to take off and leave you to your own devices. The thought did cross my mind, you know."

"I know," she said, her voice stronger. "But the point is, you didn't run. You didn't choose either the sensible or the selfish way out. And do you know what that means?"

"I have a horrible feeling I'm about to find out," he said in a wary voice.

"You love me," she said.

"I was afraid you were going to say that."

"You do. You can be as cynical as you want, but it wasn't professional ethics or chivalry that kept you here. You're in love with me, and you just don't want to admit it." She sounded smug, triumphant and almost supremely happy, and James didn't want to burst her bubble. There was a very good chance they weren't going to make it through the next twenty-four hours. The Calderinis were being completely unpredictable, and he had to make things up as he went along.

It wouldn't do her any harm to let her believe what she wanted to believe for a while. It might conceivably make her more malleable, though deep in his heart of hearts, James doubted that anything would accomplish that miracle. At least it would keep her more cheerful and optimistic while he figured out a way to get them out of there. Once they were safe, he'd set her straight. And set himself straight in the bargain.

"Aren't you going to say anything?" Sally demanded. "Aren't you going to tell me I'm crazy? Or even better, admit that I'm right? Why are you just sitting there?"

"I'm just sitting here, lady, because I happen to be tied up," he shot back, relieved not to have to answer her demand. He didn't want to have to comment on her ridiculous assumption. "It wouldn't do any harm if you wanted to come over and untie me."

"Oh, Diamond," she said in a guilty, love-filled voice that tore at his gut. Then she must have half crawled, half flown across the space that divided them, for she was flinging her arms around him and pressing her head against his stomach.

He put up with it in silence for a moment only because there was something unbelievably wonderful about being hugged by Sally MacArthur. And then he drawled, "Not that this isn't real nice, but I'd like to do something about getting us out of here. I can't while you're draped across my lap."

"I don't know, Diamond. I might die happy like this."

"I'd rather live."

She detached herself with a pragmatic sigh. "I guess I would, too." Feeling her way, she crawled around behind him and began busying herself with Alf's fiendish knots. "When did you first realize you loved me?" she asked in a conversational tone.

"January 1999," James said, hoping to prick her bubble just slightly by naming an impossible date.

Wrong answer. "I can wait," she said cheerfully. "Do we get to sleep together until then?"

"Damn it, Sally, could you just concentrate on getting me untied?"

"I'm doing the best I can. I don't think you want to move in with me. Isaiah might like you, but he's a little old-fashioned. He'd probably come to the bedroom door with a shotgun and a parson. No, I think we ought to live at your place. I must say, it looked pretty bland when I followed you that morning when we first came north. I would have thought you'd live someplace a little more colorful. Maybe we could find something we both like. Near the water, with a lot of character."

"Who says we're going to live together?"

"Well, it makes sense." She moved back around on her knees, looking up at him. "After all, the sex is wonderful, and it would be silly to do without until 1999 just because you're so pigheaded."

"Could you please just untie me?" he begged, feeling like his head was about to explode.

"Honey, you're untied."

He yanked at his hands and the ropes fell free. She was already working on the knots at his ankles, but he brushed her hands away and made short work of his bands, mildly embarrassed that he'd been too absorbed in her ridiculous conversation to even notice that she'd loosened the bonds.

A moment later, he was free. He moved as far away from her and temptation as he could get, stretching his cramped muscles, pacing the pitch-dark area they were confined in. As far as he could tell, there was no source of light and the door had no handle on the inside.

"Are we going to get out of here?" Sally asked from her position on the floor. She hadn't moved while he scoped out the place. She sounded oddly at ease.

"Certainly," he snapped, certain of no such thing. "We're just going to have to wait until morning. There's a small window set up high in the wall—that should provide us with enough light. Right now it's too damned dark to see more than a few inches in front of me." He felt his way back to the uncluttered center of the storeroom, moving past the rows of shelving to where Sally sat.

He almost fell over her in the darkness. He squatted down beside her, putting his hands out, telling himself he had to touch her, to make sure she was all right. That was his first mistake.

His hands rested on her shoulders—soft shoulders, melting beneath his hard hands. She rose up on her knees to meet him, putting her arms around his waist and holding onto him in the pitch darkness. He could feel the tension, the fear in her body, a fear she'd tried very hard to disguise.

"Diamond," she said in a quiet voice, "do you think you could just pretend for a little while? Pretend that you love me? I'm a little... frightened."

God, what a sap, what a sucker, what a complete and utter fool he was! He cupped her chin, tilting her face up to his. He couldn't say the words; he still had that much sense of self-preservation. But the way he kissed her, leaning down and brushing his lips across hers, softly, clinging, a reassurance and a benediction, was just as bad.

She sighed then, as some of the tension drained from her body, and her arms tightened around his waist. "If you can't tell me, James," she whispered, "could you show me?"

The floor was cool, cushioned linoleum beneath them as he lowered her to her back. The cotton sweater came off over her head with her assistance, the almost nonexistent scrap of a bra followed. He kissed her, every square inch of her warm, smooth, lush body as he uncovered it. He kissed her collarbone, the soft place behind her ear. He kissed the inside of her elbow and underside of her breast, stripping off his own clothes in awkward haste.

He tried to tell himself he was doing this for her, to reassure her when she was frightened, but he knew that was a lie. He was doing it because he couldn't help himself. It didn't matter that to touch her again would be compromising his independence, his way of life, his very soul. It didn't even matter that she might end up getting even more hurt than he was. There in the darkness on the cool linoleum floor, the only thing that mattered was the moment, the feel of her smooth skin beneath his hands, the tiny little cry she made when he put his mouth on her breast, the restless squirming of her body as he shoved her jeans down her legs and tossed them away in the darkness.

He wanted to take his time. He had no idea what time it was, but chances were they had a long night ahead of them. He wanted to stretch it, make it last, but the more he kissed her, the hotter his own need burned. She threaded her hands through his hair, caressing him as he gently suckled her breasts, and her breath was coming in rapid gusts against his hair. He pulled away, ignoring her little cry of protest, to move his mouth down, across her slightly rounded stomach.

She realized what he intended a moment before he did it. She made a strangled sound, "Don't," as his mouth found her, and she arched off the floor, digging her heels in.

He held her hips, inexorable, as spasms ricocheted through her body in immediate release. The sound of her choked whimpers of pleasure almost made him explode, and when he finally pulled away, he had every intention of pulling her beneath him and sinking his body into hers.

She stopped him with shaking hands and barely controlled breathing. "No," she said, pushing him onto the floor, onto his back, leaning over him. He couldn't see her expression in the darkness, but he knew it as well as he knew his own heart. She'd be determined, a little dazed and very very sure of herself.

Damn, she was good with her mouth. The little clumsiness only added to the delight, as she kissed his flat male nipples, his stomach, drew her lips across the scars and bruises and war wounds he'd suffered in the past fifteen years. And then she took him into her mouth, her silky hair falling around her face, returning the intimate caress he'd given her, and he was afraid he was going to explode beneath her tender, untutored ministrations.

When he could finally bear no more, he pulled her away with more force than necessary. "Not that way. It's not. . . fair. . . ."

"But I wanted it," she whispered, and he believed her. He reached for her, but she'd already climbed over his supine body, positioning herself above his aching hardness, sinking down, a bit at a time, until he thought he'd go mad with the sheer pleasure of it. Once more, he caught her hips, helping her with the rhythm of it, and then he couldn't wait any longer and he thrust up into her, hard, filling her with the love he refused to admit existed, holding her as she exploded once more around him, her body squeezing tight.

And then she went limp, all the energy draining out of her in a rush as she collapsed against him. He caught her as she fell, tenderly, rolling over onto his side and taking her with him. She was gasping for breath like a landed fish, and her heart was pounding against his in triple time.

He held her very tightly for a moment, somehow wanting to absorb her into his skin, his soul. And then he loosened his grip, pushing her damp hair away from her face, following the path his fingers took with his mouth, kissing her eyelids, her cheekbones, her chin, her lips.

Slowly, by infinitesimal degrees, she calmed. Her heartbeat slowed, her breathing steadied, the trembling in her body settled down. She sighed, a deep, shaking sigh, and melted against him, wrapping herself around him like hot wax.

"We're going to surprise the hell out of Alf if he decides to check on us," she said in a rough little whisper.

"And I don't care. If he wants to get in the way of true love, then that's his problem."

"Sally," James said, his voice tight with regret, "I'm not the man for you."

"Yeah, I know. You're too old, too broke and too mean. Don't worry about it. I'll get older, I'll give away my money and I'll work on being just as sour as you."

"Sally..."

She put her lips against his and he had to kiss her. There was no way he could stop himself. "Don't argue now, Diamond. Once we're back in San Francisco and my sister's safe, you can give me the brush-off. Or you can try," she added, as if honesty compelled her to. "But for now, just shut up and kiss me."

"You better not expect me to make love to you again," he warned her, drawing his hands down to her breasts and feeling them swell in his hands. "That's one of the problems of being too old." It was a lie. He was ready for her again, and no matter how limited her experience, she probably knew it.

"Diamond, you're thirty-eight, not seventy-eight," she said. "And if you don't want me again, you'd better tell your body that. It seems to have other ideas."

He moved suddenly, pushing her over onto her back and straddling her with breathtaking swiftness. Her black hair was spread out around her on the linoleum floor, and the faint glow of the newly risen moon from the small window shone in her eyes. He cupped her face with his hands, holding her still, and she waited patiently. Waited for what he was willing to give.

As far as he could remember, no woman had ever been patient with him. They'd always been demanding, wanting what he couldn't provide, wanting it immediately.

Sally wanted those things, too. She deserved them. But she was willing to take whatever he could give her. And he could no more see her nagging him than he could imagine her as a yuppie executive. She was crazy, scatterbrained, ridiculous and adorable. And he was absolutely defenseless against her.

"You're going to be the death of me," he said, his voice rough as his insistent body pressed against hers.

She wrapped her legs around him, letting him settle into the cradle of her thighs. "Not for another fifty years," she said, running her hands up his sides.

He couldn't fight any longer. He could fight her. He could fight the lure of sex. But he couldn't fight the lure of his own hungry heart. "I don't believe in happy endings," he muttered against her mouth.

"Tough. You're going to get one anyway." And she opened her mouth against his, and for a while, there were no more arguments as their bodies were in complete accord.

SALLY SLEPT A LITTLE BIT, wrapped in his arms. Diamond slept a little bit, his head on her soft breasts. By the time the first gray light of dawn filtered in through the small, high window, Sally began to stir, aware of every little ache and twinge in her body. She looked at Diamond, still dozing, and she wanted to ignore the pain and wake him up with her mouth. She moved toward him and his eyes flew open, staring at her in unabashed alarm.

"Don't touch me," he warned.

"Why not?"

"Because you know perfectly well what will happen if you touch me, and we'd damn well better get our clothes on and see if we can get out of this place before Alf remembers we're in here."

"Do you think he's forgotten?"

"No. But we can always hope." Diamond was pulling on his clothes with rapid grace, ignoring her wistful expression. A moment later, he was out of reach, stalking around the storage room that was still mostly impenetrable shadows while she started to dress herself, less gracefully, less swiftly, her entire body one mass of aches and pains.

He was examining the door when he whirled around at the moan she was unable to stifle. "Are you all right?" he asked, frowning through the darkness.

"I hurt."

"I'm not surprised. You're not used to so much sex."

"Who says?"

"I say." He turned back to the door, cursing with his usual fluency. "There's no handle on the inside of this door. We're trapped here until Alf comes to get us."

"We can always—"

"Don't even think it," Diamond snapped, obviously in a grumpy mood.

Sally pulled her sweater over her head, pausing long enough to admire the love bite on the top of her breast. She started to struggle to her feet, then sank back down with another groan of pain.

"I have never hurt so much in my entire life," she announced. "My head hurts form where Alf hit me, my back hurts from sleeping on the floor, my...well, my entire body hurts. But you know what hurts most of all?"

"I can imagine," Diamond said with a drawl, sinking onto the floor as he abandoned his quest.

"It's not what you think. You know what hurts most of all?" She clutched at her chest, doing her best to look tragic.

"You're going to tell me," he said in a resigned voice.

"I'm going to tell you. It's not my poor bruised and pleasured body. It's not even my fragile heart that's expecting you to stomp all over it."

"Stomp all over it?" he echoed, his reserve vanishing in momentary amusement.

"Don't interrupt. It's not even my heart that's tearing me apart. You know what hurts most?"

"What?" he asked with great patience.

"My stomach."

She'd managed to drive that dark, almost tortured expression from his face entirely. "Your stomach?" he said, not bothering to disguise his incredulity.

"I haven't had a damned thing to eat since that rabbit food last night," she said in a loud, unabashed wail. "I'm starving, Diamond!"

He leaned back against the wall, stretching his long legs out in front of him, and he laughed with real amusement. "You're in luck, Sally. You were locked into the right place. This isn't just any storeroom. There's food all around you."

Ignoring her aching body, Sally leapt up, peering through the shadows at the rows of shelving. She grabbed the first thing she saw, a bag of nacho chips, and ripped it apart, sending chips flying around the room as she stuffed a handful into her mouth. Tossing the split bag to Diamond, she went foraging, grabbing anything that took her fancy and shoving it into her mouth. She ate gourmet cookies, dried apricots, semisweet chocolate and Wheat Thins dipped in raspberry preserves, making as big a mess as possible as she went, deriving a small, vengeful satisfaction from her destruction.

"I don't suppose you have a can opener on you?" she said, turning to Diamond and holding aloft a tin of caviar.

He was still leaning against the wall, munching on the nacho chips. "Nope."

"No Swiss army knife?"

"I'm neither a Boy Scout nor MacGyver. On the other hand, I don't suppose you've run across my cigarettes up there on the shelves?"

"No cigarettes. I'm surprised you aren't crankier."

"I've moved beyond cranky to downright murderous. Lucky for you I'm saving my attitude problems for Alf when he decides to reappear."

She tossed the caviar back onto the shelf, listened to it roll off the other side and reached for a box of sugary cereal. Ripping it open, she climbed down from the shelves and sat beside Diamond, offering him the box.

He shook his head, shuddering in disgust as she popped a handful in her mouth. "I worked up an appetite," she said defensively.

"I know you did. I wonder how many residents of the spa get to eat caviar and presweetened cereal," Diamond said, crunching into another nacho chip.

"They're probably part of Barbie's private stash. Diamond, don't you think—" Before she could finish, he'd put his hand across her mouth, silencing her.

"Someone's coming," he hissed in her ear. "Do exactly as I tell you."

She nodded, her eyes wide, and he released her mouth. "Go behind the shelves and lie on the floor," he ordered, barely making a noise.

"Why?"

"I don't want you to get shot."

She shuddered. "I didn't realize you still had a gun."

"I don't. But Alf and his buddies do. Do as I say."

"You're going to take them on without a weapon?" Her whisper got a little louder.

"Do as I say," he said, a little louder himself. "I can handle myself.

"I'm not moving," she said, stubborn and quite loud. "I'm not going to let you get killed in some noble attempt to escape. And don't you threaten me."

"I'm not going to," he said between gritted teeth. "No matter how much I love to. Please," he said, the request sounding more like a warning.

"No."

He stood up, shaking his head as the sounds of footsteps outside the door broke through her panic. "It's too late now," he growled. "Just keep out of the way, and—"

"No," she said, flinging herself against him, wrapping herself around his body like a leech. He wouldn't dare try anything foolhardy if she were in the way.

She simply ignored his fluent curses as he tried to pry her loose. The door opened and Alf stood there, the expected large and nasty gun resting comfortably in his meaty hand.

"Isn't this cute?" he said. "I should have tied you both up."

"What are you going to do, Alf?" Diamond said, trying to sound dignified with a female wrapped around him. "Hasn't this game gone on long enough?"

"Not quite. Not until we have the real falcon."

Sally couldn't quite swallow the little gasp as her worst fears were confirmed.

"We don't know where the real falcon is," Diamond said.

"Now that's just too bad. I guess you'll have to explain that to Don Salvatore. I wouldn't want to be in your shoes then. In the meantime, I've brought you a visitor. Another unwilling guest of Desert Glory's hospitality." He shoved a small, slight figure into the room and slammed the door shut.

Sally released her stranglehold on Diamond, rushing toward the small, sagging figure, catching her as she began to sink to the floor. "Lucy!" she cried. "Thank God you're here."

Chapter Seventeen

"Lucy, darling, have they hurt you?" Sally asked, holding her sister's frail body in her arms.

Lucy looked up, her face woebegone. "Not...not much," she said in a faint voice. "Oh, Sally, I'm so glad you're here. I've been so frightened. I never realized what a brute Vinnie was."

Sally paused for a moment, startled. "A brute? Vinnie? I never would have thought it. You don't mean to say he's hurt you? Actually abused you...?"

Lucy took refuge in another bout of easy tears. James watched the performance, marveling at it, and marveling at how gullible Sally was, taking in every bit of it. "He hasn't actually hit me," Lucy was saying. "Not that it would show. He's just been...so cruel. I'm afraid he's going to kill me."

"My poor baby," Sally crooned, ready tears of sympathy in her own eyes. "I won't let him hurt you, and neither will Diamond. If Vinnie dares to touch you, I'll scratch his eyes out, and Diamond will beat him to a pulp."

"Leave me out of all this bloodthirsty stuff," James said, moving back to the wall and sinking down again.

"Diamond!" Sally protested, shocked and disappointed. "My sister's been hurt, and you're just sitting there being cynical."

"There's not much else I can do at this point until Alf decides to open the door," James pointed out. "You're making more than enough fuss over her for both of us."

Sally glared at him, her tender protestations of love obviously forgotten in the heat of the moment, and then she turned back to her sister. "When did you first realize that Vinnie was after the falcon?"

Lucy obviously wasn't the sort to reply to a straight question. She looked more like her mother than Sally, with the same hard eyes and ash blond hair. She obviously liked lies as much as Sally did, for she was throwing herself into them with a real enthusiasm. There was a difference, however, between her fabrications and Sally's. Sally made up stories mostly for the fun of it. Lucy's lies were for her own advantage.

"Sally, if he doesn't get the real falcon, he's going to kill all of us. He's sworn he will, and I believe him!"

Sally frowned. "Vinnie isn't the killer type. I suppose he's capable of putting a contract out on someone—"

"What makes you think you know more about Vinnie than I do?" Lucy demanded with a certain sharpness that hinted at jealousy. "You never took him seriously. You never cared for him, never even slept with him...."

"And you did," Sally said quietly. "Oh, Lucy, did you love him?"

"She still does," James drawled, deeming it time to interfere with this touching soap opera.

"That's even worse. To love a man who's planning to kill you," Sally said, her blue eyes so like Lucy's, and yet so much more real, filling with easy tears.

"He won't kill me if you tell him where the real falcon is," Lucy said, tossing James a hard glare over her shoulder before returning her attention to her gullible sister. "He's supposed to present it to the Bho Tsos this afternoon in some stupid ceremony. Don Salvatore's arriving this morning, along with his own private army, to witness the deal. If the falcon isn't there, it all falls through."

"So what?" Sally asked, and James was relieved to realize she wasn't being quite as trusting as he'd thought.

"Then the Bho Tsos are going to be very angry and insulted, and the Calderinis are going to be very angry and disappointed, and you and I are going to be very dead. And your pet private detective won't be able to save us."

"How did you know who Diamond is?" Sally asked almost casually.

"Vinnie said something. I guess his father warned him."

"Was that before or after he threatened to kill you?"

Lucy looked up at her sister, her huge eyes swimming in tears, her pale, pretty face defenseless and touching. "Sally," she begged in a sweet, pleading voice, "don't you believe me?"

"Oh, I believe you, Lucy," Sally said, brushing her sister's hair away from her tear-damp face, just as she must have when they were little and sweet sister Lucy fell and skinned her knees. "I believe that the Calderinis want the real falcon and would do just about anything to get it, up to and possibly including murdering me and Diamond. I believe the Bho Tsos will call off the deal if they don't get the real one. But I'm not too sure where you fit in with all this."

"Sally!"

"You and I haven't grown up with too great a respect for telling the truth," Sally said in a meditative tone. "Probably due to Marietta's influence, I suppose, or maybe some internal flaw. But that doesn't mean we can't change. Our lives may depend on it, Lucy. Tell me the truth."

Lucy fluttered her big blue eyes, and her full lower lip trembled enough that even James found himself beginning to believe her. "I'm telling you the truth!" she cried.

Sally's rueful smile was a revelation. She released her comforting hold on her sister and moved across the room, sinking down beside James and taking his hand in hers. He could feel her trembling slightly, and he realized what an effort it had cost her. "Don't waste your time in here, Lucy," she said, resting her head against James's shoulder. It was a nice weight, solid, warm. "Trust me, it's quite uncomfortable. You'll be much better off with Vinnie in his luxurious quarters. You smell of expensive shampoo and perfume, Lucy. If you were being held prisoner, you wouldn't be in such good shape. Go away and spin some lies for Vinnie. Maybe he'll believe you."

The tears in Lucy's eyes vanished. "So you've found true love and that's changed everything," she said in something close to a sneer, taking in Sally's position of trust, leaning against James. He could feel the tension in Sally's body, could feel the tension in his own. Vinnie might not want to hurt Lucy, but James certainly was tempted. He felt a very primitive violence toward anyone who wanted to hurt Sally.

But he didn't move. Sally held him still. "That's changed everything," she agreed.

"Well, I've got news for you. I've fallen in love, too. With Vinnie. And he loves me." Lucy's voice was defiant.

"I'm happy for you."

"I don't believe you. You're jealous!"

Sally laughed, an unfeigned sound of amusement. "Lucy, I have Diamond. What would I want with someone like Vinnie? I didn't want him when I could have him. I certainly don't want him now."

"You could never have him. He was just stringing you along, playing you for a fool while he was trying to get the falcon."

"I thought as much," Sally said, unperturbed. "I'm glad his feelings for you are more sincere."

"You don't think he loves me!" Lucy shrieked.

"I said I'm glad that he does," Sally said patiently.

"If he doesn't get the falcon, our future is ruined!" Lucy wailed.

"Why?"

"This deal with the Chinese has been years in the making. If it falls through at the last minute, all because Vinnie couldn't come up with the goods, then his future with the family will go up in smoke."

"Wouldn't that be for the best?"

"Where is the falcon?" Lucy shrieked.

"I don't know," Sally said, her voice very calm and steady, but her hand shook in James's.

"I hate you," Lucy screeched. "I've always hated you. You're mean and stupid and ugly and I hate you, I hate you, I—"

James had had enough of this. "If you don't shut your mouth, Miss MacArthur, then I'm going to have to shut it for you. And since the only thing I can find to gag you with would be a crumpled up bag that used to hold nacho chips, I don't think you'd find that very pleasant."

Lucy shut up, her blue eyes wide with astonishment as she realized he'd do exactly that. Blessed silence reigned in the storeroom as it grew marginally lighter.

"It's not MacArthur," Lucy said suddenly, in a small, defiant voice. "It never was MacArthur, and it certainly isn't now. It's Calderini. Vinnie and I were married last week."

"Congratulations," James drawled. "Sally and I wish you the best of luck. Count on monogrammed towels from the both of us."

"Go to hell," Lucy snarled, glaring at the two of them.

"After you, Mrs. Calderini," James replied, stroking Sally's hand.

JAMES'S WATCH HADN'T worked in days, and Sally's thin Rolex had disappeared at some point after Alf had knocked her on the head. If Lucy had any idea of the time, she wasn't about to divulge it, so the three of them sat in limbo as the minutes, the hours crawled past.

"I have to go to the bathroom," Lucy announced suddenly, breaking her sulking silence.

"Join the club," Sally said. "I've had to go for the last three hours. This place doesn't come equipped with a private bath."

"Well, I'm not going to sit here any longer and suffer. If you want to die, then that's your choice." Lucy surged to her feet, went to the door and started pounding on it. "Alf, let me out of here! At once!" she shrieked.

"You say she's your younger sister?" James murmured.

"Hard to believe, isn't it? She's always been more mature," Sally said with a ridiculous note of maternal pride.

"I'd say she's more nasty than mature."

"I suppose you could say that, too," she admitted.

Apparently, Alf had gone off duty. No one appeared to answer Lucy's strident demands, and when she began kicking the steel door, James decided he'd had enough.

"If you don't stop that, Mrs. Calderini, I'm going to lift you up and stuff you through the window. I don't expect you'll fit, but I'll put you out head first so we don't have to listen to you shrieking."

Lucy turned on him. "That's the second time you've threatened me, Mr. Diamond. Sally might be impressed by such caveman tactics, but I, for one, am not."

"I'm not trying to impress you, Mrs. Calderini. I'm trying to terrorize you."

"You'd better believe him, Lucy," Sally piped up. "Diamond can be an absolute pig if he wants to be."

"Thank you, dear," James murmured.

"You're welcome, darling," she replied sweetly.

"You two make me sick," Lucy spat out.

James didn't even bother to glance at her. Sally was looking up at him raptly, her big blue eyes shining with a certain guarded adoration. He decided he liked that. Particularly the guarded part. He wouldn't want a woman who was stupid enough to trust anyone implicitly. Given his profession and his nature, he'd never be completely trustworthy in all matters. But he suddenly realized he could be in the area that mattered the most. The area of the heart.

"I sure the hell hope we get out of this mess," he murmured, leaning his head close to hers.

"Why?" she asked. "So you can ditch me and get on with your life?"

"So I can ditch your caterwauling sister and find a real bed where we can spend a couple of days in undisturbed peace."

He liked the light that came into her eyes at the thought. He liked the way her mouth curved into a shy smile. Hell, he liked everything about her, up to but excluding her sister.

"Then I guess we'd better make it through this mess, somehow or other, shouldn't we?" she said, kissing him lightly.

He deepened the kiss gently, and for a moment, they were so absorbed, they didn't hear the heavy, metal door swing open.

"Now ain't love grand?" Alf drawled. "Sorry I had to dump the broad in here to cramp your style, but we ran out of holding places."

"Don't bother, Alf," Lucy said, rising and brushing herself off with haughty dignity. "They didn't believe me." She started toward the door, but Alf's meaty hand shot out, forestalling her.

"Where do you think you're going, little missy?"

Lucy's entire body was rigid. "To Vinnie."

"Nope. You're staying put. The rules of this particular game have changed."

"Vinnie couldn't . . . ?"

"Vinnie didn't. Don Salvatore has taken over, and he's not too pleased with his son and heir. Vinnie's being read the riot act right now, and you're to be kept on ice until the Don decides what to do with all of yous."

"I'll be dead of a burst bladder before he decides," Sally announced in a pragmatic voice.

"The good news is that Don Salvatore is a gentleman. He doesn't believe in holding ladies under adverse conditions. You'll be escorted back to your rooms and locked in. He'd like your word of honor that you won't try to escape. Not that I'd believe it, but the old man has a certain old-fashioned respect for women."

"I'm not going anywhere without Diamond," Sally said flatly.

"Diamond stays here."

"Then so do I."

Alf looked torn. Clearly, executive decision making wasn't his forte, but just as clearly, his orders hadn't been engraved in stone. "You wanna give me your word, copper?"

"Sure, Alf," James said in a lazy drawl. "I won't try to escape. Cross my heart and hope to die."

Alf spat on the linoleum. "Up and at 'em, then. You haven't got much time."

James hadn't really expected he'd be able to get the drop on Alf once they reached the hallway. For one thing, the gun in Alf's hand was much too big, and James couldn't count on being able to keep Sally safe. For another, the expected backup was waiting, a solid phalanx of armed suits waiting to escort them to their rooms.

"A lot of muscle for two women," James observed.

"Yeah, well, you were supposed to go, too. I just thought you deserved the storeroom," Alf said, his dark, piggy eyes gleaming with hatred.

"I don't know. I have a certain fondness for that storeroom," James said, taking Sally's hand and squeezing it lightly.

"Disgusting," Alf muttered.

It was too much to hope they'd be taken back to their original rooms. Even if they had been, someone would have gone through their baggage and found the knife James had hidden in Sally's suitcase as extra insurance. Instead, they were locked into two small rooms that must have been reserved for the cleaning staff.

Alf did his best to put the two sisters together, but once more, Sally was having none of that. Once more, Alf backed down and the volubly protesting Lucy was shoved into one room while James and Sally went willingly enough into the other next door.

James leaned against the door and surveyed the cubicle. "I wouldn't call this much of an improvement. There's no window, the door's locked and the bed looks more like a cot."

"There is, however, a toilet and shower," Sally said, heading straight for them. "I'm counting my blessings."

It took all his self-control for James not to join her in the shower. The very sound of her voice, the thumps as she moved around in the tiny shower stall made him hard as a rock. He had to stop thinking with his glands if he was going to get the two of them out of there in one piece, and he had to stop considering whether that tiny cot was really too small.

When she finally emerged from the bathroom, he'd ascertained that there was no way out of the locked cubicle. He looked up when he saw her, frowning as he took in her pale appearance. She'd put her rumpled clothes back on, and her damp hair framed a face white with strain and exhaustion.

"I thought you'd reappear in a towel," he said, moving toward her.

"I decided that might be a bit dangerous. We have to concentrate on getting out of here first."

"You're smart," he said, "and you're gorgeous." He kissed her, hard, and then moved past her to the bathroom.

By the time he emerged fully dressed after his shower Sally was sound asleep, curled up on the tiny cot. He wanted to wrap himself around her, to simply hold her for a while. And that knowledge was the most disturbing of all.

He wasn't ever going to be free. Oh, they might very well get out of this particular mess. He might even be able to get rid of her, drive her away with his complete lack of charm and financial stability. He could start drinking with a vengeance, maybe take up smoking unfiltered cigarettes.

But he didn't think that would get rid of her. The only way he was going to get rid of her was to tell her to go. And when, not if, he did that, he was still going to be haunted by her memory for the rest of his life.

The door was flung open abruptly, and Sally sat up in bed, startled out of sleep.

"Too bad." Alf chuckled unpleasantly. "I was hoping to catch you with your pants down."

"Too bad," James echoed, deciding then and there that Alf wasn't going to get through this unscathed.

"Get on your feet, girly. You're wanted."

"She's not going anywhere without me," James announced.

"Don't get excited. You're going, too. All hell's breaking loose and the Chinese want some answers."

THE FORMAL MEETING between the Calderini crime family and the Bho Tsos was being held in a banquet room that looked better suited to stag parties than high-level criminals. The Bho Tsos were seated at one side of a long table, men only, all of them looking completely disgruntled. At a smaller table sat the wives, with the Dragon Lady firmly in control. She was looking straight at Sally when she entered, and Sally could feel a cold shiver run down her back. She thought Vinnie was essentially harmless and that Don Salvatore not much more than a sadistic lech, but the Dragon Lady scared the hell out of her.

The Calderinis were at the opposite side of the table, Don Salvatore in the middle, a cowed looking Vinnie beside him, and various midlevel functionaries flanking them. All eyes were on Diamond and Sally when they entered the room. Lucy was already there, sitting in a corner like a naughty little girl.

Sally could feel the tension in the room, the tension radiating from Diamond. She had to be very careful, she thought, or Diamond might make another grand gesture that could get them killed. The phony jade falcon was sitting in the middle of the table, directly in front of Mr. Li and Don Salvatore, and with a sudden surge of energy, Sally pulled away from Alf and sauntered over to it. She reached between Don Salvatore and Vinnie and picked it up, surprised as always by its light weight.

"Do you gentlemen have a problem with my father's falcon?" she asked brightly.

Mr. Li hissed in disapproval, sounding like a fat snake. "We have a problem. The falcon we are looking for was stolen from our country by a thief and a scoundrel. Your father, Miss MacArthur. We want it back."

"You have it." She put the falcon back on the table.

It jumped as Salvatore pounded his fist down. "He does not have it. This is a phony, commissioned by you from Derek Dagradi at the School for Fine Arts. You have no secrets from us, Miss MacArthur. We want to know where the real one is."

"If I had no secrets from you, then you wouldn't be asking," she pointed out with deceptive calm.

Diamond moved then, putting a restraining hand on her elbow. "Sally, watch it," he muttered. "You're not playing with amateurs here."

"Listen to Mr. Diamond, Miss MacArthur," Don Salvatore said. "He's come up against us before. If you don't cooperate, things will go poorly for you. And most particularly, for your baby sister."

"No!" Vinnie protested, unquelled by his father's glare. "She's my wife and I won't let you touch her."

"Marriages like that can be dissolved."

"Not mine!" Vinnie said stoutly. "She's pregnant."

Silence filled the room as everyone, the Bho Tsos and the Calderinis, turned to stare at Lucy. "Whose child is it?" Don Salvatore asked finally.

Vinnie lunged for his father, knocking the banquet table. The falcon went rolling across the damask cloth, Lucy started screaming, and the Bho Tsos began shouting.

In the midst of all this, the Dragon Lady rose to her full, impressive height and made an announcement in Chinese. It was short and dignified, and had the effect of silencing the place. Everyone was standing, glaring at each other. Mr. Li was taking a step backward, tugging at his suit jacket, when the swinging doors on the lobby side of the banquet room opened.

"Who the hell is that?" Don Salvatore demanded in a rage, his white hair standing on end.

Alf was already racing toward the door, but he was too late. An elderly figure backed into the room, pulling something behind him. The doors swung shut behind him, and the man turned, wheeling his burden in front of him.

"Oh, God," Sally muttered weakly as she recognized Jenkins holding the handles of the wheelchair Isaiah used when he was feeling fragile, or at least, when he wanted to give that appearance.

Isaiah himself was in fine shape, dignified, erect in the chair, his faded eyes glinting with malice. And resting in his lap, beneath his arthritic hand, lay the Manchurian falcon.

"I believe you were looking for this?"

Chapter Eighteen

Dead silence filled the room. Mr. Li moved from behind the table, walking very slowly toward Isaiah's erect figure. "So," he said. "We meet again, Mr. MacArthur."

"We do, Mr. Li," Isaiah said with equal dignity. "It has been many years."

"Many years. You have come to return the falcon to its rightful owners?"

"No, I wouldn't necessarily say the Bho Tsos happen to be the rightful owner of a national treasure like this one," Isaiah said.

"Consider us a representative of the government," Mr. Li said solemnly, an unimaginable glint of humor in his small, dark eyes.

"That would take a stretch of the imagination. Nevertheless, I believe I'm up to it. Assuming my daughters and my future son-in-law are allowed to leave safely."

"Vinnie and Lucy are already married," Sally piped up, before Diamond's hand on her arm could silence her.

Isaiah didn't even glance her way. "I was referring to Mr. Diamond, the private detective." James didn't even bother to wonder how the old man knew who he really was. Obviously, Isaiah MacArthur was a lot more savvy than anyone had given him credit for.

Mr. Li cast a polite glance at Don Salvatore, who nodded with equal dignity. "They are free to leave."

"Then," said Isaiah, lifting the falcon in his swollen hands, "I present to you the Manchurian falcon." He placed it in Mr. Li's slightly trembling hands, and out of the corner of his mouth, he muttered to Sally, "Get the hell out of here."

James grabbed her arm, awash with the sudden sinking suspicion that things were still not what they seemed. He'd just begun dragging a reluctant Sally away from the cluster of men when Mr. Li let out an enraged shout.

"*This* is not the real falcon!"

Immediately two of the Calderini henchmen stepped in front of Sally and James, barring their escape. Sally tried to stare at her father, and Isaiah shrugged. "I tried."

"Where is the real falcon?" Mr. Li demanded, positively vibrating with rage.

"I have no idea. I had this one commissioned from the same man who made the other copy. Your guess is as good as mine as to where the real falcon is."

"You cannot play us for fools," Mr. Li warned. "People do not trifle with the Bho Tsos and come out unscathed. I owe you a debt of vengeance, Isaiah MacArthur, and I rejoice at the chance to pay it." He started toward the wheelchair-bound man as the rest of the crowd watched in fascinated horror. James tensed, ready to step between Li and Isaiah and probably get a bullet in his ear for the trouble. But he had no choice—if he didn't do something to stop it, Sally would.

Suddenly a voice stopped Mr. Li in his murderous tracks. "Behave yourself!" The Dragon Lady said firmly, and Mr. Li hung his head like a naughty little boy.

Isaiah swung himself around in his wheelchair to stare at the woman in surprise. "Why, Bambi," he said, his voice soft with wonder. "I didn't know you were still around."

"Bambi?" Sally echoed in fascination.

The Dragon Lady was a master at dramatics. She strode around the table, her thin, elegant body that of an empress. "I have prospered, Isaiah MacArthur. As have you. I would wish we could share memories together, but this is a day of business, and I'm afraid sentiment is of no value. Where is the falcon?"

"Bambi, I would give it to you if I had it. I truly have no idea where it has gone to," Isaiah said sadly.

"Maybe a random thief?" Sally suggested, but Don Salvatore simply glared at her.

"We would know if anyone had taken something the Calderinis wanted. We would have it by now."

"Then who—"

There was a noise at the door as one more unwanted guest wanted to join the party. Suddenly it all fit together in James's brain, and he laughed with pure pleasure.

The sound of his laughter shocked the room into silence. "What's so damned funny, boy?" Isaiah demanded grumpily.

"Isn't it obvious?" he countered. "Don't any of you know where the damned falcon is?"

"If you know, you'd better inform us immediately. Unless you'd like to lose your fingers one at a time," Don Salvatore said pleasantly.

"I imagine the person who took it is the same person who's making such a fuss right now. If I were you, Don Salvatore, I'd tell Alf to call off his goons and let her in."

"Her?" Several key players echoed as Don Salvatore snapped his fingers imperiously.

"Her," James verified, as a familiar figure sauntered into the room.

"Good God, I should have known," Isaiah moaned, sinking his head into his hands.

"Hullo, mother," Sally said, resigned.

"Hello, darling." Marietta was another player, milking the scene for all it was worth, and she even managed to put Bambi the Dragon Lady in the shade. She was stunning, dressed in black and crimson, a huge black bag over her arm. She had a cigarette holder that was at least a foot long, with a lit cigarette at the end, and it took all James's strength of mind to ignore it and concentrate on the real falcon.

He almost tackled her for it. Instead, he held still, his hand still protective on Sally's arm, as Marietta reached into her bag and drew forth still another falcon.

To his untrained eyes, it was identical to the other two. But Mr. Li drew in a deep, reverent breath and held out his hands for it.

James was never quite sure how it happened. Mr. Li reached for it; Marietta released it; Bambi lunged for it; Isaiah jerked his wheelchair; and Sally's foot poked out. Mr. Li stumbled; Bambi floundered; Marietta fumbled; and the falcon went flying through the air like a football.

"I've got it," Vinnie shouted, feinting back for the pass, arms overhead like a tight-end receiver. Everyone watched in silence as the statue hurtled toward him, turning over and over in the air. Everyone watched in silence as Vinnie leapt for it. And missed. And the Manchurian falcon crashed to the floor, smashing into a million pieces.

The silence was as intense as a scream. Finally, Sally leaned forward to stare at the rubble, and said in her most prosaic voice, "I never realized jade was so fragile."

Mr. Li straightened himself. He snapped his fingers, and even Bambi pulled herself to attention. "We are leaving," he announced. "The deal is off. If we wish to have a piece of the northern California gambling concession, we will simply take it. In the meantime, the sooner we get out of your benighted country, the happier we will be." He marched toward the door without a backward glance, and the assembled Bho Tsos followed, leaving behind only Bambi.

For a moment, she didn't look like a dragon lady at all as she knelt beside Isaiah's wheelchair. "We should never have grown old, Isaiah," she said in a soft, musical voice.

"You will never grow old, Bambi," Isaiah said, touching her cheek. A moment later, she followed the others, back erect, breathing fire.

Don Salvatore moved slowly, an old man. "I should kill you all for this," he said heavily. "But then I would have to kill my worthless fool of a son, and even I cannot do that. You." He turned to the hapless Vinnie. "You are too weak for the life we lead. Go back to Yale Law School, finish your degree and then come work for me. Maybe you're better at juggling numbers and legal matters than you are at juggling priceless art objects." He glanced over at Lucy's cowering figure, then sighed. "And bring your wife back to the house so that we can welcome her. But not," he said fiercely, pointing at Sally, "that one. She is a plague and a bane."

"I agree," Vinnie muttered, glaring at her.

"So do I," James couldn't resist adding.

Sally stood by her father's wheelchair, and to James's surprise, she didn't even raise her head to glare at him. Her shoulders were bowed, and for the first time, she seemed truly numbed by the events. He wanted to put his arms around her, to lift her chin up and kiss her, to tell her he was only kidding, that she'd done well even if she'd almost gotten them killed. But he didn't move.

It was his chance to break free. Probably his last chance. He couldn't afford to let it pass him by.

The Calderinis marched out, following the old man single file, leaving only Vinnie behind. Alf was the last to leave, and as he did, he turned to glance at James.

James nodded as a silent agreement passed between the two. A cease-fire may have been called between the other warring factions. The battle was still hot between these two men.

"Well, Marietta," Isaiah said finally. "You still manage to surprise me. Why in heaven's name did you steal the falcon?"

Marietta took the handles of the wheelchair from Jenkins's capable hands. "Would you believe me if I told you I heard the Calderinis were after it and I was trying to protect it for you? But when it came to the safety of my daughters and our precious falcon, I had to make the only decent choice."

"Not for one moment," Isaiah replied.

Marietta shrugged, looking very young and very naughty, and James could see where Sally got her love of fantasy from. "Would you believe I heard the Calderinis were after the falcon and I thought I could make a tidy little nest egg by delivering it to them?"

"That sounds more likely. What made you change your mind?"

"I didn't. I knew their reputation well enough to realize my daughters weren't in any real danger. I imagine I could have gotten quite a nice sum from them," she said with misty-eyed regret.

Isaiah reached up and patted her hand consolingly. "Never mind, dearest. You'll find some other get-rich-quick scheme. And don't forget, your daughter just married into a very wealthy family. There must be some profit to be made from all that."

"You always were able to look on the bright side of things, Isaiah," Marietta said fondly, pushing him toward the door. "Every cloud always has a silver lining."

Sally lifted her head for a moment, and James could see a trace of her old fire. "There's even better news, Marietta," Sally called after her rapidly disappearing parents. "Lucy's going to make you a grandmother."

Marietta's scream of anguish echoed long after the doors swung shut. Vinnie had gone to Lucy's side, wrapping her in protective arms, neither of them the slightest bit aware of the other people in the room. James looked at Sally, at the wary, hopeful expression in her eyes, and he hated to douse that flame. But he had no choice.

"Looks like your sister will have her happy ending," he drawled, wishing to hell he had a cigarette. He'd almost forgotten how much he was needing one, but right then, he would have killed for one. Something to keep his hands and eyes busy as he broke Sally's heart.

"What about you?" Her voice wasn't much more than a whisper, but he heard every word, spoken and unspoken.

"You know me. I don't believe in 'em," he said, cool as menthol. "Listen, I need to get back to town. I've got too many other things hanging fire. If you don't mind, I'll take the car and you can catch a ride with one of your parents."

Sally opened her mouth to protest, but that defeated expression blanked over her face and she nodded. "You'll send me your bill?"

"Including seventy-five dollars for my car," he said, wanting to coax a smile out of her.

It didn't work. She looked up at him, and there were tears swimming in her eyes. "Goodbye, Diamond."

He was no good for her, and he knew it even if she didn't. "Goodbye, kid," he said, sounding like Bogart. And he left her standing in the middle of the room, the worthless shards of the priceless falcon at her feet.

"WHY DON'T YOU COME with me? It doesn't do you any good to sit around moping. If that man is foolish enough not to love my daughter, then he's not worth having."

Sally glanced up at Marietta with her customary listlessness. It had been ten days since their return from Glory, California. Ten days of listening to Lucy's blow-by-blow account of her morning sickness, the luxury of the Calderini family compound and what a stupendous lover Vinnie was. Ten days of Marietta and Isaiah flirting and fighting. Ten days of Jenksy's worrying and cossetting and fussing over her. Ten days without word from Diamond.

"You're leaving?" Sally asked her mother, not really surprised. Her mother never stayed in one place for very long—it was one of her major failings and one of her major charms.

"For the Amazon. I have a need for lush, tropical climates. Your father and I aren't going to make a go of it, you know."

"I never expected you would," Sally said, staring out the window into the rainy afternoon. It was a gloomy day in late September. The rain was relentless, and the gray chill filled her soul.

"So why don't you come with me? I know I haven't been much of a mother, but I promise you, I can be a hell of a good companion. We'll have fun."

Sally looked at her with great patience. "Mother," she said, "I don't want to have fun."

Marietta looked startled. "I do believe that's the first time you've called me Mother in years."

"Diamond told me I shouldn't judge you. He's probably right." Sally sighed. "Besides, I don't have the energy to be angry anymore."

"Well, maybe James Diamond isn't as big a fool as I thought he was. Though if he's stupid enough to leave you, he can't be all that bright."

Sally leaned back on the window seat, stretching her long legs out in front of her. They were getting skinnier. For some reason, she hadn't felt like eating, or sleeping for that matter, since they returned from the Calderinis' pseudo spa. At least Diamond had returned her car, though she would have given anything if he'd brought it himself instead of sending it with Frankie the pimp. He still looked like a seminary student, but the assessing looks he'd cast over the MacArthur mansion had been professional, indeed. She'd wanted to count the silver once he'd left.

Diamond hadn't even sent her a bill. And she wanted one desperately. Not so that she could pay it and put some sort of closure on that section of her life. She wasn't nearly so rational and well adjusted.

She wanted the bill because she wanted something of his. Something that belonged to him, even a piece of paper, something that bore his handwriting. She wanted a bill so she could refuse to pay it and make him come and try to collect. She wanted any part of him she could have. And apparently, she could have nothing.

She sighed, glancing up at her mother. Marietta was dressed for travel in a crushed silk suit and rakish hat with a pair of oversized sunglasses on her perfect nose. "Are you leaving now?" Sally asked, rousing herself to curiosity.

"Right this minute. If you think I'm going to wait around while Lucy blossoms, you must be crazy. I'm not ready to be a grandmother. Maybe in another twenty years or so, but not now. I'm simply going to consider the Calderini bambino my godchild."

Sally knew she should be angry with Marietta's blithe self-absorption, but instead, she laughed. "You're hopeless."

"You're certain you won't come? You don't need to pack, you know. We could have a marvelous time shopping."

"No, thank you, Mother. Maybe some other trip."

"You think he'll come back?" Marietta asked shrewdly.

The very thought stabbed hope through Sally's heart. "No," she said, truthfully enough. "But there's a chance in a thousand I'm wrong."

"So you'll sit and wait like some creepy old maid, mourning your lost love?"

For a moment, some of Sally's old energy reemerged. "Of course. For as long as a month, maybe. Then I'll go after him."

Marietta smiled her brilliant, heart-stopping smile. "That's my daughter. Say goodbye to Isaiah for me. I can't do it."

"He doesn't know you're leaving?"

"Oh, he knows, all right. I just haven't told him. He and I came to an understanding years ago. He knows me better than I know myself. I'm just afraid he might have started to hope..." She let the thought trail off, and for once in her life, she looked faintly regretful.

"I'll tell him."

"I left him a little present. Tell him that, darling. And give him my love."

Marietta never hugged Sally or touched her if she could help it. She didn't that day, either. She simply waved, an airy little wave, and ran out the front door.

Sally could imagine the present Marietta had left for her tolerant ex-husband. A stack of bills. A subpoena. Maybe even one of her absolutely awful paintings. The message and the gift could wait.

Night was falling around the old house when the yellow headlights pierced the gathering darkness. Sally watched with her usual apathy, still ensconced on the bench, as the headlights drew closer up the drive. It was some sort of old car, the kind she'd seen in movies, pulling up under the bright lights in front of the house.

Her heart started to pound, loud and hard beneath her breast, and she swung her legs off the window seat. By the time she reached the front door, the car had stopped and someone was walking up the front steps.

She couldn't see his face, but she'd know that body anywhere, even dressed in an old-fashioned dark suit, wing tips and a fedora.

She wanted to run to him, but she couldn't. She was rooted to the spot at the top of the steps, waiting for him.

He looked up and saw her, and she could see the trace of uncertainty on his face. "I looked like hell for an old Chrysler like Marlowe used to drive," he said in a rough voice. "But this '42 Packard was the best I could do. I figured with a swell dame like you, I oughta go for the best."

"James," she said in a broken little voice. "You really do love me, don't you?"

He'd almost reached her. "I thought you'd already figured that out. Who else could make me give up cigarettes and hooch?"

"You said you wouldn't love me till 1999." He'd reached the top step. His face was back to normal now, the bruising gone, and once more, he had his artistic stubble, his beautiful face, his infinitely clever mouth.

"I'm a quick learner. So what's it gonna be, doll? Marriage to a shamus like me, or a life full of empty pleasures? Name your poison."

"Diamond," she said happily, "I'm yours." And she went into his arms, wrapping herself around him, home at last.

She didn't know how much time passed before she heard Jenkins's gentle harrumph. Dazedly she disentangled herself from Diamond, pleased to see that he looked just as shell-shocked as she did. She'd knocked his wonderful fedora off and discovered his hair was still too long, but she liked it.

"What is it, Jensky?" she murmured happily, not bothering to look away from Diamond.

"Your father wants to see you. And may I be the first to offer the two of you my best wishes?"

"You may," Diamond said. "Maybe I'd better ask the old man's permission. Where is he?"

"In the study, sir. And if I may say so, he's been waiting for this quite impatiently."

Sally took Diamond's hand, bouncing along the hallway cheerfully as they headed for the study. "I can be your secretary, Diamond. Hard-boiled detectives always have secretaries who're in love with them."

"Yeah, but they're usually blond."

"I'll dye my hair."

"I'll fire you."

"That's the nice part about it," she said happily. "You can't fire your wife."

"What have I gotten into?" Diamond asked of no one in particular.

"Miss Sally's clutches, sir," Jenkins replied gravely, opening the door to the study.

Isaiah was sitting at the desk, an odd expression on his face. He barely acknowledged their arrival. "Your mother's left," he said abruptly.

"Yes," Sally said, suddenly less giddy. "She told me you knew she was going."

"I figured she would. She always does."

"Yes, she always does. She told me she left you a present. Is it something quite ghastly?" Sally took a step toward her father, still holding tight to Diamond's hand.

Isaiah simply shook his head in bewilderment. "I'm not sure what to make of it. She left me this." And his gnarled old hands lifted up a piece of gray-green sculpture. One that looked oddly familiar, and yet different.

"It's not..." Diamond said.

"It is," Isaiah replied, staring at it in wonder and disbelief. "The Manchurian falcon."

HARLEQUIN®
OFFICIAL SWEEPSTAKES RULES

NO PURCHASE NECESSARY

1. To enter, complete an Official Entry Form or 3"× 5" index card by hand-printing, in plain block letters, your complete name, address, phone number and age, and mailing it to: Harlequin Fashion A Whole New You Sweepstakes, P.O. Box 9056, Buffalo, NY 14269-9056.

   No responsibility is assumed for lost, late or misdirected mail. Entries must be sent separately with first class postage affixed, and be received no later than December 31, 1991 for eligibility.

2. Winners will be selected by D.L. Blair, Inc., an independent judging organization whose decisions are final, in random drawings to be held on January 30, 1992 in Blair, NE at 10:00 a.m. from among all eligible entries received.

3. The prizes to be awarded and their approximate retail values are as follows: Grand Prize — A brand-new Mercury Sable LS plus a trip for two (2) to Paris, including round-trip air transportation, six (6) nights hotel accommodation, a $1,400 meal/spending money stipend and $2,000 cash toward a new fashion wardrobe (approximate value: $28,000) or $15,000 cash; two (2) Second Prizes — A trip to Paris, including round-trip air transportation, six (6) nights hotel accommodation, a $1,400 meal/spending money stipend and $2,000 cash toward a new fashion wardrobe (approximate value: $11,000) or $5,000 cash; three (3) Third Prizes — $2,000 cash toward a new fashion wardrobe. All prizes are valued in U.S. currency. Travel award air transportation is from the commercial airport nearest winner's home. Travel is subject to space and accommodation availability, and must be completed by June 30, 1993. Sweepstakes offer is open to residents of the U.S. and Canada who are 21 years of age or older as of December 31, 1991, except residents of Puerto Rico, employees and immediate family members of Torstar Corp., its affiliates, subsidiaries, and all agencies, entities and persons connected with the use, marketing, or conduct of this sweepstakes. All federal, state, provincial, municipal and local laws apply. Offer void wherever prohibited by law. Taxes and/or duties, applicable registration and licensing fees, are the sole responsibility of the winners. Any litigation within the province of Quebec respecting the conduct and awarding of a prize may be submitted to the Régie des loteries et courses du Québec. All prizes will be awarded; winners will be notified by mail. No substitution of prizes is permitted.

4. Potential winners must sign and return any required Affidavit of Eligibility/Release of Liability within 30 days of notification. In the event of noncompliance within this time period, the prize may be awarded to an alternate winner. Any prize or prize notification returned as undeliverable may result in the awarding of that prize to an alternate winner. By acceptance of their prize, winners consent to use of their names, photographs or their likenesses for purposes of advertising, trade and promotion on behalf of Torstar Corp. without further compensation. Canadian winners must correctly answer a time-limited arithmetical question in order to be awarded a prize.

5. For a list of winners (available after 3/31/92), send a separate stamped, self-addressed envelope to: Harlequin Fashion A Whole New You Sweepstakes, P.O. Box 4694, Blair, NE 68009.

PREMIUM OFFER TERMS

To receive your gift, complete the Offer Certificate according to directions. Be certain to enclose the required number of "Fashion A Whole New You" proofs of product purchase (which are found on the last page of every specially marked "Fashion A Whole New You" Harlequin or Silhouette romance novel). Requests must be received no later than December 31, 1991. Limit: four (4) gifts per name, family, group, organization or address. Items depicted are for illustrative purposes only and may not be exactly as shown. Please allow 6 to 8 weeks for receipt of order. Offer good while quantities of gifts last. In the event an ordered gift is no longer available, you will receive a free, previously unpublished Harlequin or Silhouette book for every proof of purchase you have submitted with your request, plus a refund of the postage and handling charge you have included. Offer good in the U.S. and Canada only.

HQFW-SWPR

HARLEQUIN OFFICIAL SWEEPSTAKES ENTRY FORM

4-FWARS-4

Complete and return this Entry Form immediately – the more entries you submit, the better your chances of winning!

- Entries must be received by **December 31, 1991.**
- A Random draw will take place on **January 30, 1992.**
- No purchase necessary.

Yes, I want to win a FASHION A WHOLE NEW YOU Classic and Romantic prize from Harlequin:

Name ______________________ Telephone ______________ Age ________

Address ____

City ______________________ State ______________ Zip ______________

Return Entries to: **Harlequin FASHION A WHOLE NEW YOU,**
P.O. Box 9056, Buffalo, NY 14269-9056

PREMIUM OFFER

To receive your free gift, send us the required number of proofs-of-purchase from any specially marked FASHION A WHOLE NEW YOU Harlequin or Silhouette Book with the Offer Certificate properly completed, plus a check or money order (do not send cash) to cover postage and handling payable to Harlequin FASHION A WHOLE NEW YOU Offer. We will send you the specified gift.

OFFER CERTIFICATE

Item	A. ROMANTIC COLLECTOR'S DOLL (Suggested Retail Price $60.00)	B. CLASSIC PICTURE FRAME (Suggested Retail Price $25.00)
# of proofs-of-purchase	18	12
Postage and Handling	$3.50	$2.95
Check one	☐	☐

Name ____

Address ____

City ______________________ State ______________ Zip ______________

Mail this certificate, designated number of proofs-of-purchase and check or money order for postage and handling to: **Harlequin FASHION A WHOLE NEW YOU Gift Offer,** P.O. Box 9057, Buffalo, NY 14269-9057. Requests must be received by December 31, 1991.

FASHION A WHOLE NEW YOU WIN CARS.TRIPS.CASH!

ONE PROOF-OF-PURCHASE

4-FWARP-4

To collect your fabulous free gift you must include the necessary number of proofs-of-purchase with a properly completed Offer Certificate.

See previous page for details.